NIGHT WHISPERS

"Erickson skillfully navigates the fraught task of portraying the mind of a stalker with multiple personalities . . . The narrative is shadowy and suspenseful, leaving the reader with a creepy, unsettled feeling of expectation."

—*Publishers Weekly*

ASPEN

"A deliciously juicy romp through the winter playground of the wealthy and powerful . . . A complex and truly interesting heroine . . . Suspenseful and tumultuous . . . a sharply plotted page-turner." —*Publishers Weekly*

Praise for the novels of RITA Award–finalist
Lynn Erickson

ON THE EDGE

"Erickson's suspenseful romance takes readers into the dangerous world of mountain climbing and makes the trip worthwhile." —*Booklist*

"*On the Edge* will excite romantic suspense fans from the first stop on a mountain's side to the final climax. Meredith is an interesting heroine whose pangs of guilt feel genuine . . . Lynn Erickson keeps fans on the edge." —*BookBrowser*

ON THIN ICE

"Ms. Erickson really delivers a first-rate story with characters who'll have you begging for more. They're so well-drawn readers will even feel sympathy for the villain. I highly recommend this book to anyone looking for a great story." —*Old Book Barn Gazette*

"Erickson creates masterful suspense with *On Thin Ice* . . . Fascinating characters . . . As the tension builds and the pages turn faster and faster, the reader will be swept away in a dangerous world." —*Midwest Book Review*

"A highly suspenseful novel. Erickson makes you feel as though you're walking the tightrope with Ellie as she searches for the killer . . . a must-read." —*Rendezvous*

continued . . .

Searching for Sarah

"Erickson builds suspense by expertly weaving romance into multiple thrilling story lines." —*Publishers Weekly*

"Intricate suspense and deft characterizations make *Searching for Sarah* a top-notch thriller. Don't miss out." —*Romantic Times*

"Ms. Erickson teases the reader like a cat is teased with a piece of string. The reader follows the string through all the twists and turns of this well-plotted story all the way to the surprise ending." —*Rendezvous*

The Eleventh Hour

"Fabulous romantic suspense . . . the lead characters are charming . . . Counterpoint to the sizzling romance is a brilliant who-done-it." —*Painted Rock Reviews*

"Layers of depth . . . what a ride!" —*Rendezvous*

"A thrilling read . . . exciting . . . compelling relationships . . . a winner." —*Romantic Times*

IN THE COLD

LYNN ERICKSON

BERKLEY SENSATION, NEW YORK

If you purchased this book without a cover, you should be aware that this book is stolen property. It was reported as "unsold and destroyed" to the publisher, and neither the author nor the publisher has received any payment for this "stripped book."

This is a work of fiction. Names, characters, places, and incidents either are the product of the author's imagination or are used fictitiously, and any resemblance to actual persons, living or dead, business establishments, events, or locales is entirely coincidental.

IN THE COLD

A Berkley Sensation Book / published by arrangement with the author

PRINTING HISTORY
Berkley Sensation edition / June 2003

Copyright © 2003 by Carla Peltonen and Molly Swanton
Cover design by Ann Marie Manca
Cover art by David Stimson

All rights reserved.
This book, or parts thereof, may not be reproduced
in any form without permission.
The scanning, uploading, and distribution of this book via the Internet or
via any other means without the permission of the publisher is illegal and
punishable by law. Please purchase only authorized electronic
editions, and do not participate in or encourage electronic piracy of copy-
righted materials. Your support of the author's rights is appreciated.
For information address: The Berkley Publishing Group,
a division of Penguin Group (USA) Inc.,
375 Hudson Street, New York, New York 10014.

ISBN: 0-425-19069-2

A BERKLEY SENSATION™ BOOK
Berkley Sensation Books are published by The Berkley Publishing Group,
a division of Penguin Group (USA) Inc.,
375 Hudson Street, New York, New York 10014.
BERKLEY SENSATION and the "B" design
are trademarks belonging to Penguin Group (USA) Inc.

PRINTED IN THE UNITED STATES OF AMERICA

10 9 8 7 6 5 4 3 2 1

This book is dedicated to Roger Mestler, modern-day miner, who showed me through the Compromise Mine, and to all the visionary, hardworking miners of Aspen's silver boom days.

ONE

The wheelchair always got him.

Shiny, high-tech, lightweight, with big wheels that tilted in. He still wasn't used to the thing, even though over a year had gone by since his friend Joe had been confined to it. Joe, still the same from the waist up, exactly the same it seemed, despite the accident. Handsome, dark and ascetic looking, a Spanish hidalgo with an easy smile. But from the waist down, inert. Nevertheless, he envied the wholeness Joe possessed.

"So," he said, putting on the face, the relaxed but cocky one that Joe was used to, "how's it going?"

"Pretty good," Joe said. "How you doing, Chris?"

They were sitting at the table under a striped umbrella on Joe's backyard patio. It was a hot day, normal for July in Denver. Hot and so arid the sweat dried on you before you had a chance to feel sticky. Chris often thought in terms of somnolent lizards on sun-heated rocks when it got like this. Denver in the summer.

"Oh, you know." Chris shrugged.

"No, buddy, I don't know. You've been back for how long—six months? You've been evasive as hell. You looking for work?"

Chris squinted through his sunglasses out over the backyard, where water from a Rainmaker sprinkler caught the sun, swirling glittering drops. All he could see was grass and water and the tall redwood fence that divided Joe's backyard from his neighbor's. No help there. He narrowed his hazel eyes and mentally phrased his reply.

"Well?"

"I'm not presently looking, no. I told you, after that bundle I won, why work? I'm taking it easy."

Joe shook his head then took a pull on his beer. "Yeah, well, you laid most of it on me," he said softly.

"A mere pittance. Don't worry, I kept more than enough for myself. I might be crazy, but I'm not stupid."

"Still, I feel like . . . you know, a charity case or something. Someday you might need the extra cash. I can't help it, I worry about you, Chris."

"Well, don't."

"Come on, this is *me.* I know when you're off."

"Off?" Chris laughed.

"You know what I mean. You're faking it, man. Even right now you're faking it."

Chris felt the cloak of insouciance slipping, tried all his mental tricks, every last one that he'd learned, but the veneer peeled away like scorched skin. He ran a hand over his face, feeling the dried salt on his forehead. "Shit."

"All right, for chrissakes, tell me," Joe said.

"It's just that . . . damnit, sometimes I . . ."

"Spit it out."

He leaned an elbow on the table, rested his forehead in a hand. "I don't know. It's like sometimes I wake up at night . . . and I don't remember who I am. I get this adrenaline rush—'Who am I tonight? Did I give anything away?' and I lie there and I go through all of them, all the roles, all the bullshit, and I have to concentrate to remember who I am. And I . . . Christ . . . sometimes I don't know."

Joe reached out and put a hand on his arm. "It's a good thing you resigned. And you'll get over it, Chris. In time. Believe me, if there's one thing I learned, you get over things in time."

"Sure."

"It's better you left when you did. If you stayed, you could have got yourself killed. Or one of your task force partners."

"Yeah."

"Did they offer you counseling?"

"I didn't want any goddamn counseling." If only Joe knew, if only he knew. *Counseling.* Right, like the Newark Police Department was going to offer him counseling after what he'd done. He was lucky they asked him to resign instead of prosecuting his ass.

"Sometimes it helps."

"It won't help me."

"Okay, have it your way. You always were a stubborn son of a bitch."

He looked over the top of his sunglasses and forced a crooked grin. Yeah, that was better.

"So, no plans?" Joe said.

"Nope. I'm kicking back and enjoying my downtime."

"You're bored out of your mind. Admit it."

He could tell from his friend's tone, from the expression on his face, that Joe didn't believe a word he said.

Joe never had been able to hide his feelings, not when they were kids, not now. Joe was worried sick, afraid any day Chris was going to eat his gun.

Thank God Joe's wife came out just then to see if they wanted more beer. He couldn't handle the scrutiny another second. He shouldn't have said anything at all. Stupid, but the fear festered inside, the fear, the horror, the panic in the dark hours before dawn. The time when old people, sick people, those with a feeble grasp on life died.

"How you guys doing?" Charlene asked. A pretty lady, a little chubby, auburn curly hair and big brown eyes. Joe had met her in high school and never looked at another woman.

"I'm okay," Joe said. "Chris?"

He tilted the bottle and drained the last of the warm brew. "Another would be great."

Funny, he couldn't stand sitting there with his friend's pitying gaze on him, but he'd asked for another beer to delay his departure. There must be some deeper meaning in that, but for the life of him, he couldn't figure what it was.

Then he almost laughed out loud at himself. *Hell,* sure he could figure it out. He wanted to confess, get the weight off his chest; he wanted forgiveness and absolution and understanding and all that crap. He wanted one person, one stinking person in this whole ugly world he did not have to pretend with. One person who knew what he was, what he was capable of doing. And then maybe he'd remember who he was.

Charlene came out with another bottle of Coors, the glass already sweating in the heat.

"Thanks," he said.

"Hot, isn't it?"

"Sure is."

"You guys don't want to come in? It's much cooler inside."

"Maybe later," Joe said.

"You two arc nuts," she said fondly, then trailed a hand along Joe's arm as she turned to go in the house.

She loved him. Even though, barring a miracle, he was confined to a wheelchair for life, she still loved him. Chris felt a moment of pure envy. Joanie had quit loving *him* just because he'd moved the family to Newark for the job with the task force. At the time the relocation had seemed like a great idea, a solid advancement in his career, and there was New York City, with all its culture and excitement, on their doorstep. Well, the big plan had backfired. She hated Newark. She hated what he'd become. And just when he had needed her the most, she'd taken his son and gone home to Denver. *Nothing like loyalty*, he thought bitterly.

"How's Rich?" Joe asked as if reading his mind.

"Fine. I promised to go watch his Little League game this afternoon." He shook his head. "How do kids play in this heat?"

"We did." Joe smiled.

"We were nuts, like Charlene said."

"Nah, we were just young. But, hey, weren't the summers in Newark worse than here? You know, humid."

"They were that. Unbearable. You walked from your air-conditioned house to your air-conditioned car to your air-conditioned office. Hell, even the wiseguys' dumpy Italian restaurants were air-conditioned." As he said it, a scene flashed unbidden in his brain, the smoky back room of a pizza parlor, the smell of dough and garlic and tomato sauce, a skinny, dark-haired man at a table, daintily eating pizza with knife and fork. An impassive bodyguard. And fear slicing through his guts. Stark terror. He'd almost given himself away.

"Hey, I said . . ."

"Huh?"

"I said, what's Joanie doing now?"

"Oh, yeah, Joanie. She's selling real estate, would you believe it?"

"I knew she got her license. Charlene, well, you know, they were friends."

Damn straight they were friends. All those years being the wives of cops, it bred a closeness stronger than family. Of course Charlene was still friends with Joanie, especially since Joanie was back in Denver.

"You probably knew about her new career before I did," Chris said lightly.

"Maybe Charlene did," Joe said carefully.

"Joanie likes it because she can schedule time for Rich."

"You bet."

A ticking silence fell between them. He played with the label of the beer bottle, scratching at a sodden corner with a fingernail.

"Charlene's looking for a job," Joe said. "Part time. Now that things have calmed down around here." What he meant was, now that he was out of rehab and able to manage by himself at home, now that she wasn't afraid every second he was going to die or that their health insurance had paid out the maximum and there was no workers' compensation because Joe had been off duty when the accident happened.

"She doesn't have to work, does she?" he asked.

"She wants to," Joe said. "And this fall I'm going to start taking computer classes. I've been sending out feelers. Talked to a guy at the Denver Building Department.

They might hire me. I sure could inspect buildings for handicap accessibility, right?"

That was Joe, always putting the best spin on things. "You sure could, buddy."

"It'll work out."

"It usually does." Yeah, things worked out, but with some help. And where was he going to find that help?

Joe adjusted his position in the wheelchair. "Have you thought about getting back on the force here? They need good men in the downtown office. It'd be a piece of cake compared to Newark. And, hell, you were the best. You can ask for burglary, something like that."

He almost choked on his beer. No force in the world would hire him. Not anymore. But he couldn't tell Joe why not, because then his carefully constructed house of cards would collapse. And he would die before he'd tell Joe or anyone where the money had really come from. "I don't think so. I'm considering another line of work."

"Oh yeah?"

"A car dealership maybe. Something like that."

"A car dealership? You and John Elway, right?"

"Why not?"

"It must be quite an investment," Joe said.

"Don't worry, I told you . . ."

"I know what you *told* me."

"Christ, Joe." He took a swig, then dangled the long-necked bottle between his thumb and index fingers. "Get off my ass."

"I'm still worried about you. Charlene is worried about you. Hell, Joanie's worried about you. And then you tell me this stuff about not knowing who you are."

He set the bottle down on the glass tabletop. "I shouldn't have said a word. Now you're going to hold it over my head and bug me. You're like a broken record, buddy. It's just *sometimes,* Joe. Doesn't everybody go through some bad shit in their lives?"

"Sure they do. But they don't go through it alone. They ask their friends and families for help."

Chris looked out at the tall redwood fence again. "I'm okay." He twisted his lips into a smile. "You know me, I exaggerate. Jesus, I tell you I had a nightmare, and you go weird on me."

"Is that so?"

"I'm the same guy. Look at me. I'm your old friend, Christopher Judge. I'm fine."

Lies, all lies. He lied well. It was his life's achievement.

Joe said nothing, but the sympathy in his dark eyes drove a dagger in Chris's chest.

How much did Joe suspect? If Joe came out with it right now, and asked Chris exactly where the money had come from, would he confess? Was he hoping and praying Joe knew what he'd done?

Fuck the system, he thought. The money would have gone into some corrupt cop's pocket. At least with Joe, the money was doing someone good.

He upended the beer and swallowed the last of it. In this weather you could drink three beers lickety-split and not even have to piss. The dry air sucked the moisture from you like a vacuum.

"Gotta run," he said. "Little League calls."

"You going to be okay?"

"What, me worry?" he said, their boyhood joke. From *Mad* magazine. Old issues they'd saved up to buy at a secondhand bookstore.

"Chris."

"What?"

Joe did something with his hand to one wheel of his chair, and he was close to Chris, their knees touching. *He* could feel Joe's knees, but Joe couldn't feel them. Chris pushed his chair back and stood.

"Cut the bullshit," Joe said, looking earnestly up at him.

He must get a crick, always having to crane his neck up like that, he thought. "Hey, buddy, I'm fine."

"Get some professional help."

He stepped back. "I don't need professional help."

Joe shook his head, his gaze holding Chris's. "You know you can call me anytime. You need to talk, whatever. I'm here."

"Likewise," he said, abruptly chipper and cocky and lying better than ever.

His car was a furnace. He had to open the windows so he could breathe until the air-conditioning kicked in. He sucked in hot air, his hands slippery on the wheel, his armpits damp, back sticking to the seat. Shit, shit, shit. Damn Joe and damn Charlene. Damn Joanie, the new real estate whiz kid, damn everyone.

He headed to the park where his son, Richard, had his Little League games. He fought the sinking sensation he got when he knew his act wasn't good enough. Disillusionment pinioned him, despair impaled him. He was empty. No faith in anything or anyone. No direction in his life. He'd betrayed his oath, lost himself in the deadly maze of undercover work. Maybe he really was the criminal he'd pretended to be all that time. Maybe there was no Chris Judge left in him, and it wasn't an act at all.

He parked near the chain-link fence of the Little League field, got out, took a deep breath of dust-dry, hot air, pushed his dark glasses up on his nose. The sun was beginning to descend over the mountains to the west, but the cool evening would be a long time coming. The trees hung dusty and dispirited; the grass was worn. But dozens of little boys in matching T-shirts and helmets ran around the bases, yelling, sliding, sweaty, and filthy before the game even started. Mothers in shorts and tank tops and sun visors watched and whistled from the bleachers, even a few fathers, although most men were still at work at this hour.

Not him, of course.

From across the field he spotted Rich, waved to make sure his son knew he was there, then watched as the boy raced toward him. Ten years old, tall and wiry for his age, with the same unruly light brown hair and hazel eyes as his father, the wide mouth and smooth features of his mother.

"Hi, Dad," he said, panting.

"Hi, Rich. What position you playing? Third base?"

"Shortstop."

"Excellent."

"Coach wants to try me there. He says I have quick hands and eyes."

"That's great."

"I'm not such a great hitter, though."

"Practice is all it takes."

"But you weren't a good hitter, either, you told me."

"That's true. I was a lousy batter. Never could get the weight shift down."

"I have to go now. Warm up."

"Sure, go on, champ."

Rich grinned, an instantaneous glimpse of his mother, then he ran back to his position in the field.

Joanie arrived a few minutes after the game had started. Incongruous in a skirt of pale gray, a white silk short-sleeved blouse, the jacket of her business suit obviously left in her car. She'd come from work.

"Hello," she said. "I'm glad you could make it."

"I said I'd be here. I told Rich I would."

"Of course."

She looked lovely, serene and blond, her hair pulled back into a bun, a high clear brow and a mobile mouth.

"You think I'd lie to him?" he asked, bristling.

"No, no."

"All right."

They sat together to watch their son play ball. They could still have been married; they could still have been in love. But they weren't.

They spoke of inconsequential matters, the closing she'd just come from. How well Joe and Charlene were doing. And their kids, Toby and Beth. Joanie never asked him the questions Joe had asked, never impinged on his independence, never wanted to know when he was going to look for work. He knew she felt that she'd given up those privileges when she'd packed up and left. Which was good.

He smiled and he cheered Rich's spectacular play that resulted in a third out. He patted his son on the back after the game, praised him, politely refused to go to McDonald's for dinner with the team. Acted just like a regular father, divorced, but so what? There were lots of divorced fathers around.

He left Rich and Joanie to walk across the field to where his car was parked. A carefree wave, an insouciant grin.

He drove away, turned right because it was easier, although his apartment was to the left. But it didn't matter, he was in no rush to go home.

He'd carried it off. He knew he had. He always knew

when his performance had been seamless. He drove, heading toward the setting sun, carried along like flotsam in a river of traffic. No one would know, to look at him, an ordinary guy, average size, average coloring, average everything. No one would know that inside he was terrified he'd never see his son again.

He drove, and he reacted automatically, breaking, turning, accelerating. Into the fiery eye of the sun, wondering how he'd find the guts to go on.

Or if he even wanted to.

TWO

Ashley Marin's life was a tangle of obligations. She was on summer vacation from her job as a math teacher at Aspen High School. And while most of her colleagues looked forward to the three-month hiatus, time for fun, for family, for educational travels, for kicking back and relaxing, Ashley had even less time than usual.

She had a house full of people: her daughter, Lauren, rebellious and sulky, a normal fifteen-year-old. Pauline, her mother, widowed and in the early stages of Alzheimer's disease, stubborn and difficult. She refused to go into a nursing home, didn't qualify for assisted living. Luckily, Pauline had sold her own house and there was enough money to pay for a live-in couple to care for her. *Lucky,* Ashley thought. *Hah.*

"I want to know what for dinner," Luda Rostov demanded that summer afternoon.

"Whatever you want," Ashley said reasonably.

"You tell me."

"Um, how about spaghetti? Something easy. And a salad."

The caretaker muttered in her native Russian tongue. "What?"

"Spaghetti. Okay," Luda said.

Ashley breathed a sigh of relief. The woman could be difficult. Sassy. *This not way things done in old country* lurked unspoken behind every grimace, every muttered imprecation. Luda was mousy blond, with a pinched face, rawboned, as if she'd starved back in Russia and couldn't put weight on no matter how much she ate now.

Her husband, Vladimir, was easier to get along with, very patient with her mother, Pauline. A big man, barrel-chested, very Slavic in appearance. He'd been a hospital orderly in Moscow, and Ashley was fortunate to have found him. But then, fortunate was a relative term.

Life was indeed complicated. Lauren and Pauline drove her crazy. Luda did, too. Vladimir was okay, but he was *there* constantly. She had no privacy, no quiet time. Her place was crowded, not that it was a very big house to begin with, and she was always being thrown curveballs—not enough in the refrigerator, her check-book mislaid by Pauline, her best silk blouse "borrowed" by Lauren and stained, bills to pay, a roof that she knew would leak again come winter, a new math syllabus to prepare for fall.

And her ex-husband, Robert, wealthy, with his young trophy wife, Elaine, a new baby, his superior manner and bulldozing technique, relentlessly pushing for custody of Lauren.

Well, he wouldn't get her. *Over my dead body,* Ashley had thought more than once. She had said it right to Robert's face, too.

Robert owed her two months of child support. God,

he was a tightwad. He could easily afford it, but he liked to keep Ashley in his debt, keep her off balance, the poor relation.

"Now, if Lauren lived with *us,*" he said, "you wouldn't have to keep reminding me to pay you. Wouldn't it be simpler, Ashley? And Elaine would *love* to have her."

Needling, tormenting her, as deliberate and tenacious as Chinese water torture.

It was a warm afternoon, not hot—it rarely got hot at 8,000 feet in the Rockies. Off to the west, wreathing Mt. Sopris, clouds amassed; perhaps there would be a thunderstorm later in the day. Although sometimes the clouds built and hovered and growled, then miraculously dissipated so that the evening was clear and cool and fresh, the stars diamond bright.

Lauren was at her friend Hayley's house that afternoon. The girls had gone to play tennis in the morning, then Hayley's mother had kindly invited Lauren to stay.

One down.

Pauline was taking a nap.

In the kitchen Luda rattled pots and dishes. *I'm here,* the noise said. *I'm working hard.* Vladimir had retired to his side of the duplex. Three more taken care of.

The house Ashley lived in with her menagerie was the only thing she'd gotten in the divorce settlement. On paper it was worth close to a million dollars, maybe more, due to the outrageous real estate market in Aspen. In truth, it was thirty years old, shoddily built, small and crowded. What was known as a bulldoze job. The value lay in the land, the quarter-acre plot of land Robert had purchased years ago as an investment.

The house was a Pan-abode, a cheap, fake-log style that had been popular in mountain communities in the sixties and seventies. Years ago it had been converted into a duplex, three bedrooms on her side, two on the Rostov's side. And a detached garage, built later than the house, with a small apartment over it, a "bandit" unit. So-called because Aspen zoning rarely allowed rental units in residential neighborhoods. The bandit unit was presently for rent, advertised in the *Aspen Times,* and she hoped and prayed some nice young person would move in and provide her with extra cash. Of course, that would mean an addition to the Marin menagerie.

She took the book she'd been reading off the cluttered coffee table in the living room and slunk away to her bedroom, the only retreat available to her. She'd painted the original dark brown interior logs of the Pan-abode white, to lighten up the place, hung pictures and brightly colored photographical lithographs of Navajo woven rugs, which were sold by a local entrepreneur.

She'd taken a few of her favorite possessions from Robert's pretentious starter castle when they'd divorced: a fine Navajo rug for the living room, a couple of pieces of Pueblo pottery, two marvelous Remington photographs and three expensive goose-down comforters, one for each bedroom in her cramped new digs.

Her bedroom. Muted colors, relaxing, a big window overlooking the backyard. The window was essential. No curtains or blinds—no one could see in—it had sections that swung open. And she kept it open all the time, even in the winter.

She took a deep breath, climbed onto her bed, because the only chair in the room was spindly and uncomfortable, and lay back against the piled-up pillows.

Alone at last.

Her book was a family saga, triumph and tragedy,

easy to start and then put aside. She opened it and began
to read, jerked as her eyes closed and her head sagged.
God, she was tired. Just a few minutes . . . She glanced
at the window, reassuring herself. Yes, it was open, and
outside aspen leaves rustled in a slight breeze, robins
clucked, chickadees whistled, magpies chattered. A dog
barked. Her next-door neighbor Jay was a car mechanic.
A Jewish mechanic. She could hear him hand-throttling
a car engine in his dusty front yard. Jay did nothing to
hide his illegal home business; he merely tiptoed around
county regulations.

"Just helping some friends out with their car troubles," he'd say amiably.

The neighborhood Ashley lived in was a small, out-
of-the-way enclave of older houses. It was hard to find,
isolated yet less than a mile from Aspen's Main Street,
nestled in the aspen and cottonwood trees at the base of
Smuggler Mountain. Hidden, really. You'd never know
it was there unless you followed the winding, potholed
private road.

The county didn't plow the road in winter; Jay used
his own pickup to clear the snow. Never charged a cent.
They were all good neighbors. There was a ski instructor
and his wife. Jay and his dog and the dozens of cars that
constantly arrived limping at his doorstep. On the far
side of Jay was a longtime couple, children grown and
gone, who owned one of the more popular local eateries.
People like that. Not rich, not second homeowners, not
here on vacation. Ordinary people, the lifeblood of the
community, the ones who ran Aspen when the tourists
were gone.

She left her bedroom door ajar, a habit now. The door
and the window. So she could get out if she became
desperate.

She was claustrophobic, diagnosed, signed, sealed and delivered. A textbook case. She also suffered from post-traumatic stress disorder. She hadn't been born that way, hadn't even known what the terms meant until she was sixteen years old. She'd worked with a therapist for years, knew all the definitions of her condition.

> *Exposure of the focus stimulus almost invariably provokes an immediate anxiety response. . . . The person recognizes that the fear is excessive or unreasonable. . . . The phobic situation is avoided or else endured with intense anxiety or distress. . . . The avoidance or anxiety anticipation in the fear situation interferes significantly with the person's normal routine.*

The awful panic attacks were better now, not as frequent, not as debilitating. She figured her phobia was a burden she had to live with, a chronic but mostly controllable disease like arthritis or ulcers or asthma. People led full, satisfying lives with these ailments, and she could, too.

Mostly this was true—she'd gotten out of the hospital, evaded the media hype that had surrounded her that long-ago summer, returned to her parents, finished high school. She'd gone to college at the University of Arizona, in Tucson, because she'd sought the wide-open spaces, the big sky, a large part of existence there lived in the open air.

And she'd found she was an orderly person, literal-minded and logical, seeking the security of routine. Not for her the ambiguities of literary analysis or historical movements.

Mathematics. The clear, straightforward beauty of

equations and geometrical proofs. She was considered a bit strange, a nerd, a girl studying math. Almost as bad as if she'd chosen engineering. But the study of numbers gave her a kind of peace.

She'd returned to her hometown of Aspen, met Robert, barely had time to catch her breath before she'd been married and pregnant with Lauren.

She rested there on her bed, feeling the faint summer breeze stir the fine hairs on her forehead, hearing the birds—a steller's jay now, raucous and loud, the clang of a tool on metal—Jay working.

She guessed Robert had swept her off her feet. Older and utterly in control of his life. She guessed that's what had attracted her, sucked her in. An insecure kid like her, fair game for Robert Marin, just starting his own software company. Talking mergers and IPOs and user-friendly software, flying back and forth between Aspen and Silicon Valley. Older than Ashley, but good-looking. Blond and clean-cut.

What had he seen in her? A young, naive girl with a phobia. A girl whose family was considered valley locals, quite middle-class, really, in a town crammed full of the elite. Her father had been a ski bum in the early sixties, her mother a vacationing student from the University of Denver, who'd met the ski bum turned ski instructor and been married within a few months. Luckily Ken and Pauline Lacouter had enough good sense and foresight to purchase a century-old dilapidated clapboard house in the heart of town. Purchased it for a song and dance forty years ago and then watched the property value skyrocket.

Nevertheless, Robert still considered Ashley of questionable stock. He had thought her easy to mold into the kind of Barbie doll he required to validate his success.

And when she had no longer fit the mold, he'd dumped her. Even tried to use her claustrophobia as grounds for gaining custody of Lauren. Thank God that hadn't worked.

Yet.

She put her book aside and rested her head on the pillows. What she craved was peace and quiet and her daughter's love and respect. Order and harmony. She kept thinking about all these years she'd hung on to the hope that her phobia would be cured if her life were peaceful enough. And yet she'd somehow contrived to create a fragmented, stressful existence for herself, filled with eccentric needy people and a rebellious daughter.

Sometimes she imagined she was in the abandoned mine again, in the dark and clammy blackness. She'd start awake in the middle of the night, feeling the rock walls closing in on her. Her mouth dry, her heart pounding, unable to catch her breath. Pure panic. But she'd learned to calm herself with the phrase whispered over and over: "So what? It's a dream. It's not real. So what?"

It was true, as her therapist had assured her, that the attacks would come less often. She'd learned to handle them: certain mental stratagems, breathing exercises, yoga, imaging. Robert had so disliked her nightmares he'd finally moved into another bedroom. Lauren referred to her attacks as freaking out. As in, "Mom's freaking out again." Accompanied by eyes rolling in scorn. Her mother turned defensive and mean, because she was unable to help her daughter, never had been able to help her after the kidnapping, and possessed no tools whatsoever with which to handle her child's suffering.

"God, Ashley," her mother would say. "Your generation is so self-indulgent. Names for every tic and every pain. In my day we didn't talk about those things. We just went on." As if scolding would cure her daughter.

But there was in Ashley a wellspring of unquenchable optimism—things would get better. Her phobia would recede, her mother would turn nicer, her daughter would outgrow rebellion, Robert would give up trying to get custody of Lauren, her most promising student at school would apply and be accepted by Harvard or Yale, the garage apartment would be rented.

She slept, a slim, girlish figure on the earth-tone bedspread, dark eyes closed, dark hair spread on a taupe-and-peach pillow, an innocent amid chaos, uncorrupted by her kidnapping ordeal twenty years before, by divorce and money problems and recurring panic attacks. She slept.

Until the room grew close and hot, and the dream crept out of the depths of her subconscious, reenacting the horror of that long-ago time. It was dark. She couldn't see anything, could only hear water dripping, smell the rock and damp. Shivering, terrified, left alone to die. The walls of the mine moving soundlessly, closing in on her. Crushing her. Buried alive. She was panting, her heart racing, fear ate at her. She curled into a ball to stave off the inevitability of being crushed. She couldn't breathe, she couldn't . . .

Her body convulsed into wakefulness. Her book slid and fell onto the floor with a sharp slap. She sucked in a deep lungful of air, as if she were drowning, sat bolt upright.

Panic, familiar but no less horrifying. "So what," she whispered. "It was a dream. So what."

She stood, shaky. The door. The door was shut. Who . . . ?

She pushed it open and swiftly crossed the living room to the front door. Outside, standing on the porch, gulping in air. Thank God no one had witnessed her headlong rush to freedom. Although, of course, they'd all seen it before.

The panic subsided; she knew it would. It always did, and she had to hang on to that. She stood there, face raised to the afternoon breeze, and sanity returned like cool water being poured into a glass.

What time was it? How long had she slept? Who had closed the goddamn door?

She went back inside. Her mother was sitting in her favorite armchair reading. Looking normal as anything despite the fact that she'd been reading the same page for a month. And Luda was banging around in the kitchen, speaking to Vladimir in Russian. Ashley always wondered what they said, but when she asked they both looked at her with blank and icy suspicion.

"Hi, Mom, did you have a good nap?" Ashley asked.

Pauline looked up from her book. "Oh yes, fine." She held the paperback up, one finger marking the page she'd been on. "You know, I think I read this before, but I can't remember how it ends."

"Some books are worth reading more than once."

"That's the beauty of not being able to remember. Everything is new," Pauline said sarcastically.

"Oh, Mom."

"Give me a few years, and I'll be back to *Winnie the Pooh*, and loving every word. That is, if I remember how to read."

There was no magic pill for what ailed Pauline. Certainly the doctors had tried every Alzheimer's remedy as soon as it received FDA approval. As yet nothing had helped. One minute she was fully rational and in charge of her thoughts. The next, she'd subside into memory lapses that caused her to alternate between paranoia, fear

and anger. It seemed as if she'd remember an incident
from thirty years ago better than she recalled the events
of yesterday. Other times she was simply confused about
everything.

"Tell your father dinner is on the table," she'd said
just last Monday. Ken Lacouter had died eight years ago.

Then Pauline would be her old self. "I miss your father so much," she'd say, and she'd reminisce about his
ski instructor days on Aspen Mountain.

Today, right now, she was apparently her old self. "I
saw you running out of the house," she said slyly.

"Um," Ashley said.

"Another one of your dreams?"

"Um." She didn't want to discuss it.

Her mother crossed one leg over the other. Trim an-
kles and calves, still shapely at sixty-eight, the cruelest
irony. Her body could last thirty years more, but her
brain probably wouldn't. "Maybe one of these days I'll
forget why you have your attacks," she said in a decep-
tively pleasant tone. "Wouldn't that be nice?"

"Mom."

"Okay, okay."

"Did you happen to close my bedroom door?" she
asked casually.

"Who, me? Goodness, no. I know better than that."

Ashley went into the kitchen. Luda was stirring a big
pot of bubbling tomato sauce.

"Hi," Ashley said, feeling, as always, an intruder in
her own house.

"Your mother very good this afternoon," Vladimir
said. He was eating pickled herring out of a jar. The
scent of fish, the sharp tang of vinegar mixed with garlic
and tomatoes.

"That's good," she said. "Um, Luda, did you close my bedroom door?"

Luda turned from the stove. "Yes, I close it."

"Why?"

"Close everything, hot air, like sauna, good for you. I would have closed window, too, but I would wake you up."

"Luda, I've asked you"—she drew a breath—"I've asked you never to close my door. You know that."

"Humph. I forget."

Like hell she forgot. "Please don't do it again. You know I'm claustrophobic."

"Yes." Luda turned back to the stove.

Ashley sighed. The woman had some bizarre beliefs, Russian peasant suspicions. Open windows and doors let in dangerous vapors and werewolves.

Shortly after four o'clock, Ashley reminded Vladimir he was supposed to pick Lauren up at Hayley's house at five, across town in an area called Pitkin Green, an upscale neighborhood at the foot of Red Mountain. Lauren couldn't drive yet, but she'd be able to get her permit in a couple of months. She was going to sign up for Drivers Ed in the fall, and she'd take her driver's test in the spring when she turned sixteen. Having a license would certainly make things easier. On the other hand, Ashley only had one car, an older Jeep Cherokee that Jay kept running. Maybe Robert would buy Lauren a car. Did she dare suggest it? Perhaps the idea should come from Lauren. Yes.

At six-fifteen Vladimir arrived back and parked in front of the house. *What in the devil had taken him so long?* Ashley registered. He came in through the front door, his brow furrowed.

"Where's Lauren?" she asked.

"She not there."

"What?"

"She not with Hayley."

"Well, where is she?"

He shrugged heavy shoulders. "No one know. Maybe she taking bus home?"

"But she's not here, is she?"

"No."

"Oh, for God's sake, where did that kid go now?"

"Mrs. Hodges upset." That was Hayley's mother. "She say to call her."

She phoned Betty Hodges, angry. *As if I don't have enough problems.*

"Ashley? Oh dear, I'm so sorry. I reminded Lauren of the time. It was a few minutes before five. She called okay, and I heard the girls giggling, then the front door banged shut. I assumed Lauren walked out to the end of the drive."

"She's usually good about the time, I know, but . . ."

"It must have been five-fifteen, maybe later, when your man beeped in front of the house. I sent Hayley out, and they both came back in and that's when I found out Vlad . . . Oh, what's his name?"

"Vladimir."

"Yes, Vladimir had been waiting all that time on the road. I can only think Lauren walked out and caught the bus downtown. You know the Hunter Creek bus runs every fifteen minutes, and . . ."

"Yes, I know. Oh, damn Lauren. She knows better than that."

"She hasn't even phoned?"

"No. I don't suppose she said anything about going downtown to Hayley?"

"Of course I asked Hayley first thing, but I'll ask her again."

Ashley waited then while Betty cocked her hand over the mouthpiece and called out to her daughter. When Betty came back on, she said, "Hayley swears up and down Lauren said she was meeting Vladimir and going home."

"Thanks, Betty."

"Let me know, okay, Ashley?"

Damn Lauren. She paced the living room, thinking.

"Teenagers," her mother remarked.

"This isn't like Lauren, though, Mom."

Pauline went back to her book, unruffled. Ashley found Vladimir in the kitchen.

"Lauren here?" he asked.

"Not yet. Vladimir, are you sure you were there to meet her on time? Mrs. Hodges says Lauren was outside just before five."

"I stop for gas, like you say earlier."

"Yes, right, I did."

"But I wasn't late. Lauren just not there."

"I don't know how you missed her on the road," she reflected out loud. Then she had a thought. Maybe Lauren hadn't waited for Vladimir on the road. Maybe she walked up that footpath instead and . . .

The kid went to her father's house. The problem was Ashley absolutely could not call and ask, because that would give Robert more ammunition to use against her. *See,* he'd say, *this woman is an unfit mother, loses her child, doesn't even know where she is.*

Okay, so she'd call but not exactly ask if Lauren was there.

She dialed the number she knew so well, the house above Pitkin Green on Red Mountain that she'd decorated with loving care, the house that the new wife had ripped apart and redone, all in super modernistic stainless steel and glass and commercial carpet and marble in the foyer. *Italian* marble.

"Hello?"

"Oh, hi, Elaine. This is Ashley."

"How are you, Ashley?" Elaine gushed.

"Fine. Hey, I was just wondering, um, I forgot if Lauren was having dinner with you or me tonight?"

"Well, certainly not us, because we're going to that benefit at Harris Hall."

"Oh, right, of course. How could I forget that? It's just that Luda wasn't sure, you know."

"That Luda," Elaine said sweetly.

"Okay, thanks."

"How *is* Lauren?"

"Oh, she's fine. Just fine. Thanks, Elaine."

She wasn't really worried about Lauren. Nothing much could happen to kids in Aspen. Crime was rare—mostly traffic infractions, disorderly drunks in the bars, plenty of white-collar crime like embezzling. But kids could come and go as they pleased, walking or riding the free buses or bicycling. It was still a small town, and you rarely went anywhere without running into a friend.

So, she wasn't concerned. But she *was* angry. Lauren knew better than to pull a stunt like this. She was rebellious, yes, and smart mouthed, fighting for independence from her mother with every hormonally charged cell in her body. Ashley remembered what that felt like, sure she did. Although her adolescence had been cut short, beheaded, shot in the heart. But still, she remembered.

Where had the girl gone?

She leaned down and tapped Pauline on the shoulder,

getting her full attention. "Mom, I'm going downtown to look for Lauren. I'll take my cell phone. If she calls or comes home, phone me. You know my cell phone number?"

"Yes, dear. It's written on the phone book cover if I forget."

"Okay. And tell her she's in deep caca for this one."

Ashley repeated the directions to the Rostovs.

"So dinner be late?" Luda frowned and wiped her hands on a towel.

"You and Mom can eat. Don't wait for me or Lauren."

She turned the car around to head out the private road, jockeying carefully so as not to hit Jay's collection of indisposed vehicles. She grasped the wheel tightly, her knuckles white, her mouth a straight line. Damn kid.

She drove down Main Street, scanning the sidewalks. Plenty of teenagers among the throngs crowding the town, but no Lauren. Up Mill Street to where the brick-paved pedestrian malls began. She finally found a parking place and walked back to the center of town, looking at every person, checking, discarding. There were groups of teenagers, as usual, near the Paradise Bakery cookie shop, girls flush with their new figures, in shorts or tight jeans and tank tops. Boys, awkwardly adolescent, in baggy-kneed pants and T-shirts. Tourists milled, carrying bags that read Banana Republic and Pitkin County Dry Goods and Manrico Cashmere. Locals going to their night jobs as waiters and bartenders. Students from the Aspen Music Festival playing a Dvorak string quartet, the notes sweet as honey on the early evening air.

No Lauren.

Well, this had been a dumb idea. Lauren could be anywhere, at another friend's house, in a store idly perusing clothes. Anywhere.

So Ashley drove home empty-handed. Still angry but beginning to feel the stirrings of uneasiness. No one from the house had called on her cell phone, so Lauren wasn't home yet. Where was she?

She got back at seven-thirty. The sun was low in the west, its rays stretching along the valley floor, sending long shadows across the driveway and the house. The air was cool, the way it always got in the mountains, no matter how hot the day had been. The clouds were gone.

"No Lauren, huh?" Pauline said. She was watching television.

"No."

"Well, she didn't call and she didn't come home. That little scamp."

"Boy, is she going to get it when she gets home," Ashley said.

"Why don't you sit down and eat your dinner?"

"Later. I think I better make some phone calls."

"The police?"

Ashley whirled on her mother. "Good God, no, not the police. What are you thinking, Mom?"

She called every one of her daughter's friends that she could think of. Embarrassed, growing more uneasy as each call failed to turn up her child.

The phone rang right after she hung up from the last call, and her heart beat like a wild thing. *Lauren,* she thought, *let it be Lauren.*

"Oh, Ashley, I was worried, and I wondered if . . ."

"Betty?"

"Did Lauren come home yet?"

"No, she hasn't."

"Oh, God, I should have told her to stay right in the house till her ride got here."

"It's not your fault."

"I feel so awful," Betty was saying.

"It's all right, Betty. How could you know she'd pull this?"

"Please, call me when you find her. I'm so upset."

So am I, Ashley thought.

It grew dark. There was no one else to call, nothing to do. She couldn't eat, even though her stomach growled. Couldn't think, couldn't stop her heart from beating a heavy cadence.

Her anger bled away, replaced by apprehension. Where was Lauren? She'd gone over every word they had said to each other that morning, searching for a clue. Had her daughter been mad? Had Ashley set her off unknowingly with an innocent remark?

She paced, watching the phone as if it were a poisonous snake. *Ring, damn you.*

The worst thing, the most awful, frightening thing, was that she herself had disappeared one day just like this. Her mother had gone through precisely the same torture, the fear and worry and not knowing. She'd never before thought of her ordeal from her mother's point of view. No, always her own. And now *she* was the mother, and her little girl had disappeared.

But, of course, the situation was entirely different. There was no comparison. Lauren hadn't been kidnapped. That simply didn't happen.

At nine-thirty, Luda and Vladimir stole quietly to their side of the duplex. Pauline kept glancing at her, on the verge of saying something but held silent by the expression on her daughter's face.

"Well," she finally said, "I'm going to bed, Ashley."

"Okay, Mom."

"You should go to bed, too."

"I'll wait for Lauren."

"Isn't she already in bed?"

"No, Mom. You remember. She was at Hayley's."

"Oh, yes, of course. Then you went to town to pick her up. Yes, I remember now."

"Goodnight, Mom."

Then it was ten o'clock, dark out, and still she sat on the couch, or paced the living room floor, watching the phone, jumping at every sound, every creak of the house, the water rushing through pipes in the bathrooms.

Where was Lauren?

Should she call the police? *Should* she? But she knew the police would only tell her a person was not considered missing for twenty-four hours. Besides, she had a deep and undying distrust, a contempt for the authorities. They hadn't helped *her,* had they? No, she would not call them.

Robert? No, *no.* Never. He'd blame her, he'd have her declared unfit, he'd take Lauren from her in a heartbeat.

She sat again and then she paced again and then she went outside and stood there, hugging herself, listening to the night as if the darkness could tell her where her daughter was.

From far off she heard the warbling call of a coyote, then an answering wail from across the valley. She shivered and went inside.

Eleven, eleven-thirty. Where was her daughter?

Just before midnight her cell phone rang. She froze and her heart contracted and she snatched at the thing, almost dropping it.

"Lauren?" she said into the receiver.

"Well, no, it isn't your kid, but she's here. Oh yes, she is, *Ash-lee,*" a voice said.

For an endless moment she stood in her silent living

room gripping the phone, her mind paralyzed. Then sudden horror ripped through her, and she sank to the floor, still holding the phone, crushing it, her fingers hurting. Huddled on the floor. She knew that voice.

THREE

He sat in the dark in a chair, fully dressed, unable to sleep even though it was past two in the morning. Powerless to stop the scenes from replaying in his mind, sucked down by memories, he turned his old service revolver slowly over and over in his hands.

Who was he? A loser, a corrupt ex-cop? A friend, a father, an ex-husband? Johnny, the petty criminal hanging around the fringes of the mob? An undercover cop who was so good at his job he'd lost his way?

Which man was he?

He'd been exceptionally adept at undercover work. Something about him . . . He was of average height, his features well contoured, and he often caught women's eyes, handsome, a bit wicked-looking when he was in his cocky mode. But if he let his expression go lax, his features slid into undistinguished mediocrity. He had light brown hair, hazel eyes that could appear amiable or intense, a perpetual five o'clock shadow on a jaw that could be slack or pugnacious.

It wasn't just his looks, though. His face was an asset, but more important was an inborn talent—a pliant personality. He could *be* Johnny Tutello. He truly *was* Sal's friend.

But, he'd discovered, there had to be some truth in a persona if it was to be convincing, some congruity between mask and man. Undercover work made him aware of his alternate selves, and one of those alternates had gone wrong.

He sat there, sweating and suffused with self-pity, and recalled an incident from the past, one that had scared the shit out of him. The beginning of the end?

He'd finally been invited to an important meeting, trusted enough to attend, although relegated to an insignificant position.

"Just listen," Sal Damato had said to him. "Just shut your trap and be nice and polite and listen." Sal, his best friend in the organization, his mentor, the one he'd betrayed more than anyone else.

"Okay," he'd replied. "Hey, fine, I'm honored."

The Long Island and Manhattan family heads were gathering in Newark for a summit. A big deal. So Chris's task force leader wanted it on tape. Insisted.

His leader was a spit-and-polish FBI agent, a man who never sweated, never had a hair out of place. Chris had once seen him standing in front of headquarters in a nor'easter, no hat, coat or umbrella, and the slashing rain had neither dampened his gray suit nor blown a hair astray.

Special Agent in Charge Maxwell Hearn. Not Max. Never Max.

The North Jersey Task Force was made up of five

squads, each consisting of two Newark cops, two DEA agents, one state trooper and one Feebie. Chris had been one of the cops in Squad Two, the undercover man. It had taken him more than a year to ingratiate himself with Sal and a couple of other wiseguys, but he'd done it. He was in.

Max had made him wear a wire for the big meeting. He'd never worn one before—too dangerous—but this time he went to the office and let them tape the wire to his torso, showed him how it worked, assured him they'd be down the block in a Bell Atlantic van listening, recording every word the godfathers said.

He sat there alone in his featureless apartment in Denver and he pumped sweat, and he felt the barrel of his gun, the heft of the weapon, the glistening cool oiliness of the metal, and he was just as scared as he had been that night.

Because for the first time ever in his months with Sal and the mobsters in Newark, they were frisking every man who went into the meeting room, the head office of New Jersey Waste Solutions.

"It's 'cause the big boys are coming," Sal had told him, almost apologetically.

"I'm not letting those assholes put their hands on me."

"Sorry, Johnny"—that was his undercover name, Johnny Tutello—"but you got to."

He'd sweated then. Christ, they'd find the wire and off him on the spot, stuff his still-warm corpse into the trunk of one of their Cadillacs and dump him in the Jersey Pine Barrens. Okay, okay, he'd thought, desperately casting about for a solution.

"Come on, Johnny," Sal had said, getting impatient.

What should he do? Make an excuse and leave? Brazen his way through in the hope no one would find the wire?

Right ahead of him was the doorway to the office, two bodyguards waiting for him. Inside lay the goal of the North Jersey Task Force, all the men and hours and planning. . . .

"Fuck, Sal, listen, I just got a terrible bellyache. I gotta go to the can." He'd faked doubling over, but the sweat on his face was genuine.

"Hell of a time, Johnny."

"Sorry, I really gotta go."

In the cramped and foul bathroom, he'd sat on the toilet seat, head in his hands, breathing hard, sick, really sick. Tears squeezed out of his eyes, and he stood, pulled his shirt up, ripped the wire off, hurting, pulling out hairs. Ripped it off, wadded it up and stuck it to the bottom of the toilet tank.

Rinsed his face, slicked back his mussed hair with shaking hands, tucked his shirt in and went out to be frisked and stand silently against the wall of the office while the big guys talked about drugs and extortion and payoffs.

He sat in his apartment, remembering. Then, disturbing the quiet, shrilling, interrupting his reverie, his phone rang. The sound seemed to come from an immense distance, and at first he didn't realize what it was. Then a small, still-rational part of his brain tested the sound, decided on its origin and posed the questions: What the fuck? A phone call at 2 A.M.?

But it didn't matter. He had more important things to think about than a phone call. He'd let his machine pick up. He stroked the grip of his revolver—a beautiful and powerful tool that could dispense oblivion with efficiency and impartiality.

The clip was in and he'd pumped a round into the chamber. He was ready. All he had to do was make the final decision, the one Joe Garcia was afraid he'd make. So easy, one small twitch, and his suffering was over. Then it wouldn't matter who he really was.

The ringing continued, three, four, five times. Then a click and the machine took over.

Just pull the damn trigger. Why wait? Did he truly think things were going to get better?

His own voice, tinny and alien: "You have reached Chris Judge's number. You know what to do."

Hell, he didn't care who it was. Some doofus, probably a wrong number, intruding on the low point of his life. Or maybe the low point had been when he took the drug money.

Whatever.

He turned the gun barrel around and stared down into its unblinking black eye.

The voice pulled at his consciousness—a female—talking. Scared, he registered. Near tears. Panicky. *Shit.*

"Chris, are you there? I know it's late. I'm so sorry. Please, I have to talk to you. Please, Chris, are you there?"

He felt as if he'd been bludgeoned, shot through the heart with an arrow. *That voice.* He knew that voice. He'd know it if a hundred years had passed, a thousand. It was emblazoned on his brain.

Ashley Lacouter.

He forced himself to rise from the chair, stiff, shaky, his muscles complaining. He set the revolver down very carefully on the coffee table and moved toward the phone. Words were still emerging from the answering machine, disembodied, filling the room with an emotion that was achingly familiar to him.

Fear.

". . . Chris, I got your number from Information, and I didn't know what else to do. It's my daughter, Lauren. She's been kidnapped. Oh God, Chris . . . ?"

His hand reached out and his fingers closed around the receiver. Somewhere in his head he knew that picking up the phone would change the direction of his life. It would be some kind of turning point, as his encounter with Ashley had altered the direction of his life twenty years before.

But he lifted the receiver from its cradle anyway, lifted it up to his ear, heard the machine click off, said, "Hello, Ashley," but only a croak emerged, and he had to clear his throat and try again.

"Chris, Chris, is that you?"

"Yes, it's me."

"Oh, thank God," she cried. "Chris, I was afraid you weren't there or . . . or . . ."

"I'm here."

"I didn't know what else to do. I'm sorry . . . did I get you up?"

"Don't worry about it."

"Oh . . . oh, I . . ."

"What's this about your daughter?"

"Lauren, she's fifteen, and today . . ."

He didn't hear the rest; he thought: a fifteen-year-old daughter. My God, how could that be? Ashley's only . . . but no, that had been years ago, and he knew she'd married. That rich software mogul Robert Marin. Sure, he knew that, but he didn't know she had . . .

"Chris?"

"Yeah, uh, say again?"

"Lauren, she disappeared this afternoon, and I

thought, I figured it was a teenage prank, she'd be home sooner or later, and I waited . . ."

"Um, hold on. Where are you calling from?"

"Aspen. I still live in Aspen."

"Okay, so your . . . Lauren didn't come home."

"I waited. Since six this evening, no, yesterday evening. And then"—he heard a sob—"I got a phone call. Oh, Chris, a man, he said he had Lauren."

"When?"

"The call? Around midnight. He said . . . he said, oh God, he said he had her and no one would ever find her and he'd call back . . ."

"Money? A ransom?"

"No, no, nothing like that. But . . . Chris, his voice. I know his voice."

He straightened, his fingers tight on the phone.

"I'm sure it was Davey Potts."

"Jesus."

Davey Potts. The name came roaring out of the past, a punch in the solar plexus. One of the men who'd abducted Ashley twenty years ago. But he was in prison. . . .

"Okay, Ashley, calm down. Potts is in prison."

"No, Chris, he was released."

"You're sure?"

"Yes, I'm sure. Look, I'll tell you everything, but he's got Lauren, and I . . . Chris, can you help me find her?"

"Me?"

"Can you do it? Can you take time off, whatever, come up here? Chris, I have to find Lauren."

"I can't help you, Ashley. Call the police. They'll bring in the FBI if it's a kidnapping."

"*No.* He said he'd . . . kill her, he'd know if I called the cops, and he'd . . ."

"Ashley . . ."

"But it's more than his threat. You know what happened last time. The police, the sheriff, the FBI. The goddamn *army* couldn't help me."

He wanted to tell her he was a loser, a disgraced ex-cop, unemployed, useless to himself or anyone else. He wanted to tell her, the one person on earth who needed him.

"You've got the wrong man. I can't do anything."

"You found *me*."

"Pure chance."

"You're the only one I trust. I know you're a policeman. I hear . . . you were in Denver and you moved, and I can't believe you're back when I need you. God, Chris, don't make me beg."

I know you're a policeman. He felt like vomiting. Should he let the lie stand?

"Chris . . ." She was crying now, sobs making her voice shudder. "My little girl."

He thought of his son, and how he'd feel if a sick jailbird like Potts kidnapped Rich.

Maybe that made up his mind. Or maybe it was Ashley's tears; he hadn't been able to withstand them two decades ago, couldn't now.

"Ashley, stop crying. Look, I'll drive up in the morning. I don't know what I can do, but I'll drive up."

"Oh, thank you, thank you. I'm so afraid. What if . . . ?"

"Your daughter is okay. If Potts did it and called you . . . Ashley, you hear me?"

"Yes." The barest thread of sound.

"He wants to make you suffer. So he won't do anything yet. He wants it to last."

"Oh God."

"That's in her favor. Trust me on that."

"You're the only one I do trust," she said quietly.

"Your daughter's . . . uh, Lauren's father?"

"No. We're divorced and . . . and . . ." She sighed. "It's a long story. But I don't want him involved."

Divorced. "Ashley, I'll be up in a few hours. Will you be all right?"

A wry laugh. "No, but what choice do I have?"

"Where exactly do you live?"

She told him, gave him directions, which he wrote down on the back of an envelope.

"Hang in there."

"Okay."

"Get some sleep."

"Right."

"Try to get some sleep, Ashley."

"When will you be here?"

"I'll leave as soon as I can."

"Chris . . ."

"Yes?"

"I'll be waiting."

"Will I recognize you?" he asked.

"Will I recognize *you*?"

Good question. "See you soon, Ashley."

When he hung up, the silence in the room reverberated. Ashley Lacouter. Ashley *Marin.* A fifteen-year-old daughter. Davey Potts.

His mind started filling with plans and possibilities, questions, a million questions. He'd been in Vice and then Narcotics. He'd been an undercover cop, never dealt with kidnapping. But he knew the lore, the stories, the statistics—all cops did.

What if he got Ashley's daughter killed? But, hell, he was only going up to Aspen to help her out, explain how all kidnappers threatened to kill their victims if the cops got involved. He could at least afford her moral support.

Davey Potts. Interesting, back on his old stamping grounds. Up to his old tricks. What about his father, Jerry? He'd forgotten to ask Ashley about Jerry.

He went to the coffee table, looked down at the revolver. It seemed diminished, an inert lump of steel. He leaned over, snicked the safety on.

He stood there, the room still dark but for a rectangle of brightness from a streetlight spilling in the window. Then he smiled grimly to himself and said out loud to the empty room, "Guess this wasn't a good day to die."

FOUR

The night seemed to last forever. She sat with her cell phone close by, paced the floor, sat again. Dozed a couple of times, jerking awake, remembering snatches of dark, terrible dreams. Her mind shuttled among horrors, each worse than the last.

Davey Potts. He'd been in prison for twenty years. His father, Jerry, had been in prison as well. The two of them, vicious miscreants. Survivalists, living a squalid and primitive existence in a log cabin in the mountains near the tiny town of Marble, only sixty miles from Aspen, but worlds away in lifestyle.

Davey had been close to her age back then, his father around forty. Both of them washed-out looking, colorless hair and eyes, sun-reddened skin where it was exposed. Shrewd and wiry and exceedingly knowledgeable about hunting and fishing and living off the land. Davey's mother had been dead by then, so there were only the two—father and son. And they'd decided they needed a woman to keep house for them.

She sat in her living room waiting, one table lamp laying down a lonely circle of light. Night sounds outside, aspen leaves rustling, a coyote's wail, the drone of vehicles on the main road, fewer and fewer as the hours wore on. The hum of her refrigerator.

Lauren. Please be all right.

She'd learned later at the trial that Jerry Potts had come up with the idea when he'd read a news article about two men who'd done precisely the same thing, kidnapped a girl to tend to them.

It had been Ashley's misfortune to be on a camping trip with her father and another girlfriend when the Potts men had put their plan into motion.

She knew Jerry Potts was dead now; he'd succumbed to emphysema in the prison hospital four years ago. Davey had come up before the state parole board several times since then, and she'd dutifully gone to testify to the board that he should remain in prison. But this last time—in the spring—she'd gone and she'd given her story and her reasoning, and they'd released Davey anyway. Because he'd been so young when the kidnapping had been committed and because his father had been the real perpetrator.

But she knew the true Davey Potts, and she knew he was worse than anyone realized. He was vicious.

They'd grabbed her when she went into a copse of aspen trees next to the campsite to relieve herself. Snatched her so quickly and silently she didn't quite comprehend what was happening. Her father and her friend never heard a sound, didn't even know she was gone for some time, and by then she was being hustled along the trail out to a dirt road, blindfolded and tied and stuffed like a sack of flour into the Pottses' rattletrap old pickup.

She'd cried and begged, but they'd paid her no mind. They'd driven for what seemed like hours, then dragged her along a dark trail and into . . .

That was where her mind stopped short.

She'd found out much later where they'd taken her— The Close Call, an old, played-out silver mine from Aspen's heyday a hundred years before. It was on Taylor Pass, up the Castle Creek Valley outside of Aspen, and she'd never been up that valley since.

The kidnapping and imprisonment had been the turning point of Ashley Lacouter's life. The Potts men had held her the rest of the summer and into the late autumn, until elk season, when hunters infiltrated the mountains, and one hunter had heard her and found her and rescued her.

She learned later there'd been a hue and cry at her disappearance, unheard of since the serial murderer Ted Bundy had jumped out of a second-floor window in the Aspen courthouse and gone to ground for several days.

Her father had called the local sheriff, who'd brought in the Aspen police, the state police, then the FBI; they put her name and description out on the wires, in the local papers, in the Denver papers. Those paths led nowhere, but they continued to comb the country where Ashley and her father and friend had been camping.

By then, of course, the trail was cold, and she was imprisoned in a dark mineshaft, left alone for days at a time, with a kerosene lamp and food and a bucket.

And now Davey Potts had stolen Lauren, her daughter, her baby. In revenge, she was quite sure. Because once she'd been rescued she'd identified Jerry and Davey and testified against them in the trial. She'd been single-handedly responsible for the guilty verdict and their incarceration.

Now it was payback.

The night dragged on, and then the sky lightened in the east, a pearl-gray gleam that drove the black shadows into their hiding places. Birds began their daily conversations; cars could again be heard on the main road. She was cold, sitting there for so long. She shivered and pulled the plaid throw from the couch around her shoulders. She focused on one thing: Chris would be here soon. He'd save Lauren the way he'd saved her.

Her cell phone rang at five minutes to seven. She jumped, knocking her wrist against the corner of the table, not feeling a thing.

"Hello? Hello?" she gasped.

"Good morning, Ash-lee."

"You're Davey Potts, aren't you? Where's my daughter? Don't you hurt her, do you hear me?"

"I didn't call to listen to you carry on."

"What do you want?"

"I want you to wonder what I'm doing to cute little Lauren."

Vomit rose in her throat. "Don't . . . don't do anything to her."

"I'll do whatever I feel like. I was in that damn prison a real long time."

"Lauren's father is rich. He'll pay a ransom. How much do you want? Just tell me, and . . ."

"It's not about money, Ash-lee."

"Let me talk to Lauren."

"No."

"You know . . . you know you can't get away with this."

"Sure I can."

"You didn't last time. And now it'll be worse. Now that we all know . . ."

"I sure hope you haven't called the cops," he said calmly, his voice more mature but undeniably familiar, with a bit of Colorado twang and a new overtone of sophistication, his prison education.

"No, no, and I won't. But her father . . ."

"You'll keep him under control, I'm sure."

"Is she okay? Don't do the same thing to her, that mine, don't, please, you can have anything, take *me* instead, but not Lauren."

"Good-bye, Ash-lee." Click.

She stared at the phone then put it down carefully. *Lauren, Lauren.* Oh dear God. And what would she tell Robert? He'd hire detectives and lawyers and probably publicists. He'd get Lauren killed. No, no, she couldn't think that. She had to keep this from Robert—maybe that wasn't fair, but it had to be that way—for a while, at least.

Chris. Chris was coming.

Then she cried, trying to muffle the sounds, curled up on the couch, both hands over her mouth, her body wracked. *Lauren, oh God.*

She was composed by the time Luda entered the back door to cook breakfast.

"You don't make coffee?" Luda remarked. Ashley put the pot on every morning.

"I forgot."

"You want me to make it?"

"Sure, go ahead." If Luda noticed that she wore the same clothes as she had yesterday, the woman said nothing. She also said nothing whatsoever about Lauren. Did she think Lauren had returned in the middle of the night? Did the woman even *care*?

She poured herself a cup of coffee and watched Luda begin her daily commotion in the kitchen.

Luda slid two slices of bread into the toaster and turned to Ashley, finally broaching the subject. "I punish that little girl if she mine."

And Ashley realized the woman did not know Lauren was still missing, much less kidnapped. How much should she tell her? God, she wished Chris would get here.

She took a breath. "Lauren isn't home," she began.

Luda's eyes widened and she started to say something, but Ashley put up a hand. Then Vladimir walked in the back door. "I set sprinkler, but hose need replacing. You want I should go hardware today?" he asked, rinsing his hands in the sink.

They were going to find out sooner or later. They'd certainly know that something terrible had happened when Chris arrived. She was sure Vladimir would keep his counsel. But Luda? If the woman said one disparaging word, Ashley knew she'd begin to scream and she wouldn't be able to stop.

The decision of exactly when to tell them the truth was forced on her when the kitchen phone rang and one of Lauren's friends was on the line.

Ashley held the receiver in her sweating palm and thought with lightning quickness considering her frazzled state of mind. "Oh, Shelly, gosh, didn't Lauren tell you? She flew out to visit her father's parents in California. . . . Um, I'm not sure, maybe for a week or so." *A week.* She felt the phone slipping from her grasp. She didn't know how she'd make it through twenty-four hours, much less a week. "Oh, okay, Shelly, I'll be sure to tell her to call you."

When she was off the phone, Luda was glowering at

her. Even Vladimir was watching her closely. "Look," she said, and she cleared her throat. "I have to tell you both something, something very upsetting. And I don't want any advice. I'm frantic enough as it is. Lauren is . . . she's been kidnapped."

Their reactions were nearly identical. Both of them froze, their expressions at first blank, then puzzled. Finally they seemed to digest what she'd told them.

Luda sank onto a chair, speechless, and Vladimir leaned against the sink and began to shake his head. "It's because I get gas. She disappear when I get gas?" he asked, his voice stricken.

Ashley nodded slowly. "But it's not your fault. Don't for a minute think this is your fault."

He didn't say anything. He only stood there rooted to the spot, shaking his head.

"You call police?" Luda asked.

"I, ah, have a policeman coming, yes. An old friend."

"He find Lauren?"

"He . . . yes, yes, he'll find her," Ashley told her, because the alternative was unthinkable.

Now where *was* Chris?

It occurred to her, as she sat down at the table in her sunny kitchen, that her daughter could be in a mine, in the dark and the constant fifty-three-degree temperature, water dripping interminably, as if the bowels of the earth were squeezing out tears. *No,* she couldn't go there.

It was nearly eight, and Pauline was stirring when Ashley heard car tires crunch on the gravel driveway outside. She rose too quickly, bumping the table so that her coffee sloshed over, and went to the front door. A black Mustang convertible was pulling up. The vehicle halted, and a residue of fine dust rose from its wheels and hung in a shaft of morning sun. The door opened, and a man ducked out, straightened, turned toward the front door when he heard it open.

She stopped on the porch and looked at him. Was this Chris? It had been so long. . . . A man of slightly over medium height, medium build, brown hair, a face . . . yes, a familiar face, but one from the past, and now, she thought, it was leaner and more marked. He wore a light blue polo shirt and wrinkled khakis; his car was dusty and it bore New Jersey license plates.

"Chris?" she asked, her voice tentative.

He took a step toward her, then another. "Ashley." He didn't smile.

"It really is you."

"Were you expecting someone else?"

"No, no." She walked across the porch and down the three steps to the driveway. She was shaky, her knees going liquid.

"Any developments?" he asked.

Up close, she could see his hazel eyes—how could she have forgotten the way they burned with golden light? "Yes," she whispered, "he called again."

She felt her knees give way abruptly, so that she sat down on the steps. He was there in a heartbeat, leaning over her. "Ashley? Are you okay?"

The sound of his voice brought back a rush of memories. How could she have forgotten that, too? He had an amber voice that slid through you like thick honey. .

She forced herself to reply. "No, I'm not okay. Of course I'm not okay. Oh, Chris."

He put his hands under her arms and helped her up. She was embarrassed and grateful for his help, terrified and relieved all at once. His hands encircled her arms, and they were so warm and strong that she wanted to collapse against him, wanted to feel his arms around her,

the way they'd been when he carried her out of the mine,
craved the security and reassurance of him.

But that was not why he was here. His eyes searched
her, concerned. There were new lines in his face, deep
brackets around his mouth, a day's growth on his
cheeks, vertical grooves between his brows. He looked
tired, too, but then he'd driven half the night. His maturity was arresting, his features finished now, not the
unformed youthfulness of twenty years ago.

She took a step back and felt his hands release her,
felt a sense of loss.

"Better?" he asked.

"Thanks. I . . . uh, I haven't slept, I haven't eaten. I
must look like hell."

"You look great."

She gave him a sad smile. "Well, I guess you've always seen me at my worst." She swallowed. "Listen, I
have to warn you. I have a houseful of weirdos. My
mother, Pauline . . ."

"I remember her."

"But she's . . . she's forgetful."

"Okay." Reasonable.

"And there's a Russian couple who live here, on the
other side of the duplex. Luda and Vladimir." She
pointed. "They help take care of my mother."

"I see."

"I'm not sure you do. But you will. Come on inside.
There's coffee."

"Sounds good."

She filled him in on the cover story she'd come up with
to explain Lauren's absence then introduced him to Luda,
who gave him a grim-faced nod, and Vladimir, who shook
his hand and didn't seem to want to let go.

Pauline emerged from her bedroom, her hair uncombed,

her expression bewildered. *Uh-oh,* Ashley thought, *she's having a bad day.*

Her mother had no recollection whatsoever of Chris. But she evidently thought he was quite good-looking, also held his hand too long when they were introduced. Flirted mildly. Humiliated Ashley to death.

"Mom," she said. "Have some breakfast. Chris and I have a few things to discuss."

Privacy. Dear God, where could they talk?

The empty apartment over the garage came to mind. It might as well be of some use. She took the cell phone, led Chris up the stairs and opened the locked door.

"We can talk in here," she said. "I'm trying to rent it out, but right now . . ."

"Sit down. You're beat," he said. "And tell me everything, from the beginning."

She sank down onto the couch, a functional piece in a striped nubby-textured synthetic fabric. Chris sat in the single worn armchair, leaning forward, elbows on his knees, hands clasped.

"Okay," she said, drawing in a breath. "Yesterday at five, Vladimir drove over to Hayley Hodges's house to pick Lauren up . . ."

She told him the sad tale, trying to repeat Davey Potts's exact words. It didn't take long—there was no middle or end to this story yet.

Chris was silent when she was done. He stared into space for a moment, thinking. She watched his face intently as if she would find an answer there.

"So," he finally said, "you're *sure* it was Potts?"

"Yes. And the call came in on my cell phone. Not the regular phone."

"So you couldn't get caller ID?"

She shook her head.

"And is your cell phone number unlisted?"

"Well, yes, but lots of people have it."

"So, Davey Potts, you know he was released from prison?"

"Three weeks ago."

"Jerry died in prison?"

"Yes."

"I didn't follow them," he mused. "I could have, I guess, but I got an offer in New Jersey, and I figured it was all finished."

"So did I."

"All right, let's back up here. Could this friend of Lauren's, Hayley, could her family have anything to do with her disappearance?"

"No, absolutely not. And I told you, it was Davey."

He held up a hand. "We have to cover every possibility, however remote."

"Sorry, of course."

"What about Vladimir?"

"Good God, no. He loves Lauren. Plus she was already gone when he got to Hayley's."

"Luda?"

"Luda hates the world, but she'd never harm Lauren."

"Okay, your ex-husband?"

She shook her head. "Robert adores her. In fact, he's been trying to get custody of her ever since our divorce."

"How long have you been divorced?"

"It was right after Dad died, eight years ago."

"And Robert wouldn't have stolen Lauren, left town with her? Called you and disguised his voice to make you think she was kidnapped? It wouldn't be the first case of parental kidnapping."

"Robert hasn't left town. He's remarried and has a new baby. And Elaine, his wife, told me yesterday evening that they were going to a big-deal benefit concert in Harris Hall. He'd never miss that. Not Robert Marin, pillar of the community. Oh, not him."

"He's a wealthy man?"

"Yes."

"Why wouldn't a kidnapper call him for a ransom? Why you?"

"I don't know. All I can think of is that it's for revenge, like I told you."

Chris was studiously silent. He rose and walked around the apartment, and she followed his movement with her eyes. He was heavier than he'd been as a college student, but still slim and erect. His hair, always unruly, showed no gray—he'd be, what? Six years older than she was, which made him around forty-two. He looked the same yet different, as if something had shifted irrevocably inside him. Life, she supposed.

"Chris . . ."

"Yes?"

"I never thought, I never even considered your family when I called."

"I'm divorced," he stated flatly.

"You, too," she said softly.

He shrugged.

"Children?"

"A son, Richard, ten years old. He goes by Rich."

"Um."

"My wife didn't like Newark. Didn't like my work. Hey, it happens to cops all the time."

"I'm sorry."

"It's okay. Now that I'm back in Denver I see Rich a lot." He stopped moving and faced her. "But this isn't about me."

"No."

"It's about your daughter."

Futility swept her, and she put her face in her hands. "I don't know what to do."

"Call the police."

She lifted her eyes. "No. You didn't hear his voice. He'll kill Lauren, he'll . . . oh God."

He waited.

"Robert doesn't know yet," she whispered.

"What?"

"Robert doesn't . . ."

"Jesus, Ashley."

"I know. But you don't understand about him. I told you, he's trying to get custody of Lauren. If he knew, you see, don't you, he'd say it was my fault, I was a bad mother. He can hire lawyers, take me to court. I can't tell him, Chris."

"He's going to find out."

"I thought . . . maybe you'd find her, and I wouldn't have to . . ."

"Ashley."

"I know, it's crazy. *I'm* crazy."

"You're not crazy. You're a desperate mother. But you're going to have to tell your ex."

"Later."

"Do you know where Potts lives? Where he went when he got out? If he has to report to a parole officer?" His eyes pinioned her, golden and searching.

"No."

"We can find out. Rather, the authorities can find out."

"Chris, please, don't make me call them. It's far too risky. And you know, you of all people know—how completely, how *useless* they were."

"This isn't the same."

"Yes, it is!"

"Ashley, I'm no good to you, I can't do anything. . . ."

"You can. You *can*." She started to cry, tears overflowing, sliding down her cheeks, her nose running.

"Ashley," he said helplessly.

"You have to find her!" What if Potts had already put Lauren in a mineshaft? She couldn't bear the thought, couldn't. . . . She felt herself sinking into the old panic, the terror and the closeness of death, dank and black and dripping, the walls moving in on her, no one hearing her screams.

FIVE

He saw her change in front of his eyes, from a desperate mother to a shivering, fearful creature that he recognized. He'd seen her like that the day he'd stumbled across her in the mine when she was sixteen. He'd seen her like that later in the teen unit of the hospital, where he visited her.

The new Ashley, the one who had greeted him when he drove up, had been unfamiliar. Mature, very beautiful, with a graceful way of moving and new curves and shorter hair. But her eyes were the same—dark and deep and very sad. Oh yes, once he'd gotten close to her, he'd recognized her eyes.

When he'd rescued her, he'd held her tightly; wrapped in a blanket, he'd half carried her into the cold sunlight and to his father's Jeep. If he released her for a moment she cried and clutched at him. He'd known instinctively what to do then.

But now?

Dare he touch her, embrace her, try to comfort her?
This woman, who had an ex-husband, a child, a household full of responsibility, was not the lost sixteen-year-
old he'd known.

"Ashley," he said quietly, and he put a hand on her
bowed back. "Come on. We'll figure this out."

"I want my daughter back."

"I know, I know. But it's going to take some time."

"She may not have time."

"He's going to drag this out, *if* it's Potts, if you're
right. I told you that. It's a waiting game."

"I don't know if I can stand it, Chris. I'm so afraid.
What if . . . ?"

He kept his hand on her shoulder, feeling her softness
and warmth through the white blouse she wore. He
turned his hand over and ran his fingers down her arm.
She didn't seem to notice.

"You have to stay strong," he said, "for Lauren's sake.
She needs you now more than she ever did. You have
to sleep and eat and keep your mind clear. That's the
most important thing you can do."

She said nothing, head drooping, dark glossy hair
hanging around her face.

"Ashley, did you hear me?"

"Yes," she whispered.

"You can do it."

"I'll try."

"All right. Now, there's nothing more we can do but
wait till he calls again. If you went to the police . . ."

"No, stop trying to convince me. You can't."

"All I'm saying is, *if* you went to them, they'd bypass
caller ID and put a real trace on your phone. We'd be
able to tell where he was calling from." He frowned.

"Unless he's using a public phone or even a cell phone. Then it gets damn tricky."

She nodded.

"The thing is, the cops have the authority to order the traces, and I don't." He thought a moment. "When did he call last?"

"Around seven."

He checked his watch. "Okay, he probably won't call again this soon. Why don't you get some rest?"

"What about you?"

"I'll be fine."

"I never told you, but I thought at first that you were Superman," she said.

"What?"

"In the mine. I was so messed up, and then you were there, like magic."

"That's me, Superman."

"Chris . . ." She looked at him with red-rimmed eyes. "Will you stay? You must have a job you have to go back to. I never asked, I never asked about your life. It was very selfish of me."

"I'm retired from the force," he said, knowing she wouldn't recognize the irony in his tone. "No job, no family."

"Can you stay then? You can have this apartment all to yourself."

"You don't want to rent it out?"

"That can wait. For now, for as long as you need it, it's yours."

"I don't know if I can help you," he said. "I told you. . . ."

"I don't care what you told me. I don't trust anyone else. Chris, you were in law enforcement, you know what to do."

Irony piled on irony. *He knew what to do.*

"Okay, a day or so, that's all I can promise. We'll see."

He got her to eat a piece of toast, the kitchen empty now, her mother watching TV. Pauline had forgotten who he was already; introductions had to be repeated.

"Lauren?" Pauline said, puzzled. "She's at school, isn't she?"

"Yes, Mom, that's right," Ashley said, and he knew she couldn't bear to repeat Lauren's plight over and over again.

"I'll keep your mother company," he said. "Take a nap."

"A nap? God, Ashley, isn't it too early for a nap?" Pauline said.

"It's okay, Pauline," Chris said. "Ashley doesn't feel good."

"Is it that damn summer cold that's going around?"

"Maybe."

Pauline waved her hand, dismissing Ashley. "Go on then. We'll sit right here and chat. Right, Cliff?"

"Chris."

"Chris."

"For Christopher."

"In the year 1492 Christopher Columbus sailed the ocean blue," Pauline chanted.

He must have fallen asleep watching *All My Children.* He woke with a start, his neck cramping. Running a hand over his stubbled jaw, he sat up. What time was it?

He heard voices in the kitchen. Pauline, Vladimir and Luda. Was Ashley still asleep? God, he felt like death warmed over.

They were eating sandwiches around the table.

"We let you sleep," Luda said.

"Thanks. Uh, anyone see Ashley?"

"She still in room," Vladimir replied.

"I don't know why that girl is so worn out," Pauline said. "Low blood sugar or something. She never eats a damn thing."

He wanted to defend Ashley, but it would be a waste of time. Obviously Pauline found solace in being critical of her daughter.

Luda got up and put together a sandwich for him without asking. Set it on the table, put down a glass of iced tea. "Eat," she said.

Charming, he thought. She reminded him of the women in a TV commercial years ago, a spoof on Russian fashions. "Russian evening gown," the voice-over would intone, and a peasant would strut down the runway in a burlap sack.

Ashley woke up after lunch, coming out of her bedroom, looking confused, her eyes puffy, her hair mussed, her clothes wrinkled.

"Any news?" she asked breathlessly.

He shook his head. "No."

She stood there, swaying on her feet, put a hand to her head.

"Luda, could you make Ashley a sandwich, please?" he asked.

Luda grumbled in Russian, then in English: "Dishes all done."

"Please, Luda."

"I'm not hungry, Chris, honestly."

"You got me up here from Denver. You'll do as I say. All right?"

She slumped. "Fine. Okay."

After that there was nothing to do but wait. Chris

knew about the waiting game; it was something police had to learn. But Ashley had no tools to help her pass the time. It killed him to see her sit, her body taut with anxiety, her hands clenched into fists.

He made her go for a walk that afternoon.

"What if he calls?" she asked.

"Bring your cell phone."

They headed down the road, past the mechanic's place, past a new house, just completed, that belonged to a local couple who competed in triathlons, and an older house occupied by some restaurant owners. A quiet neighborhood nestled in aspen trees, the private road meandering and full of potholes.

"Tell me about New Jersey," she said.

"It's not very interesting."

"It'll keep my mind occupied. And it probably is interesting."

The day was warm, with a breeze and stark white cumulus clouds piled up over Independence Pass at the end of the valley.

"Newark," he said after a pause, "well, it has a reputation, which is true, but there are other sides to the city. Nice neighborhoods. It's not such a bad place."

"Why did you move there?"

"I transferred because I got a great offer, and I thought I could do more good there. The stakes are higher. More excitement, definite career advancement. I was in Vice in Denver, and it was a natural fit. The DEA is very active in Newark."

"You were in the DEA?"

An old black lab, its muzzle white, came out of a driveway to sniff at them. Idly, Chris stroked his head. "I was on the Newark police force, on one of the special task force squads."

"That sounds dangerous."

He looked away. "Yeah, sometimes."

"But you retired?"

"Uh-huh."

"Why?"

"I burned out, I guess."

"That sounds . . . painful."

Painful. "Um."

"But couldn't you have, say, transferred back to Denver or gone into another department or something?"

"I chose not to."

"So you're unemployed right now?"

"Yes."

"Are you looking for work?"

"Hey"—he turned on the carefree, cocky Chris—"you're sure full of questions. The cops should hire you for interrogations."

"Sorry." She gave him a look but couldn't penetrate his sunglasses.

Dinner was an uncomfortable affair, Pauline carping, Ashley quiet and distracted, Luda glowering and Vladimir stoic, watching Chris then Ashley, his eyes shifting between them.

After dinner Ashley proposed that she make up the bed in the garage apartment.

"Just give me the sheets," Chris said.

"No, I'll do it. Honestly." In a lower voice. "I can't stay here, Chris. Please."

He helped her make the bed. Hung towels in the bathroom. Got his overnight bag from the car.

"You'll be okay here?" she asked.

"This is better than my Denver apartment."

Her eyes pivoted to him. "You're joking, aren't you?"

"Sure, I'm joking."

Later they sat in his living room area, Ashley on the couch, Chris in the armchair. She placed her cell phone carefully on the coffee table.

"Can I stay here for a while?" she asked.

"Sure."

"You want to talk about anything special?"

"No. You talk. You've pumped me already."

She fixed him with her melancholy gaze that was like a dark lantern. "I haven't even started pumping you."

"Tell me about Lauren."

She laid her head on the back of the couch. "Lauren. Well, she's fifteen. Her birthday is next spring, April. It snowed the day I had her. She's fairer than I am, like her father, but she looks a little like me. She's taller than I am, though. We wore the same size for a time, but she outgrew my clothes. Which isn't all bad.

"She's got a mouth on her. Wow. You think my mother's bad? She has what we call hissy fits. Stubborn. A good student. Lots of friends. She plays tennis and rides horses and plays volleyball for the girls' high school team."

"She must be pretty," he offered.

"She is. She'll be even prettier when she's grown up."

"Do you two get along? I know the mother-daughter thing can be hard. My sister . . ."

"You have a sister?"

"She lives in New Orleans."

"Oh, now I remember. Sure, you told me."

"She has a chubby husband and three kids."

"I don't have any brothers or sisters. Of course, you know that. Sorry. Anyway, I asked my mother once why she hadn't had more kids. She said she couldn't handle more than one."

They talked on, and he could see that she was growing

drowsy. She stretched out on the couch, her head resting on an arm.

"Do you think she's okay?" she asked once.

"Yes, she is, Ashley. And we'll get her back." In truth, he knew that the danger to Lauren increased exponentially as the hours passed. The failure of the kidnapper to ask for a ransom was not a good omen, either. That meant there was other motivation than monetary gain for holding Lauren. Revenge, probably, as Ashley had already surmised.

Her eyes closed then opened.

"Go ahead and rest," he said.

They closed again, and he watched as the rhythm of her breathing changed, her face relaxed. He sat in the worn armchair, and he studied her, not moving, barely inhaling. She'd been through so much in her life, so much that was bad, and yet she'd come through it all with a mature and resilient beauty. She touched him profoundly, as she had the first time he'd seen her.

It wasn't fair, he thought. But then so much in life wasn't fair. He deserved his fate, but Ashley didn't. Neither did Lauren.

What in hell was the use of questioning what was *fair*? It happened—deal with it. That's what he had to do, help Ashley deal with this situation. He'd do what he could; maybe pull in a few old favors if it came to that. He still knew men in Colorado: the head of the Denver FBI office, the police chief, some investigators at the state attorney's office. He couldn't call any of them yet; it was too early. And he needed to listen to one of the kidnapper's phone calls, see if it really was Potts.

Then he could go to work. His brain churned, sifting

through possibilities, scenarios, all that he knew about the profiles of kidnappers.

Ashley slept. He wondered what she'd think of him if she knew the truth, his failure in his chosen profession, the corruption that he'd allowed to overtake him. She'd despise him, send him packing.

He'd never tell her the truth, though. She needed to be protected from what he'd become. She needed, right now, to have faith in him, and he'd allow her that small comfort.

His muscles stiff, he shifted position. She stirred, made a noise in her throat, and her eyelids fluttered. He froze, and she relapsed into sleep.

He watched her, and it grew late. There was a single small lamp turned on in the far corner of the apartment, not enough light to illuminate her features, but enough to bathe her in velvety shadows. Her hair had parted in the back and fallen against a pale cheek. He gazed for an endless time at the soft, fine tendrils on her neck. She truly was beautiful. Mature now, filled out in the hips and breasts, her legs still long and shapely, her feet and hands small and slim.

He'd always remembered her eyes, dark and pleading, haunted. But he'd forgotten her mouth. She had the most sensual mouth he'd ever seen. Beautifully molded, both lips soft and full, but the lower one just a little fuller. The kind of mouth a man dreamed about.

He wondered if she'd ever been happy since her encounter with the Potts men. She'd married a wealthy man—for security? But the marriage had failed. Perhaps in maturity she had realized there were different brands of security, money often being the least dependable choice.

Had she ever been at peace?

She certainly had her hands full now. A mother with obvious Alzheimer's, a Russian couple—probably illegals—who seemed more burden than help, an ex-husband who apparently pulled her chain every time he got a chance, and now a daughter who'd been kidnapped.

And he thought life had dumped on *him*.

It grew later. The cell phone sat waiting on the table. The man would call again, that was a given. And Chris would listen to the voice, decide on the next step.

What the hell was he doing here? Was he seeking some sort of redemption? Was he using Lauren's kidnapping as a personal lifeline? If so, he was not being fair to Ashley, and he could be putting Lauren in more jeopardy.

On the other hand, he had no confidence in the law enforcement authorities to help. Ashley was right, they'd ride roughshod over the family and probably fuck things up. *Shit,* he thought. What had he gotten himself into?

He stared at the woman asleep on the couch, and suddenly he wanted to run, to leave her asleep and innocent, and get in his hot wiseguy car and drive away. But he didn't. He sat there, and eventually he, too, slept.

The call came at 5 A.M., the cell phone shrilling into the silence, breaking the night into a million shards of alarm.

He shot bolt upright, but she had already grabbed the phone.

"Hello?" he heard her say.

SIX

Davey enjoyed doing the voice. He'd practiced it
enough. Even dreamed it. *The voice.* Soft, unconcerned,
even sensual. Certainly never hurried.

"Ash-lee, good morning, Ash-lee, did we sleep well?"
Oh, perfect, perfect.

She spoke to him. But she sounded real stressed out.
He warmed with satisfaction just hearing the tension.

". . . Lauren, I want to speak to Lauren, you son of a
bitch."

"Ash-lee," he said calmly, then he repeated her name
two more times for effect, only more slowly. What control. Better than perfect.

She kept talking, her tone growing shrill, demanding.
As if she had any power. He laughed into the mouthpiece of the cell phone. An amazing concept, a cell
phone. He'd heard about them in prison, seen them on
TV. But he still couldn't get over the contraptions. And
better yet, just like his cell mate had told him, they were

nearly untraceable, except for state-of-the-art technology, so state-of-the-art that only top-level government agencies possessed it.

Ashley—*Ash-lee*—was rambling on, begging him to return the kid, crying to him not to harm her, offering money, as much as he wanted, offering to take Lauren's place.

He loved this.

"Oh, Ash-lee," he said, his voice resonating beautifully in his own ears, "we can't talk when you're behaving so bad. You think about that, Ashley," he said and he clicked off.

He put the phone on the battery charger gizmo and smiled, heat spreading right down to his toes. The only trouble was the kid. Really. The fucking brat with a mouth on her worse than her mother's had been all those years ago. The mouth was silenced right now, stuck closed with duct tape. Another useful invention. But her eyes were on him. Big brown eyes, kind of like Ashley's but not near as pretty.

She made him uneasy. Well, maybe not *her*—she was under control right now—but the thought of her. She was a nuisance. He'd get rid of her. He'd wanted to ever since he'd gotten his hands on her, but it wasn't time. To keep her mother on the hook he might eventually have to let the kid speak to her. A word or two. Or maybe he wouldn't—maybe he'd just let Ashley suffer.

In prison he'd learned to read. That is, he'd known *how* to read from school, the eight grades he'd completed till his father had taken him out of the corrupt system. But in prison he'd actually read real books.

He'd learned an expression: coup de grace. Wasn't exactly sure what the words meant but he'd gotten the gist of them. And ever since then he dreamed of Ashley's torment when he took her little brat from her and the final scene. The coup de grace.

She couldn't think rationally that morning. Mindlessly, she started cleaning out the kitchen cupboards just to keep her hands busy. Chris kept trying to reassure her about Lauren, but his efforts didn't do much good.

"For God's sake, Ashley," he said, "use your head. Potts got the exact response that he was looking for. You played right into his hands. Lauren is okay. She'll be okay as long as the creep can get a rise out of you."

"Are you saying I *should* rise to the bait every time that maniac calls me? Even if he never lets me speak to her?"

"Maybe. Yeah, maybe that's the way to handle him. Let him think he has the power. Let him wallow in it. And while he's wallowing . . ."

"You'll be looking for him. You'll find him."

But Chris shook his head. "Ashley, I still don't think I'm your man. After a while, Potts is going to get tired of his game and he'll ask for money. You're going to need the FBI then. This is what they *do*."

"I *told* you, I've told you a dozen times, no. And you can't be sure Davey is going to ask for money. He wants to torture me. He *is* torturing me. And for all we know he might be planning to keep Lauren in the end, the way he and his father did with me. Wouldn't that be the ultimate revenge?"

"Hell, I don't know. You could be right. Or maybe half right. He gets his revenge and he gets money, too. He could be planning on taking a bundle from you and keeping Lauren. I'm not a profiler. I can't get into his head. But an expert . . ."

"Let's not go there." She sighed and pressed her index

fingers hard into her pounding temples. "If I could just relax and think. I know Davey."

"You *knew* him. He's just spent twenty years behind bars. You have no idea what he's turned into. And neither do I."

The only thing she could do that morning was cling to the assertion that Lauren was all right. Chris might not be a real profiler, but he was intelligent and savvy and he'd been on the streets, and surely he'd run into dozens of insane criminals. And he was intuitive. She knew that. She'd put her trust in his expertise; if she didn't she'd go crazy.

By mid-morning he was gathering information. He was slow and methodical. She understood how he worked. She herself tried to accept life's curves in an orderly fashion. Like a math calculation. You couldn't solve a problem unless you took the right steps in the right order.

While they waited for Potts to contact her again, she and Chris sat down with Vladimir in the garage apartment where they could talk in private.

She settled in an old painted chair out of Vladimir's line of sight; this was Chris's job. The Russian was on the couch, Chris across from him in the worn easy chair, leaning forward, elbows on knees, hands clasped in front of him. Earnest, concerned, but absolutely vigilant.

He began the interview gently, easing into it. Asking Vladimir about his hometown in Russia and how he'd come to Moscow and to the hospital where he'd trained.

His tone was low, with a smooth overlay like a cat's purr. Velvety almost.

She let his voice roll over her, heard the questions he was asking the Russian, and she realized what Chris was doing—befriending the man. He never broached the subject of whether or not Vladimir and his wife were legal—which they were, for a few more months, anyway, and after that Ashley didn't know what she'd do. Get an immigration attorney to extend their visas?

"So, Vladimir," Chris was saying, "you stopped to fill the Cherokee a few minutes before five?"

Vladimir's head sank. "Yes. My watch say four-fifty. It not always run on time, though." He hesitated, and she heard him groan. "If I not stop, maybe get gas after I pick Lauren up, then . . ."

"Hey," Chris said, his tone amber, "how could you have known? You can't blame yourself."

"Still . . ."

"Still nothing. Forget about it, pal. Ashley could have gone to pick her up. Luda could have. It wouldn't have made a difference."

"I was there at five. I am sure it was five. Maybe couple minutes wrong, my watch, you see? But I mostly there on time as Ashley tell me to."

"I believe you," Chris said. "And I take it Lauren was usually ready when her ride got there?"

Vladimir smiled ruefully. "Oh, Lauren very good to get ride home. Ashley"—he turned around and met her eyes—"she tell Lauren no more ride if she keep people waiting. Lauren not like to take bus."

"Um. Okay." Chris dropped his hands to the arms of the chair and crossed a leg over the other knee. He certainly had a way about him, something unimpeachable that said, *hey, you can trust me. I'm the good guy*.

He must have questioned suspects like this, and he would have been the good cop. She could see him doing that, getting them to trust him, getting them to spill their guts.

"I haven't seen the road the Hodgeses live on yet,"

he was reflecting, and she put aside her musings to concentrate on his words. "But from what Ashley told me it's a narrow road at the base of Red Mountain?"

"Yes," Vladimir said.

"Does it dead-end?"

"Yes, well, there way you can get to Red Mountain Road, but it private. Not good to use that way. Very long."

"I see."

And so did Ashley. If Davey Potts had been stalking Lauren, maybe stalking her for days or even weeks, and she walked out to the road to meet Vladimir, then Potts could have snatched her on the road and been gone before Vladimir got there.

How had Potts kept Lauren quiet in his vehicle? Tied her up? Gagged her? Knocked her unconscious?

But Ashley's tortured thoughts were interrupted when her cell phone rang. She snatched it up from her lap. Both Chris and Vladimir started half out of their seats.

Chris nodded.

She took the call. But it wasn't Potts. It was a girlfriend, a fellow Aspen High School teacher, wanting to know if she was free to go on a hike tomorrow.

"Oh, Michelle . . ." She took a breath. "I . . . I can't. Maybe next weekend?" She listened, then said good-bye and clicked the phone shut. Her heart was crashing against her ribs.

"It was a friend," she finally told him. "It was nothing."

Chris finished with Vladimir then used the landline phone in the apartment to contact an old friend of his in Denver.

"Not a policeman?" Ashley asked anxiously.

"Not anymore. But he's got lots of pals on the force and he's totally discreet. Okay?"

"Okay," she said.

He got his friend on the line immediately. "Hey, Joe, Chris here," he said. "Yeah, sure is hot, but actually I'm not in Denver, I'm up in Aspen." He paused. "Hardly a vacation. Doing a friend a favor . . . No, I'd rather not say just yet. Anyway, think you could call a connection or two and shag me an address? Great. It's on a parolee named Potts. Davey P-O-T-T-S. Right. He did twenty down at the state pen in Canon City. Got out a few weeks back and I'm assuming he's been assigned a parole officer. Oh, and hey, it would really help if you can get me a current photo of Potts. The parole officer has to have one in his file. If you could get it faxed to you . . . Hey, that's great." He paused again, and then he gave Joe the number in the apartment. "I owe you, Joe, thanks," Chris said and he hung up.

"You don't really think Davey Potts is going to be at the address he gave, do you?" she asked.

"Maybe not. But, hey, why not check? All my friend has to do is contact someone at the Department of Corrections, and they put him onto the area Potts was paroled to. The parole officer isn't likely to give out the creep's address to Joe, but an active duty cop can get it from him."

"So this Joe . . . he was a policeman?"

"The best," he said soberly.

He made a second call then. She sat quietly listening while he did his thing. "Yo, Murray," he said over the line, "Chris Judge here." There was a pause. "About six months ago, yeah." Another pause. "Well, I'm not really in the market for one. I've got a little saved up and I'm kicking back." Chris listened then laughed. "Yeah, Newark sure as hell isn't Denver. Whole different set of rules there."

Ashley continued to eavesdrop while they shot the breeze for a few minutes, Chris telling this Murray that he was divorced now but still doing Little League and Father's Day and all that with Rich. Then Chris asked, "How's life with the state attorney?"

Chris got down to business: "Say, I'm up in Aspen right now . . . yeah. No, just helping a friend. Anyway, I might need a favor, a pass to talk to an inmate or two down in Canon City." He paused. "Nah, nothing like that. It's just some parolee who's giving my friend a rough time."

He listened for a moment, then said, "Great, I'll ring you back if I need the credentials. And thanks. Say, you still have the season tickets to the Rockies? Maybe when I get back to Denver we could do dinner and a game. My treat." He paused a last time. "Okay, talk to you soon," he said.

"So much for not being able to help," Ashley said, giving him a wry smile.

It couldn't have been ten minutes later when the phone rang, and his friend Joe was back on the line. "Man, you are quick," Chris said, and jotted down the information Joe was giving him. "Thanks, I owe you big. I'll check with you later on Potts's photo. Just hang on to it for now. Hi to Charlene and the kids. I'll be in touch," he said, and he was off the line.

He swiveled around to Ashley. "Okay. The address Potts gave his parole officer is a cousin's place in Glenwood Springs."

She pursed her lips. Glenwood Springs sat at the far end of the valley from Aspen, about fifty miles from Marble, where Potts had been raised.

Chris found the number and got Davey's cousin. He also got a runaround, as far as Ashley could tell. "So when *will* Davey be back?" Chris asked. Then, "Well, do you think I can reach him tomorrow?"

When Chris was off the phone, he shook his head. "What an asshole," he said. Then he glanced at Ashley. "Sorry. But I know the type and I know the setup. The cousin is a cop-hating redneck, and I'll bet Potts hasn't been available since he got out of prison."

"What about the parole officer? Doesn't Davey . . . ?"

"Yeah. He probably does have to check in once a week and all that, and he probably has been a model ex-con, but I'll bet you anything Potts doesn't check in this week. Or next week. Or ever again."

"Wonderful." She closed her eyes for a moment.

"Yeah," Chris said.

He drove over to the Hodgeses that afternoon and talked to Betty and Hayley. Ashley had begged him not to tell them the whole story, but all he could think to say was that Lauren had taken off. "A harebrained teen-age prank."

"They didn't believe that, did they?" Ashley asked when he returned.

"They didn't know *what* to think," he said, shrugging.

"Oh God."

"Anyway," he went on, "I didn't really learn much at the Hodgeses. All I can figure is Potts must've had an eye on Lauren for some time. He waited for an opportunity to grab her, and that opportunity arose when Vladimir ran a few minutes late. It wouldn't have taken Potts long to snatch her. A few seconds. Then he was gone."

Evening came and night loomed, and still Davey Potts did not call again. They waited and waited; the hours plodded by interminably. Chris stayed close and kept reminding her that Potts was probably not going to put Lauren on the phone yet. If ever.

"He'll drag your agony out as long as he can," Chris told her.

"So I should beg? Is that what you really think, or are you guessing?"

"Hell, Ashley," he said, "it's my best guess. Okay? It feels right."

"Then I'll beg. I won't even have to fake it."

"That's a girl."

There was no way she could put into words what a relief it was to have him there. His strength was bracing. His carriage, the easy pitch of his head and tilt of his mouth seemed to say to the whole world, *Yeah, just try me.*

There were times he was serious, pensive. And when he was lost in thought, the light in his eyes dimmed, the warm gold turned dull, the muscles in his face taut, and she knew he was far away from her. He looked a little dangerous then, and world-weary, as if he'd been disappointed too often.

But then he'd come out of his reverie, his features would relax, and he'd throw her a big smile of confidence that said, *It's okay, I'm here, let me take care of you.*

Late that evening she found him sitting on the top step of the porch, where he was drinking coffee and gazing at the sky. Earlier rain had threatened, but now the black thunderheads and tall cumulus clouds lay in broad swathes across the underslung sky.

The sun was still striking the tips of the clouds, the horizon glowing sulfurous yellow; in the valley the light had long since faded, the sun well below the mountains.

"Funny sky," Chris said.

"I think there are fires burning in Utah. It's the smoke, I guess."

"Um," he said. "It sure is different."

"Yes." She eased down next to him on the top step. A cool breeze caressed her neck. "Well, it's not quite dark and Mom's actually in bed. What an evening." Pauline had been difficult all afternoon, confused as to where Lauren was. Confused as to Chris's presence. Even confused over Luda and Vladimir, as if she'd never before seen either of them.

"I take it you've had Pauline on all the new medications?" he asked.

"Every one of them."

"Nothing helps?"

"Oh, sometimes. For a week or so and then she regresses."

"Well, they're making breakthroughs every day, from what I read."

She sighed. "Yes. And Mom is early stage, so there's hope."

"Hey, there's always hope, right?" He gave her one of those carefree smiles that could melt a glacier.

"So," she breathed. "What about you, Chris? You can't be fully retired at . . . What are you, forty-two?"

"Forty-one and two-thirds."

She laughed lightly. "Okay. Not forty-two, then. But anyway, aren't you going back to work?"

She saw him shrug in the curiously yellow light. "Who knows."

"That's not much of an answer. I mean, I can't imagine being retired. I always want to teach high school. Oh, sure, it's nice having the summers . . . Well, when everything isn't falling down around my ears, that is.

But I still love September. All the new faces peering at me from behind the desks, not knowing if I'm Mrs. Cool or the biggest bitch in the school. I just love the kids. I don't know what I'd do if I didn't have my work."

"Um," he said.

"Of course my work was the beginning of the end of my marriage."

"How's that?"

"Oh, when Lauren was in first grade, I decided to get my teaching certificate, and that meant going back to school to get my master's. You can get your degree right here in the valley, but Robert had a fit. I know now he felt he'd lose control of me. But I couldn't sit and arrange flowers all day once Lauren was in school."

"He divorced you for *that*?"

"We divorced each other, really. My going back to work for what he called a 'nothing salary' was more than he could handle. Having a high school math teacher for a wife threatened him. But I stood my ground. I guess I knew, deep down inside, the marriage wasn't good. Then one day he said it was him or the substitute teaching job I got at the high school, and I said I guessed it was the high school."

"You make it sound easy."

"Easy? Divorcing Robert was pure hell. All our friends were *his* friends, this duplex was in his name and rented out, and I had to fight to get it."

"What about Marin's house? Isn't it on Red Mountain?"

"He had a better lawyer than I did." She shook her head. "But I survived and made new friends, and life somehow just goes on. And you know I've never once regretted my decision. I'll always teach. But you obviously don't miss your work."

"Um," he repeated.

"Was it Newark? Did the job there turn you off?"

"Jesus."

"Oh, I see, subject closed." She toyed with the cell phone that was balanced on her knee. She wished he wanted to talk. About anything. Talking, dealing with her mother and Luda kept her mind off the agony. Even if for only a few seconds. And she craved the relief.

What *was* Chris not telling her? She was sure his secret had something to do with that tautness that altered his face every so often.

The cell phone finally rang. She jerked back, staring at it.

Chris came to his feet. "Take a breath," he said. "And remember, play along with whatever game he wants."

"Okay, okay," she whispered, her heart hammering.

But it was a telemarketer. At this hour, a goddamn telemarketer.

Chris sat back down beside her and rested a hand on her knee. "He wants you to lose it. Save it for when he calls. Believe me, you'll make it through this and it'll be a bad dream, one you won't forget, sure, but it will be over. Nightmares don't last forever and neither will this."

She nodded. "You said that before, you know."

"I did?"

"Uh-huh. Twenty years ago. In the hospital in Denver. You said the same thing. Even the same words."

"I did, huh?"

"Yes."

"And you remember that?"

"Chris," she said, "I remember every detail and every last word."

"Huh," he said again.

SEVEN

Her phone rang the following morning shortly after nine. But again the call was not from Davey. It was the secretary at the school wanting to know if she had any curriculum changes scheduled for next fall's classes.

"Ah, yes," Ashley said, collecting herself, weakness rippling through her. "But I can't get them to you this week. Next week, okay?"

"The deadline is the tenth, Ashley. Can you have them here by then?"

"Oh, sure, yes, no problem."

Maybe she'd do them now, she thought. Anything to occupy her mind.

Lauren.

Was he feeding her? Was she warm at night? Was she terrified? Or was she reacting as Ashley had done, with false bravado and an internal wellspring of hope that someone would find her any minute?

But the minutes for Ashley had dragged into hours and days and weeks. Months.

She rushed outside to find Chris sitting on the passenger side of his car, door open, glove box open, maps strewn on the front seat.

"Chris, we have to find her. We have to find her soon. She won't be able to bear it. I know she won't! Lauren talks big, but I'm so afraid she isn't as tough as I was. Kids nowadays, we spoil them so badly, and . . . What are you doing? You aren't leaving? *Chris?*"

"No, Ashley, I'm not leaving. Take it easy."

"Oh God, I saw the maps and . . ."

"Hey, I'm just taking a look at some of the roads around here."

"There aren't many real roads. Just Highway Eighty-two between Glenwood Springs and Twin Lakes on the other side of the pass."

"*Back* roads."

"Oh. You mean Jeep roads. Then you think he's taken Lauren . . ."

"I don't think anything yet. I'm just looking at a map."

"But . . ."

"As soon as I do have an idea I'll let you know. Okay?"

"Well, yes, sure. So, does that mean you'll stay?"

He'd been wearing his sunglasses. He took them off, dangling them from one hand, and met her eyes. "There might be a couple more things I could look into."

"A couple things?"

"Maybe. Soon as *I* know, you'll know. Now, that's all I'm willing to say."

"Okay," she said. It was enough. More than enough. She felt suddenly as if he'd climbed into a phone booth and emerged in his cape and mask. Superman. He'd find her child. He would. There was nothing Superman couldn't do.

She would have pressed him, wouldn't have been able to stop herself, but her neighbor sauntered up just then, a greasy rag in hand, his old stained baseball cap turned backward on his frizzy hair. He was wearing shorts and dirty tennis shoes and a bright red T-shirt that read Lake Powell.

"Jay," she sighed.

"Oh, hey, Ashley, how's it going?" he asked. But his gaze was fixed on the Mustang. "New wheels?"

"Actually," she said, "the car is Chris's. Chris Judge, this is Jay Rose, my neighbor. He's drooling over your car. Aren't you, Jay?"

"Not exactly drooling," Jay countered. "Maybe a little curious."

Chris stood and smiled. "Yeah, she's pretty nice."

Before Ashley could tell her neighbor they were busy, Jay had managed to get Chris to pop the hood and they were both eyeing the engine as if they'd never seen one before.

Then, twenty minutes later, as Jay was finally heading home, she spotted two bicyclists peddling up the pothole-filled road, dog loping alongside.

"Oh no." She felt the blood drain from her face.

"Huh?" Chris said.

"It's Robert and bimbo." She whistled out a breath. "My ex-husband and his trophy wife, Elaine. God, and he's got the baby in a backpack. What am I going to tell him, Chris?"

"Look, maybe I can handle . . ." he began, but Robert and Elaine were already there, climbing off their five-thousand-dollar mountain bikes.

They both looked like Tour de France competitors, dressed top to bottom in spandex and what Lauren called mushroom-head helmets. The first time Lauren had seen her dad's new helmet, she'd sneered, "Oh my God, that is *so* uncool."

Their dog, Sandy, a golden retriever whose color was nothing like sand, leaped up onto Ashley with muddy paws.

"Goddamn it, Sandy, *down*." Robert grabbed the dog's choke collar and yanked hard on it. "Sorry, Ashley, she's been to class, but I'm afraid she's dumb as a stick."

But Ashley wasn't paying the least bit of attention to Sandy. She was thinking furiously: What was she going to tell Lauren's father?

Chris introduced himself, shaking Robert's hand and then Elaine's, even letting the baby, who was still in the pack on Robert's back, toy with his fingers. ". . . An old friend of Ashley's from Denver," Chris was telling them.

"Funny we've never met before," Robert said. "Judge. Chris Judge. Um."

But it wasn't in the least odd, Ashley thought. Chris was a part of her life she'd always held close. Too special to share. Even with her husband.

"We thought Lauren might want to ride up Smuggler Mountain with us." Elaine gave everyone a big white smile. "Do you think Luda could get some water for Sandy?"

"Ah, sure," Ashley said, then she called out to Luda to please let the dog inside and give her a bowl of water.

"So where is Lauren?" Robert said, adjusting the backpack.

Ashley winced inside.

"Ashley?" Robert said, studying her face.

She sucked in air. "We need to talk," she said. "Alone. Maybe Elaine could take the baby for a few minutes, and we'll walk down the road a bit and . . ."

"What the hell is going on?" Robert removed his sunglasses and helmet, hung them from the handlebars of his bike.

"Please," Ashley said. "Just give Elaine the baby and take a walk with me?"

Usually Robert Marin would have insisted on an answer right then and there. But the edge in her voice, the desperation, must have given him pause, and he shrugged the backpack off and handed the baby to Elaine.

"What about our ride?" Elaine protested, nuzzling the infant with her bow-shaped mouth.

Robert threw his wife a look, and she fell silent.

They left Chris and Elaine and the baby and started down the road. She could feel the tension and annoyance emanating from her ex-husband. She'd always felt his impatience with her.

"Okay, Ashley," he began, "what's the trouble? *Obviously* it's Lauren. And I can tell right now I'm not going to like it. Is it drugs? A boyfriend? She better not have gotten herself goddamn pregnant. Christ, I've warned you about how lax you are with her. If you'd just let me . . ."

"Robert," Ashley cut in, "please, will you *please* let me explain? It's nothing like that. Lauren is . . . missing."

Telling him the truth was torture. He was so upset, so furious, that his skin took on a sick pallor and the veins pulsed in his forehead.

"Holy God in heaven," he hissed, "the same man who kidnapped you has my daughter? Jesus, let me think. I can't even begin to think here. I mean, what did he do, tell you his name?"

She shook her head. "No, nothing like that."

"Then how the hell do you know it's him!"

"I . . . It's his voice."

"His voice."

"Yes. And the way he says my name."

"And that's it? You're basing . . ."

"Robert," she said, "it's Davey Potts."

He frowned and stared at her, then said, "For argument's sake, say you're right. What I want to know then is how you could let that crazy inmate take my daughter! How did he get her? Where the hell were *you*?"

She told him every detail. But before she could explain about not calling the police, he demanded to know where the FBI was. "Shouldn't they have set up a base at the house? Who the hell's in charge? I want to talk to him right this minute."

"I . . ." She swallowed. "I didn't call the police or the FBI."

"You *what*?" he sputtered.

"I called . . . Chris."

"Chris? That man back at the house? Well, who the hell is *he*?"

"A . . . friend."

"A friend? You called a goddamn friend when my daughter's life is at stake?"

"Chris *is* a policeman."

"What do you mean a policeman?"

"Just that, Robert. He's very experienced."

"Who's he with? I don't understand. And I want an explanation."

"Look, Davey Potts has threatened to . . . to kill Lauren if I go to the police."

"Jesus . . . But of course he would say that. It's probably just a bluff."

"Fine. Whatever. But I'm not willing to take that chance with Lauren's life. Are you?"

He rubbed his arms over the shiny spandex as if he were chilled. "All right, all right, I need to think here. *Jesus.* But who is this man with? If you haven't called the authorities, then . . ."

"He was with the Denver police, then transferred to Newark. I don't see what that has to do with anything. He's helping."

Robert raised a brow. "And just where do you know him from? Chris . . . Judge. Right? Where would you know a cop from . . ." Then suddenly he nodded. "Oh, *oh,* now I know why the name's familiar. He's the man who found *you.*"

Ashley was stunned. How did Robert . . . ?

"Don't look so baffled," he said, "your mother told me. You had some sort of a teenage crush on him." He laughed scornfully. "So now I guess you think this man can save Lauren, too. For God's sake, Ashley, isn't it time you grew up?"

She swallowed her outrage and said reasonably, "Robert. I really don't want to argue. The police screwed up my case and I won't risk that happening again with my . . . our daughter."

"Ashley, listen, I understand how you feel, but . . ."

She lifted a hand and shook her head. "I'm asking you to trust me on this. It's only been forty-eight hours. Davey hasn't even asked for money yet."

"God," he whispered, and he stopped walking and sank onto a boulder by the side of the road, dropping his forehead into a hand. "I can't believe this. *Lauren.* I just can't believe it. And you didn't even tell me."

"Because I knew how you'd react. Robert, I know Davey. I know if I go along with this sick game he's playing Lauren will be okay. I just . . . know that."

He looked up at her. His stare was haunted. "You know that, do you? You know that for a fact?"

"He's doing this as payback for the years he spent in prison. And his father died there. He blames me."

"That's just insane."

"Yes, I agree. And I'm sure he'll get around to the money thing. But he wants me to suffer. He isn't going to release Lauren until I've hit bottom."

"It's a nightmare," he whispered, "a nightmare."

"Yes. It is. And when the time comes, you'll have to help with the money. I don't have it. I can't even borrow it. I had to take a mortgage on the house last year. The apartment . . . But that doesn't matter. You can come up with cash, can't you?"

"Of course. Of course I can."

"It may not come to that. Chris has a few ideas, and . . ."

"Chris," he spat out. "Not the FBI. Just a nobody . . ."

"He *is* a cop. I told you. I want you to promise you won't interfere, I mean by calling the police or anything like that."

"Ashley, you're wrong. You're handling this all wrong. I won't promise you anything of the kind. Lauren is my daughter, for the love of God."

"Our daughter."

"Of course. And if she had been with me, had supervision . . ."

"Let's not go there right now. I'm asking you, no, I'm *demanding* that you give me a little credit and let me handle this. Just a few days. Say two more days. Will you give me that?"

But he still wasn't willing to promise even a day. "I have to think. Christ, I'm in shock here. And I want to know a whole lot more about this Chris Judge who you're putting all your faith in. You better believe I do."

"Fine, Robert. Do what you have to. Just don't call the authorities."

"You know, Ashley," he said, coming to his feet, "you aren't a well person. You . . ."

"And let's not go *there*, either," she fired back.

They started toward the house. In between the barbs he threw at her and sudden spurts of fear for Lauren's safety, she was beginning to wonder if he wasn't right. Maybe she was sick. Maybe she'd been faking it all these years and her judgment was impaired. And what did she really know about Chris? Her experience with him dated back twenty years. Maybe she had made a wildly misguided decision when she phoned him—a fatally wrong decision.

They walked into the house to find the baby crying and Luda shooing the dog from the kitchen.

"That woman is crazy," Elaine said, trying to soothe the baby while she paced the living room holding the tiny thing bundled in her arms.

Pauline was confused and undone, taking refuge in her bedroom. And Vladimir was nowhere to be seen. He never could deal with a ruckus.

Ashley closed her eyes momentarily, opened them. "Listen," she said to her ex-husband. "Just a couple days. Let me do it my way, and if we haven't made any progress, we'll call the police, the FBI, we'll have to risk it. And I'll keep you informed. I'll phone you every hour, if you want."

He glared at her. "Goddamn right you will." Then he

whirled on his young wife. "Can't you keep that kid quiet?"

They finally left. Ashley stood trembling on the porch and watched as Robert picked up his titanium bicycle with one hand. Showing off. Oh God, and Chris was witnessing the whole thing. Then Robert turned to Chris and she heard him say, in that clipped corporate voice of his, "Okay, I'm giving you a little while, but I'll be checking up on you. This is my child were talking about."

Chris stood quietly, relaxed, his expression impassive. "I'm well aware of that. I've got a kid myself."

"Don't screw up, fella, that's all."

"I'll try not to," Chris replied mildly.

Robert turned away to put the baby in the pack and whistled the dog out of the house. Elaine was pouting because he'd yelled at her. Ashley waited on the porch for them to leave. She was unable to stop shaking. Inside Luda was talking to herself, and Ashley could hear the TV in Pauline's bedroom turned up full blast to drown out the commotion.

She wanted to scream. To scream and sob and feel Lauren in her arms. A wave of claustrophobia smothered her despite being in the open. Her heart banged too fast; she began to gulp in lungfuls of air. She swayed and sank onto her knees on the top step, clutching the railing for support.

"Oh God, oh God," she moaned, "what if I'm wrong? What if . . . ?"

And Chris was there. She felt him crouch beside her and pry her fingers from the rail and hold her hands in his.

"Oh God, Chris," she breathed, "tell me I'm not crazy. Tell me I'm doing the right thing!"

"You're not crazy. You're doing the right thing," he whispered against her hair, and after a time the air seemed to hold in her lungs again and she could feel the sun on her shoulders, warm and forgiving.

EIGHT

Chris folded the maps and stuffed them back into the glove compartment of the Mustang. *God Almighty,* he thought, this place was a circus. And Robert Marin thought he was the lion tamer. What an asshole.

He tried to imagine Ashley married to the man, in *bed* with him, but he found himself clenching his jaw. Angry, resentful, goddamn jealous. Stupid.

He had work to do, though. One step to take today, and then, after that, another. And he needed Jay the mechanic's help for the first one. He walked next door and found Jay, head buried under the hood of a battered Subaru.

"I was wondering," Chris began, "if you could take a look at my carburetor. I can see you're busy." He tipped his head at the gaggle of cars awaiting Jay's healing touch. "I think it's only an altitude thing. I want to be sure, though, don't want to blow the engine."

As predicted, Jay was delighted to get his hands on

the Mustang. "Hey, no problem," he said. "Probably the jets. Too small for 8,000 feet. It'll only take me a few minutes."

"No rush," Chris said. "But I was thinking . . . that old yellow Jeep over there? Is it yours?"

"Sure is. And the pickup and that '71 BMW."

"Um. I don't suppose I could borrow the Jeep for a few hours while you check the Mustang for me? I'd gas it up, of course."

Jay shrugged. He couldn't care less. "Key's in it. Have fun."

And that was that.

Ashley wasn't as easy to convince. "You're going up to the mine?"

"Uh-huh."

"But . . . What if Lauren really is there? Shouldn't I go with you? I *need* to be there. I . . ."

"This is just reconnaissance. It's doubtful Lauren is there. But I have to check it out. I tried his cousin's house, now I try the mine."

"But . . . but it's miles from here, all the way up Taylor Pass."

He reached out and tucked a stray lock of her hair behind an ear. Then he caught himself and stepped back. *Whoa,* he thought.

"I'm going," he managed to say, "because of the tiny chance she is there. We get that out of the way, then proceed. Okay?"

She searched his face. "I should be with you. I should," she said breathlessly, and he could tell she was having trouble getting air just thinking about the mine. He was suddenly and profoundly angry and in the mood to kill. *Goddamn those men for doing this to her.* And then he was glad that Jerry Potts was dead. He hoped the emphysema had lasted a good long time.

To Ashley he only said, "No. You aren't going any-where near that place."

She bowed her head in consent.

He drove out Ashley's road late that morning in the faded, topless old Jeep. He was wearing jeans and boots, a long-sleeved checked shirt and a dark blue wind-breaker. Ashley and Luda had filled a rucksack with a flashlight, sandwiches, soda pop and water, and he stopped in town to top the gas tank off and pick up a Forest Service map of the White River National Forest, which included hundreds of square miles of terrain in and around the Roaring Fork Valley.

He was astounded at how much the quaint old town of Aspen had grown since the last time he'd been here twenty years ago. The streets were still tidy and tree lined, and flowers bloomed in planters in front of the restored Victorian buildings. The impressive stone court-house looked the same, and a block farther along, the century-old Hotel Jerome appeared to have been renovated to its original elegance of the 1880s. The gaily painted Vic-torians were still there, bracketing both sides of Main Street, but in between them were new buildings, lots of them, some faux Victorian brick, some Bauhaus modern, some mountain elegant. They housed everything from real estate offices to thrift shops to outdoor cafes.

The town was now picture-perfect. When he was gas-sing up, he could see a gondola climbing the verdant face of Aspen Mountain—Ajax to the locals, he recalled. There were luxury hotels at the base of the mountain, too, where before there had been small family-owned ski lodges. Progress, he supposed, screwing the gas cap on. He decided it was the same Aspen, graceful and welcoming, the locals still driving their pickups with dogs hanging their heads over the tailgates, walkers and bicyclists all over the streets and pedestrian malls, music students hurrying to catch buses out to the Aspen Music Festival tent, the mountains to the north dotted with starter castles, Ajax still looming over the town, so steep and close it seemed to be a green wave ready to break. Yet Aspen had changed. Gone were the weedy lots in between buildings and the lived-in look of the original Victorians. *Yeah,* he thought, like a lot of the mountain resorts, Aspen had been gentrified.

The route to Taylor Pass took him up the Castle Creek Valley. For twenty miles the narrow, curving road was paved, ending at the ghost town of Ashcroft.

Chris was again surprised when he drove past the former mining town. On his last trip here the place had been a wreck of collapsed hundred-year-old buildings—more like shacks. Now bikers and hikers and bus tour groups wandered on paths between the restored structures. *Progress.* And he felt a pang of nostalgia for the days when the end of the valley had belonged to the deer and elk and a handful of serious mountaineers.

He and his dad had put in for their elk hunting licenses in the area because of the lack of human presence. From the age of twelve until he'd graduated from the University of Colorado, the weeklong annual hunting trip had been their bonding time.

Hunting had been no picnic. November in the heart of the Rocky Mountains was most often a brutal time of year, winter banging at the door, temperatures so frigid at night his teeth had chattered when he'd first left the campfire and climbed into his icy sleeping bag. Frequently, all over the Western Slope of Colorado, hunters had to be rescued when sudden blizzards blew in and

stranded them in their camps beneath four feet of snow.
There were occasional years when Indian summer lasted
into mid-November, and the weather was heavenly, but
then the hunting stank. Elk herds did not migrate until
forced out of the high country by the onslaught of winter.

So he and his dad prayed for crummy weather and
gritted their teeth and bore it.

"Meat on the table," his father had always said when
a good storm blew in and forced the herds to descend.

Dan Judge, Chris's dad, had been a native Coloradan,
a highway engineer who'd worked thirty years for the
company that had completed Interstate 70 through the
Rockies. President Eisenhower had begun the interstate
project in the '50s and dreamed that he'd live to see the
entire country linked by superhighways. Dan Judge had
loved to say, "Well, guess he forgot about the Rockies."
A year after the completion of Interstate 70 through
Glenwood Canyon in the '90s, Dan Judge had died of a
stroke at age fifty-seven. Muriel, Chris's mom, had
moved to New Orleans to be near her married daughter
and her three grandchildren. That had been before Chris
had Rich. Now Muriel only saw Rich a couple of times
a year. Another sad reality of divorce, Chris often
thought. Another facet of his life that left him feeling
helpless. When he and Joanie had been married, she'd
taken care of those details—Christmas visits to New Orleans, Muriel's monthlong summer vacations back to
Colorado and even once to Newark. Lots of phone calls
and birthday cards and presents.

Chris started the old Jeep up the unpaved road toward
Taylor Pass and was overcome by melancholy. Shit. He
missed his dad, and he missed his mom and sister who
lived so far away, and he missed kissing his son good-

night on the top of his head. He missed married life. He missed climbing into bed at night next to the woman he loved. He missed the security of a paycheck well earned. He missed, more than anything, the decent man he'd once been.

And Ashley was putting her faith in him. *Superman.*

Fortunately, he had to set aside his nostalgic self-pity when the dirt track began to rise sharply and he had to stop, get out and lock the hubs on the front tires. The Jeep reminded him a lot of the one his dad had kept covered next to their garage at their Denver house. Dan's Jeep had been red, but the paint was just as sun worn and the seats just as shredded. Yeah, could have been the same vehicle, he mused, swept again by a sense of loss.

There were sections of the rutted dirt road Chris recalled vaguely, especially when the evergreen forests stood sentinel on both sides of him, but when he drove through high parks and stands of aspens, nothing was familiar. Too lush and summer green. He'd always been there in the drab bareness of November.

He remembered the location of their old hunting campsite, though. It had sat on the far side of Taylor Pass below the 14,000-foot peaks that comprised the Elk Mountain Range. This was high country. As high as you could get before ascending above the timberline, where the environment was too rarefied for anything to grow.

He'd long since left behind other vehicles or hikers by the time he reached the camp and pulled the Jeep off the road, parking it next to a lodgepole pine—the same tall pine that his dad used to hang the gutted game from. Chris engaged the parking brake and sat breathing in the cool thin air and stared at the tree. His father had nailed a board to the tree thirty years ago and fixed a pulley to it in order to hang the elk. Part of the board was still there, rotting and hanging askew from a rusted nail.

And in the small clearing next to the tree, remnants of their fire pit remained. A few rocks in a semicircle, some even still blackened. Saplings had sprouted from the ashes in the center of the pit.

He stood in the bright summer sun, hands on his hips, baseball cap pulled low, and he surveyed the area.

It was smaller than he recalled. Hell, as a boy, he'd thought their campsite was enormous. A makeshift wood table set up over there. Several log seats near the campfire. Their big, olive-drab, four-man army tent with the small stove in its center. God, it had taken an hour to pitch that old tent, nothing like the ten seconds it took to pop up a nylon one nowadays.

"When are we going to splurge for a real mountain tent?" Chris had asked that last year they'd hunted.

Dan had turned to him. "This will probably be our final trip, kiddo. You'll graduate this spring and be so damn busy you won't have time."

Chris had laughed. "Are you nuts? I'll never give up this trip. Next year we get a real tent. My treat, Pop."

His father had tossed him the bundle of tent pegs. "We'll see," he'd said.

It had been their last trip.

It had also been the pivotal point of his life, the year he'd found Ashley.

The terrain Chris had covered that morning twenty years ago was too rocky for a Jeep to navigate. He stood in the middle of the campsite and tried to recall just how far the mine was. Half a mile? He remembered the route as if he'd taken it yesterday. The only difference was, that long-ago November, he'd been bundled in down and shouldering a .30-06. Now he reached around to the back of his jeans and felt his service revolver safely tucked in the waistband. He was about to pull it out and pump a round into the chamber when he remembered there already was one in there. From the other night.

He smiled thinly. "Great," he said out loud. But there was no time for morose thoughts or the hollowness that lurked below the surface. He needed to get going before he ran out of daylight.

He pivoted and surveyed the perimeter of the campsite. Yes. There was the route, through that stand of stunted pine. He headed into the forest, picking his way over deadfall and, as he moved forward, the years seemed to peel away. He was twenty-one again and his future lay brightly ahead. The whole world was at his feet.

His wristwatch read 5:30 A.M.

"Cold as a witch's tit," Dan said at his side. "You got your heavy gloves with you, kiddo?"

"Yeah, Pop, I got them."

It was eight degrees Fahrenheit out. Chris felt the cold air claw at his lungs and thought that down in Aspen it was probably twenty-five degrees. But where they were hunting and at nearly 11,000 feet it was downright freezing. Always was in the late autumn.

There was no moon. The woods were so black he had to reach out in front of him every couple of feet to make sure he wasn't going to walk into a tree or tumble into a ravine.

Ahead lay a park. He and Dan had always had luck in the high meadows. A stream trickled through the center of it, and the elk would one by one emerge from the black forest and make their way to the water. The cows and their spring calves first. Paving the way in gathering light. Then later the bulls. One or two. Sometimes three of them if the herd had not been overly culled the previous year.

The key was silence. You had to move quietly and slowly to your spot and await the dawn. You also had to be downwind of the herd. Elk had an excellent sense of smell.

But on that opening morning of elk season not a single bull showed. At seven-thirty, Chris whispered, "I think we're skunked, Pop. They must be in the ravine."

"Or still up higher," Dan whispered back. "What do you think? Breakfast, then take a hike, look for some fresh signs?"

Normally, Chris would've jumped at the chance to fill his stomach with bacon and eggs around a roaring campfire, but the hand of fate was guiding him that icy morning at 11,000 feet. "Um," he said. "You know, let's give that ravine a try. I've got a good feeling."

"Now there's a switch. Well, I gave you your chance." Dan stood up from behind the log that had shielded them and stretched, carefully shouldering his rifle. "You take the high side, sport, and flush whatever is in there down to me. I'll walk in by that boulder. You know the one?"

"Sure do. It's maybe five hundred yards down the slope."

"That's the one."

"Then let's do it. See you in a couple hours back at camp if we come away empty."

"Sounds good to me."

He wondered why he chose that particular route as he left his father and picked his way into the woods. He supposed he really did have a gut feeling that day, a feeling something was going to happen.

The woods ran up toward Castle Peak three thousand

feet above. The climb was rough, and despite his slow pace as he clambered over fallen trees, he was panting in the thin air. Getting warm, though, finally. Even sweating beneath his orange wool cap.

He'd never been on this side of the ravine, though he'd seen the country. Steep cliffs and lots of rockslides. Even a scree field. But there were level spots, too, where he just might spook up some game that would flee down into the gully. And Dan would be waiting below.

Later he would think it was a miracle he'd spotted that cut in the rocks at all. At least at the time he had thought it was a cut. He'd sidetracked to take a look and been surprised to see mine tailings and the entrance to an abandoned silver mine, with a set of rusty, twisted rails that disappeared into the dark interior. Those old-time miners sure got around. All the way up here, he'd marveled. There were mines leftover from the silver boom days everywhere in these mountains. Some pock-marking the ski slopes of Aspen Mountain itself, where the ski patrol marked the holes with orange tape. A little boy, skiing out of bounds, had fallen into one of the mines and been killed some years back. The story had run in the Denver papers.

But this was a slope mine, the kind you walked straight into, the opening in the side of the mountain. Yes, he noticed bleached and splintered wood around the mouth, probably the entrance shed in the old days. There was even an ancient silvered board with chipped painted letters on it, lying at what once had been the doorway to the shed. He bent and brushed off the years of dust and read The Close Call Mine. Those old prospectors sure had a sense of humor.

His father was waiting for him. Damn, he'd like to explore this place. You never knew what you might find inside—rusty tools, antique ones, cool items. But he didn't have a flashlight, and Dan was waiting.

Reluctantly, he turned away, searched the trees below for telltale elk movement. The sun was just rising above the shoulder of Castle Peak, shooting out long shafts of light to paint the valley in brightness. It'd warm up soon.

He'd started to move away, searching for the best path through the rocks and trees, when he heard it. He stopped, listened hard. An elk bugle? If so, it was really distant. Probably too far to bother with.

But he stood there, his breath pluming in the cold, a slanted beam of sun arrowing into the mine entrance. His lip curled at a corner. "Well now," he said, *"The Guiding Light?"*

Then he heard it again, a weak humming. Sobering, he turned, cocking his ear for the direction of the sound. A breeze rattled the tree branches, drowning the unfamiliar noise.

It resembled a human voice, a thready impossible song. And it was coming from the mine. The hairs rose on his neck. *No way,* he thought, his mind blank. Had to be an animal holed up in the mine. A bird. A . . . a coyote or a fox or . . .

There it was again. He took his rifle off his shoulder and held it pointed straight ahead. Feeling like a fool. And Pop was waiting.

He took a step toward the entrance, then another. The gaping hole was black and echoing, and the moment he moved inside, he was in an alien world, cut off from reality, from the sun and the trees and the craggy peaks. He felt a sudden horrible panic that the mine would suck him in, and he'd never find his way out.

The sound again, louder. Yes, it was coming from ahead of him, deeper inside. He could almost make out words. But, of course, there couldn't be a human being in this place.

He walked on, the light from the entrance fading quickly. His hands out in front of him grasping the rifle, he felt his way along the floor in a kind of shuffle.

A moan, a rattling, something was there. *Jesus.*

He drew damp air into his lungs, winced at the moldy smell and cried out, "Hello?" But his voice was weak and shaky, and he swallowed and tried again. "Hello?" Echoing.

The humming stopped instantly, and there was only silence, vast and complete except for water dripping in the dank coolness.

"Is anybody there?" he yelled, feeling like an idiot as his words reverberated around him.

A noise, yes. A human noise, ludicrously familiar in this cave. A sob.

"Hello? Where are you?"

Another sob, bouncing off the rock walls.

"I'm coming," he said, his heart pounding. There couldn't be anyone in here, but there was.

He forced himself to walk, like a kid playing blindman's bluff, the barrel of his rifle scraping the rock walls, tripping on the rotted rails that ran down the center of the floor. He'd have given an arm and a leg for a lousy flashlight.

Coming up against a solid wall, feeling his way around a corner in the passageway. Amazingly, there was light, a dim, flickering glow. Were his eyes getting used to the dark? Was there an airshaft to the surface here?

Light?

He moved faster, able to make out the twists and turns, the rails, the fallen rubble on the floor, a couple of other tunnels branching off. Mist hung in the air like dust, and support beams sprouted ghostly white fungus like aberrant mushrooms.

"Hello?" he tried again.

"Help!" he heard, and he stopped as if felled by an ax.

He never knew how long he stood frozen there, his emotions raging from disbelief to doubt to a childish fear of the unknown dark. But somehow he finally forced his feet to move, step by step, slowly at first, then more quickly until he was rushing headlong toward the light, his rifle slung over his shoulder now. He wouldn't need it—the voice was female.

He almost tripped over her. A huddled form in the wavering glow of a kerosene lamp. Bright blue and lumpy and . . .

"Oh my God," he heard her say, a sob.

"Jesus." He bent down. "What . . . ?"

A face turned up to him. Dirty and tear streaked with filthy tangled hair. "Please," she whimpered.

"Who . . . ?" He felt stupid, stammering, not knowing what to do.

"They'll come back," she croaked.

"Who'll come back?"

She shook her head then and cowered away from him.

"*Who* will come back?" he tried again.

She moaned, then said, "Those men. The ones . . ."

"Are you hurt?" he said.

She moved her head slowly from side to side.

"What's your name?"

It took her a moment, as if she had to think hard about that. Finally she whispered, "Ash . . . Ashley."

"Ashley, Jesus, what are you doing here?"

"They . . . they put me here."

They again.

"Okay, well, why don't you leave?"

She moved, and he realized the blue lumpy thing was a sleeping bag she was wrapped in. She held up a hand. He squinted, then recoiled in shock. A chain was padlocked to her wrist.

"Good God."

"They'll come back soon," she whispered. "Please, help me."

Who the hell were *they*? "All right, God, okay." He followed the chain from her wrist along the dirt floor to a rusty ring in the wall. Another padlock. He tugged on it. Hard.

"I tried that!" she cried. "Please, hurry!"

The kerosene lamp flared and fluttered, running out of fuel, and then it would be dark and . . .

"Okay," he said, "I'm going to break this chain, okay? I'll shoot it. But I don't want you to get hurt. Look, can you stretch your arm out and wrap the sleeping bag around it?"

"Hurry," she sobbed.

"There, like that. Turn your face away. It'll be loud, okay? Don't move. Ashley?"

She stared up at him, and he couldn't tell whether she understood. But she turned her face away to the wall, held her arm out and pulled the sleeping bag around herself, then crouched there, trembling.

He would have given anything for a less powerful weapon. The .30-06 was a big game rifle, for chrissakes, and if he didn't rip her arm half off with the force of the shot, the bullet would probably ricochet off the damn walls and kill them both.

"Hey, maybe this is a bad idea," he began, but she started crying, and he put the long barrel against the chain, angled it away from them, sent up a feeble prayer and pulled the trigger.

The recoil was terrific and the noise deafening. Dust lifted, and he was aware that her arm had jerked up— probably shot off, he thought for a horrible second. He even thought he heard her screaming, but it had to be ringing in his ears.

Still praying, half dazed from the blast, he stepped forward, the smell of gunpowder sharp in his nose. He coughed, tried to find her. "Ashley?"

He heard her crying, made his way toward the sound. "Ashley, are you okay?"

Small animal whimpers.

His hand touched her, felt for her arm. It was tucked tightly against her chest, with a foot of chain hanging from it.

"Did anything hit you? Here, let me see your arm."

But she clutched herself and wouldn't let him look.

God, what was going on here? Who had done this? Was she one of those feral children you read about?

"Ashley," he said again, trying to sound calm, reassuring. "You're free now. See?" He held up the severed chain. "Let's leave this place. Can you walk?"

She peered up at him. "What if they come back?"

"Hey, don't worry. I've got my rifle here. I'll take care of you. No one will hurt you, Ashley, I promise." Who were *they*? "Can you stand?"

She pushed herself up to her knees, and the sleeping bag fell away. A skinny kid, in her mid teens, he guessed. Filthy clothes. How the hell long had she been chained in this tomb? He took her arm and gently helped her. The way you would a frightened animal.

"There," he said. "Okay?"

"Hurry."

"Sure, here, hold on to me. That's it. Hm, just a sec, I'm going to take the kerosene lamp so we can see." He grabbed the wire handle, hurried back to her. "It's not far. Just around the corner."

She was shuddering, and he put his arm around her, his rifle slung over his shoulder, carrying the guttering lamp. His father must be thinking he'd found a trophy bull and was tracking it to kingdom come.

"Ashley, do you have a last name?"

"Lacouter," she got out.

"Where do you live?"

"Aspen." Another quavering breath.

"And do your . . . um," he had to be careful here, "do your parents know where you are?"

"No. No. No, no, no! Oh God!"

"Hey, it's okay. We'll call them. We have a Jeep, my dad and me. We'll drive you."

Her shoulders were bony and narrow under his arm, and they trembled uncontrollably. He walked her past branching shafts, around the corner of the main tunnel, and ahead he could see the round light of the entrance. "Almost there," he said.

"It's . . . it's day," she murmured.

"Uh, sure, it's about nine in the morning."

"I haven't . . ."

"Come on, a few more feet, Ashley."

She stopped short near the entrance, blinking.

"It's bright, isn't it? How long, I mean . . . When was the last time you were outside?"

"I don't know," she breathed.

This was one bizarre situation, he thought. Christ, maybe there was a reason why she was . . . But, no, there was no reason in the world to chain a girl in a cave.

Outside, she gasped and looked around. He saw that

she was still shivering and took off his orange parka and
bundled her in it.

How far was it to the campsite? A half a mile? Could
she make it?

She swayed and nearly collapsed, and he swung her
into his arms and carried her. She was light—hardly
weighed a thing—and she clung to him as if he were
the Savior himself.

He held her when they reached the campsite, and if
he let her go or even loosened his embrace she shook
and sobbed. When Dan returned, ready to give him hell
for not showing up, his father was instead stunned at the
sight of a dirty, disheveled teenager clinging to his son.
And Dan had to drive the Jeep, because Ashley was
terrified of him, and sat next to Chris, clinging desperately to him all the way down Taylor Pass and then
down Castle Creek Road to Aspen Valley Hospital.

After that it was police and phone calls and her hysterical parents and the brief but brilliant eye of the media
on Christopher Judge, college student and hero.

Later, he found out that Ashley Lacouter had been
kidnapped and spirited away to the abandoned mine and
held there for three months.

Three months.

By a crazy pair, Jerry and Davey Potts, father and
son, who wanted a woman to cook and clean and wash
clothes for them. But Ashley had refused, and her in-
transigence had prompted them to keep her in the mine.

Chris stayed in touch with Ashley. He met her parents, Pauline and Ken, and he visited her at the teen unit
in the Denver hospital where she was institutionalized.

Winter passed and spring arrived. He graduated. And
he was still visiting Ashley, who was suffering from
claustrophobia and post-traumatic stress disorder.

He was not certain when the idea to become a cop first took hold. Maybe it was when he'd rescued her in The Close Call. Or maybe the notion came from following the early pretrial activity on the Pottses' case. A defining moment occurred when he'd been prepped for his testimony at the trial. He was leaving the courthouse when one of the detectives working the case came up to him and said, "You ought to think about police work, son."

He was never sure exactly when he made the final decision. One day he was a university graduate with a Bachelor of Arts degree, heading nowhere in particular, and the next day he was applying to the police academy.

It took almost a year for the Pottses to come to trial. By then he was a rookie cop. He was also still visiting Ashley in the hospital, watching her fight her way back to mental health. Despite their six-year difference in age, they became close friends. He'd even imagined, with the brazen ego of a young man, that the teenager had developed a crush on him.

The trial took place during the first weeks of her release from the hospital. He also imagined that he helped her through those rough days. Then it was over. She returned to school, and their communication was down to a phone call a week, then one a month, then she left for college and they merely exchanged Christmas cards. For a few years.

When he transferred to Newark, he never heard from Ashley Lacouter again.

The present returned with a jolt. He stood in the mine, the beam of the flashlight on the spot where he'd found Ashley that long ago day. There was nothing there now;

dust lay thick on the floor, mist danced in the narrow beam of light.

Of course there was nothing. What had he expected, another young girl chained in the same place? Lauren waiting for him? He'd known that was a long shot. There were no signs of anyone having been there, no rubbish, no footsteps in the dust. Nothing.

Why had he really come all the way up here? Some sick urge to return to the past? To the one time in his life when he'd done something worthwhile? No, that wasn't true. He'd done a few other good things—loving Joanie, having Rich, helping Joe out with the money. Yeah, there were a few high points in his life.

But there were more low points, and they were crushing.

He turned and shone the flashlight ahead, sweeping it across the dirt floor and over the weeping rock walls. Nothing but his footprints and the smell of damp, moldy earth and the peculiar feel of dense humidity, so odd in the bone-dry Colorado climate.

He walked out of the mine and emerged, blinking, into the warm summer day. Hiking back to the old camp where he'd left Jay's Jeep, he thought about the ultimate irony of his life.

He'd chosen police work because of Ashley. Hell, he knew he'd been a little in love with the girl he'd saved. Young and idealistic, he'd thought he could create goodness in the world; saw himself as one of the guys in a white hat, dispensing justice as if he had an exclusive grasp on it.

How far he'd fallen since those heady days.

He moved down the green mountainside, the sky sapphire above, the trees sighing in a cool breeze, a creek

trickling nearby. A chickadee whistling its mating call—
dee-dee—over and over.

And he wondered where, precisely, his life had come
apart.

NINE

"What did it look like?" Ashley forced herself to ask.

He glanced at her from under sandy brows, shook his head slightly: *not here.*

She was desperate to know what the mine had been like, equally as desperate to evade the memory.

"Luda, Chris and I need to talk, okay? I'll be in his apartment if you need me."

"Da," Luda muttered, rattling dinner dishes.

In the apartment over the garage, she sat on the couch, Chris in his worn chair. She held herself erect, hands between her knees, scared, curious, expectant.

"Well?"

A corner of his lip quirked, and he scratched at his head with a finger. "It was the same."

"Chris, please."

"Dark, damp. No one's been there, no footprints, not even any trash. The same rusty rails." He shrugged.

She closed her eyes. "I remember it was so cold in

there. So cold." She drew in a quavering breath. "I was cold all the time, even in the summer when they first put me there."

"A constant temperature of fifty-three degrees, winter and summer, or so the sheriff testified at the trial."

She held herself and shivered, touched by the hand of the past. "The first time I felt warm was when you gave me your parka."

"That orange thing. I have it somewhere."

"And do you still hunt?"

"No. Not anymore. My dad died the year after that trip."

"I'm sorry. God, I'm so sorry. Did you ever tell me that?"

"Probably not. You had enough problems."

"Did you apologize for me? I mean, the way I was so scared of him? I know it was ridiculous, but I . . . I wasn't thinking straight."

"There was no need. He understood."

"Was there anything left in the mine? The chain, the ring in the wall?" She shuddered.

"All taken for evidence."

"Oh, sure, of course."

"It was just a dark old hole in the side of the mountain, Ashley."

"It was . . . and it wasn't." She lifted her eyes to his. "It was hell."

"Once upon a time, I guess, The Close Call was a happy place, made some silver baron real rich."

"No," she shook her head, "that mine was never a happy place."

"Well, the drive was all a waste of time. Lauren wasn't there, Potts wasn't there. It wasn't likely he'd go back, but you never know, criminals can be seriously stupid sometimes."

"Davey Potts isn't stupid."

"No."

She was chilled despite the daytime heat that had risen to the upstairs apartment. It was a close heat. Automatically, she glanced at the windows. Wide open. It was okay. *She* was okay. And she had to focus on Lauren. She couldn't let her illness get the upper hand. *God, not now*.

"Where do we go from here?" she asked.

Chris was watching her carefully. There was something in his expression. Something. Was he worried she'd lose it? Or did he know he was running out of options and was trying to decide whether or not to level with her?

"Look," he said. "I can't do anything tonight, but first thing tomorrow, I'll call Murray Klein again at the state attorney's office and see if he can get me in to talk to Potts's former cell mate. It's pretty common for prisoners to confide in their cell mates. The jailhouse confession routine. Potts probably planned the kidnapping for months, if not years. It could have been all that kept him going. He might have talked to his cell mate and even bragged about it. Some piece of shit inmate might know all about Potts's caper."

"You really think so?"

He hitched his shoulders. "Happens all the time."

"But . . . but why would this prisoner tell you? I mean . . ."

"Listen, he might not know a damn thing. And if he does, it's going to take some finessing to get him to talk. I'm just trying another avenue here. The first two were dead ends."

She nodded. "I wonder if it would do any good to talk to this cousin of Davey's in Glenwood Springs. Maybe he . . ."

"Doubt if we'd get anything out of him. I might contact Potts's parole officer, but that would be dicey, me not being on the force."

"What about the cabin in Marble where he and his father lived?"

"Sold years ago. Remember? Potts's lawyer got it?"

"Oh, right. I guess I knew that, too."

"I'm having to go at this the hard way, Ashley. Now, the police, hell, they could stake out the cousin's place, call up a full-fledged manhunt."

"No."

He lifted his hands, palms up. "Yeah, I know. Well, I'll try, but . . ."

She leaned forward. "You *are* helping. I knew you could. That's why I called you, Chris."

"Listen, I'm doing the most basic things, routine procedures the police would do, and they'd be able to do it without pulling in favors, like I have to."

"But Davey would know if there were cop cars parked out front. He'd know, and he'd, he'd . . ." She couldn't say it.

"Hey, Ashley, you can't be sure of that."

"I can. Yes, I can. He'd know." She blinked back tears and tried to conceal the shaking of her hands. After a minute, she said, "Okay, so tomorrow you're driving to Canon City?"

"Yes, unless Murray can't hook me up."

The following morning, before Chris had even had a sip of coffee, she confronted him. "I'm going with you."

He frowned and started to say something, but she cut

him off. "I will not stay here in this madhouse. I thought all night about it. I'm going."

He regarded her gravely for a full minute, then muttered something unintelligible, then said, "Just bring the cell phone."

Luda and Vladimir had the next two days off, their usual Thursday and Friday. Vladimir nodded when Ashley said she needed them to change their schedule. But Luda groused. "Phone ring all day for Lauren and I don't like saying this lie, this thing about her going on vacation. Not right. And Vladimir going to take me to Glenwood Hot Springs. Planned long time."

"I know, Luda. But you can go the next day instead."

"And Vladimir have dentist on Friday. He leave me alone with your mother. This not right."

Two weeks ago, Luda had been watching Pauline while Vladimir and Ashley were running errands, and Pauline had left the house and walked into town to buy yarn at Scandinavian Design. Evidently, Pauline had forgotten where she lived and gone to her old house on Garmish Street. When the occupants had come to the door, Pauline had lost it. Fortunately, the police knew her—everyone in town knew Pauline—and had given her a ride home. Luda was beside herself and muttered for days in Russian.

"I need you to watch Mom," Ashley said with an edge. "Luda, you're forcing me to point out things I'd rather not, but I've come through for you and Vladimir so many times I've lost count. Not that I *was* counting. Still, I'm beginning to wonder if you even care about Lauren."

"Humph," Luda said.

"Have Vladimir take Mom to bingo at the Senior Center on Friday. She can stay there all afternoon, and he can do the dentist. Will that work?"

"Your mother not like bingo."

"*Luda,* just have him take her there. For God's sake, she barely knows what she likes or dislikes, and she won't remember the bingo five minutes after she leaves."

"Bingo. Humph," Luda said.

When Ashley told Pauline she was leaving for a couple of days, her mother began to ramble in confusion. "What am I supposed to tell Lauren when she gets home? You better call her at Hayley's. *You* tell her you're going off with that man. This isn't my job. You're her mother." Then Pauline's face went blank.

Ashley tried again. "Mom, you remember, Lauren's not at her friend's? She's . . ." But she stopped. Even if Pauline could grasp reality for a moment, she'd forget within the hour. It was, perhaps, better to let her think Lauren was at Hayley's.

"So, Mom, I'm leaving soon. Luda and Vladimir are here, you know that, so . . ."

"You just go on. Go with . . . Chris. Oh, I don't know, maybe Robert isn't right for you. But what am I going to tell *him*?"

God. Ashley rolled her eyes. "Look, just don't say anything. I'll take care of Robert. Watch TV and don't forget to eat and take your medication. Don't make Vladimir or Luda have to argue with you. Can you do that, Mom?"

"We get along just fine, Ashley. Don't you worry about us."

"Great," she said, "great. And you have my cell phone number if you need me."

Chris had gone to call Murray Klein from the apartment, and Ashley ducked into her bedroom to throw a

few things into an overnight bag. Her brain was reeling.
The whole household was making her crazy. Canon
City, she told herself, she had to keep her mind on that
and nothing else. She had to concentrate and send up a
prayer that Chris could get Davey Potts's former cell
mate to talk. *If* Chris could finagle a meeting with the
inmate and *if* this man even knew anything. Well, she'd
focus on a positive outcome, which was all she could
do right now—focus and pray.

How long would they be on the road? A couple of
days. More if there were leads to follow somewhere else.
What to pack?

She had on a pair of khaki slacks and a pink short-
sleeved linen shirt. She hated herself in pink—the color
made her look insipid—but it didn't matter. And who
was looking at her anyway?

A sweater if it was cool at night. Jeans, underwear. A
toothbrush. She needed her toothbrush and . . . Her cell
phone rang. She snatched it up from her unmade bed
and took a breath, which didn't help at all. Where was
Chris? The apartment . . .

The phone rang again. She pressed Answer and sagged
onto the side of the bed, her knees too rubbery to hold her
up. "Hello?" she whispered.

The voice. *His* voice. "Ash-lee. How are you today?"

She bit her lip and said, "Let me talk to Lauren.
Please," she added, remembering what Chris had said.
Let Potts think he had the power.

"Now, you know I won't do that."

"Please," she tried again, "please, don't hurt my baby.
I'll do anything. How much money do you want? Just
tell me. Lauren's father is . . ."

"Just shut up and listen. My cousin doesn't like
strange men calling and asking about me. Who is that

man, huh, Ash-lee? And how in the hell"—Davey's voice turned hard for a split second—"how in the *hell* did he know about my cousin?"

"I . . . uh, I, honestly, I have no idea. It must've been . . . Robert, yes, my ex-husband must have hired someone."

"I told you to control him."

"Yes, yes, but I warned you, Robert doesn't listen to me, and I tried, really I did, but . . ."

"Anything like that happens again you can make your brat's funeral arrangements," he snarled, and then there was only dead air.

Chris found her on the side of the bed, the phone clutched whitely in both hands.

"He called," she said, lifting her eyes to his. "He called and he knows about you contacting his cousin. I . . . I told him it was Robert. But . . . Chris, we can't call his cousin again or even ask about him. We *can't.*"

"We won't."

"I hope," she swallowed, nauseous. "God, I hope this doesn't make it worse for Lauren."

"He's doing this deliberately. Enjoying every word."

"I . . . I can't bear this, this listening to him. His voice, the threats, it's so awful."

He came close and squatted down by the bed, put a hand on her back, stroked in circles, gently. "You're doing good, Ashley."

"I don't know . . . I just don't know anymore. I'm so scared."

"We all are," he said softly.

They were on the road by ten that morning, heading east on Highway 82 toward Independence Pass and the Eastern Slope of Colorado. The Colorado State Penitentiary, where Davey Potts had been incarcerated after he'd turned eighteen and left a youth facility, was situated in the Canon City prison complex, nearly four hours from Aspen.

Chris drove his Mustang with careless competence along the winding road up to the 12,000-foot pass over the Continental Divide, leaving behind the last few traces of civilization after passing Independence, a ghost town that had once been a mining boomtown. The weather was cloudy, cool and overcast as they ascended. The mountains, still white-capped, stretched away in undulating ranks at the top of the pass.

"I haven't been over this road in twenty years," Chris mused, "and here I am doing it twice within a few days."

"Do you want me to drive?" she asked. "Maybe later?"

He shot her an amused glance. "I don't think so."

"I'm a good driver."

"I remember, that was the one thing you wanted more than anything else, when you were in the teen unit."

"What?"

"Your license."

"Oh. Um, it seems so unimportant now, but Lauren is fifteen and she wants to drive desperately. She can hardly wait. I guess I remember . . ." She put her face in her hands. "Oh, Lauren." Then she straightened and hardened her resolve. "I'll try not to do that, I swear."

"Go ahead. I don't mind."

"I do."

Her phone rang again when they reached Twin Lakes, and she felt her heart thud against her ribcage.

"Answer it," Chris said.

She pressed the button. "Hello?"

"Jesus Christ, Ashley! Where the hell are you?"

"Robert," she breathed.

"Listen, you promised to keep me informed what that Judge character was doing, and I call Pauline, and she tells me you're out of town!"

"Robert, please." She felt herself start to tremble.

"Give me the phone," Chris said.

"No, you're driving, for God's sake, Chris."

"What? What? Who was that? Damnit, Ashley!"

"Look. Chris and I are heading to Canon City. He's going to talk to some of the prisoners there who knew Davey Potts, to find out if he told anyone about his plans."

"Ah, for chrissakes, of all the ridiculous ideas. *This* is how he thinks he's going to find Lauren?"

"Yes." God, she was whimpering.

"I can't believe it."

"I was going to call you when there was something definite to tell you. Honestly."

"Damnit, you shouldn't leave town without my knowing."

"Sorry."

"Any contact from Potts?"

"Yes."

"And Lauren? Did he let you speak to Lauren?"

"No. Not yet."

"What does he want? Has he asked for money?"

"No. So far it appears to be the revenge thing. But we're sure, I mean, Chris thinks Lauren will be okay as long as I . . ."

"*Chris*. What the hell does *he* know?" And he hung up.

"I hate that man," she muttered between clenched teeth.

"You didn't always hate him."

"My mistake," she said.

They stopped for lunch in the small town of Salida, perched on the bank of the Arkansas River. The Mexican restaurant Chris chose was decorated with potted palms around a splashing fountain and blue tiles and a fake parrot in a cage.

The waitresses, however, were pure Colorado teenagers, earning money over summer vacation. Their waitress was dressed in shorts and a T-shirt and sandals and had a gold stud in her nose, and at least six more edging one ear.

"Lauren wants to do that," Ashley said when the girl had taken their orders and left.

"Do what, waitress?"

"Get her ear pierced a million times."

"Oh."

"All the girls want to, but so far none of their mothers will let them. If one mother weakens, though, the war is lost."

"It's a war?"

"Sometimes."

"I'm glad I have a son."

"Well, you wouldn't see that side of a daughter. God knows Robert doesn't."

Their burrito plates arrived. Chris started in, obviously hungry, and Ashley watched him for a time. Finally, he must have sensed her eyes on him because he paused and glanced up. "You don't like the food?"

"I was just looking at you."

"See anything interesting?"

"It's funny. You're the same but you're not. You know what I mean?"

"Not exactly. I was a kid when I met you. Sure, I've changed."

"Not all that much. I think you're better looking."

"Jesus Christ, Ashley."

"What happened in Newark?" She leaned forward.

He narrowed his eyes. "My wife left me. I got burned out. I retired."

"Something happened."

"Eat your lunch."

She picked up her fork. "Does your ex-wife hate you?"

He hesitated. "No. She just doesn't *like* me anymore."

"Is she a good mother?"

"Yeah, I think so."

"Are you a good father?"

"Better since I moved back. Hey, what is this?"

"I'm trying to figure you out."

"It's not worth it, believe me."

"That's a lot of crap," she said.

"Fine. Whatever." He began to eat again, pointedly ignoring her.

She took a few bites, looked idly out the window. A flotilla of brightly colored rubber rafts was floating down the Arkansas, filled with tourists in equally garish flotation vests. River rafting was a big draw for Colorado in summer. She'd gone once with Robert and Lauren on the Colorado. It had been a great day. Lauren had loved it.

"Looks like fun," Chris said.

"Um. You ever do it?"

"Sure, in high school."

She knew she was making him uncomfortable. Was it her questions or was it simply her presence? She wished they could recapture the innocent friendship they'd had all those years ago.

She tried some more of the spicy food—shredded beef

and onions and cheese in a tortilla, covered with a five-alarm hot sauce. And she recalled, suddenly, having lunch with Chris before. She'd been given a pass to leave the hospital with him. Yes, and he had taken her to a close Taco Bell, and she'd been so thrilled to be out of jail, having tacos like a normal teenager. With a handsome guy. An *older* guy. One on whom she had a terrible crush.

If only she'd told him. Then maybe their lives would have been entirely different. He wouldn't have married his ex, and she wouldn't have married Robert and . . .

Lauren could have been their daughter, and they would still be together after all this time. They'd be happy. Just the way she'd daydreamed that long year in the teen unit. She'd prayed that he'd wait for her to get a little older, catch up to him. He was her friend and her knight on a white horse; he was Superman. A college senior, he'd seemed so old at the time. Utterly mature.

Had her crush been real? Or had he been merely the natural object of her emotions, given the situation?

She picked at the meat in the burrito, wondering why she'd never told him how she felt. Ashamed, probably embarrassed. Chicken.

Well, she hoped she'd learned from experience.

"So," she said, "you retired from the police force."

"Right."

"And you don't plan to work again, at anything?"

"I, ah, had a little luck at gambling. Won some money."

"Gambling?"

"Sure, lots of people gamble."

"You wanted to be a policeman so much, Chris. I can't believe you'd just give it up." She waited for his reply.

"It gets old, Ashley. I was young, you know, didn't realize how hard undercover work could be on me and my family."

"Undercover? Wow," was all she could say.

"Nothing serious. Some routine stuff." He drank his iced tea and wiped his mouth with a napkin. "They gave me an assignment, getting friendly with some of the mob guys. You know, small-time crooks. Nobody important."

"Did you like it?"

"Undercover? Yeah, I liked it." He seemed to reflect for a moment, turning inward. "It was a challenge. And I was good at it."

"Really."

He leaned back, and something in his eyes receded from her into the past. She suddenly wanted, *needed*, to know what he'd done. To understand what had happened to him since they'd first known each other.

"Tell me," she said softly.

"Oh, I was just thinking about this one time"—he smiled, laugh lines crinkling at the corners of his eyes—"when Sal—he was my assignment—put a contract out on his dog's psychiatrist. I kid you not. His dog was nuts, kept biting people, and Sal sent him to a dog shrink. Well, the shrink told him his mutt had unresolved issues from his youth, and he couldn't help the dog and Sal should euthanize him. So Sal scraped together five thousand dollars and asked his boss to hire a hit man to do the shrink.

"We had to talk him down, show him why he couldn't do that. No matter how pissed he was. It was a scene."

"You liked Sal."

"I did. He was a friend."

"A criminal, but a friend."

He leveled his golden gaze on her. "Let me tell you,

Ashley, one has nothing to do with the other."

"Was Sal a nice guy?"

"Yeah, you could say that. He was scrawny, bald with a big beak of a nose. He had a couple grown kids and a wife he adored. And he got up in the morning like everybody else and went to work. Only work was . . . illegal stuff, shady stuff. But he never saw it that way." He looked at her, a crooked grin on his face. "He was a helluva guy."

"It must have been hard."

"It was my job."

"And when you left, what happened to Sal?"

His expression congealed; she barely recognized him. "Yeah, well, Sal is, shall we say, deceased?"

"Oh God, Chris."

He gestured with a hand, a curiously Mediterranean movement, and she realized he had retreated into a past persona. "It's over. Finished. Hey, I got paid the big bucks for my work."

"But, that's awful. It must stay with you, I mean, the pain of doing that kind of thing."

"I knew what I was getting into. No excuses. Somebody has to do it. Like astronauts, you know, trained and ready, and they know their job is dangerous as hell, but it has to be done. A job, Ashley."

She shook her head. "No. My God, it's so much more than a job. It's your life, it's . . ."

"It's over, is what it is. Forget about it."

She leaned forward. "You haven't forgotten about it."

"What makes you think that?"

She stared into his eyes, saying nothing.

"Come on, lighten up. My past is uninteresting."

"You don't have to put on that front for me, Chris."

"Front? Jesus . . ."

"Chris."

He switched his attention to the window, only his profile visible. A strong profile, straight nose and chin, the shadow of whiskers on his jaw.

"Chris," she urged gently.

"You don't want to know any goddamn thing about that stuff. It's in the past. You don't want to know what I did or who I was then," he said bitterly, still looking away.

Oh, but I do want to know, she thought. *I want to know every last detail.*

TEN

Robert Marin leaned forward and put his elbows on the polished desktop, the phone held to his ear. On the other side of the tall teak doors that separated his home office from the living room, he could hear the baby wailing and Elaine's soothing coos. His brow furrowed in annoyance.

"Hold on, Kingston, I didn't get that. Who did you say he worked for?" Robert listened. "Uh-huh. Okay. Northern New Jersey Task Force? Interesting. And when did he leave?"

The private detective spoke for another minute.

"Really?" Robert said. "So let me get this straight. Chris Judge moved back to Denver last winter after an Internal Affairs investigation?"

Again he listened.

"Um. I'm starting to get the picture, all right. Undercover cop goes bad. Or *maybe* he does."

Mark Kingston was the best, or so Robert had been

told by his lawyer, who'd suggested the man. The P.I. was out of Denver, and he'd been FBI before an injury had forced him into early retirement. Now his home base was in Colorado, but he had connections from New York to Miami to L.A. He'd only been on the case for a day, and already had some solid info on this asshole Ashley was putting her faith in.

Kingston told him everything he'd thus far learned, even the mundane details of Judge's background: father, deceased, had been an engineer with the outfit who'd built the interstate through Colorado; mother, still alive, lived near a sister in New Orleans; wife and son had moved to Newark with Judge but returned to Colorado, where she'd filed for divorce two years ago.

"I don't care about that crap," Robert cut in. "I just want to know if this man stands a chance of locating my daughter. I don't even care if he was dirty. What did he do with this task force in Newark? I mean, did he ever work with kidnappings?"

"No. Never," Kingston told him. "Apparently, he was undercover, got in with organized crime. There was a drug bust, and a lot of missing money from a trunk of one of the wiseguys' Caddys. From what I've gathered so far, and like I said, this is very preliminary, there was never any proof of money in the trunk, just one of the wiseguys screaming bloody murder after his arrest that his 'personal savings'—I love that one—but anyway, his money was missing. Evidently, Chris Judge was the only one who had access to the vehicle before the rest of the task force took down the dealers. The IA investigated Judge and fell short as far as an indictment went."

"So why *was* he forced out?"

"Oh, hell, everyone figured he was dirty. Plus he'd

gone sour, been undercover too long. It happens. Agents can lose the sense of who they are. Good guy or bad guy. They make friends on both sides of the law, and they get bitter."

"Oh?"

"Yes, they figure out that there are as many dirty hands on the side of the law as there are on the other side. Especially with the New York–Jersey crowd."

Robert was pensive for a moment. He let out an exasperated breath and stared through the plate glass windows that overlooked the valley from Independence Pass to the four ski areas of Aspen Mountain, Aspen Highlands, Buttermilk and the slopes of Snowmass beyond. From his Red Mountain aerie, he could even see a shoulder of Hayden Peak and a wedge of majestic Pyramid Peak, mountains that ran in a jagged line of 14,000 footers, which formed the Continental Divide. In Denver his home would have set him back a million and a half. In Aspen, the place had cost him five. It was the view.

Right now that noble view was only a taken-for-granted blur in a corner of his mind.

"I have to tell you," Mark Kingston was saying. "I was FBI for eighteen years before my back injury. I worked the periphery of some kidnapping cases, and in my opinion, I think your ex-wife is making a grave error by not bringing the feds on line."

"She's adamant. I told you."

"I understand, Mr. Marin. And hey, she has a point. Cops make mistakes. More than we'd like to admit. But your daughter, Lauren, you said, still stands a better chance of being found if the FBI's on the case."

Again Robert was quiet. He sat up straight and focused. "I appreciate the advice, Kingston," he said. "I promised my ex-wife a couple of days to do it her way.

I guess that was a misjudgment. It's just so hard to think straight. Shit, I haven't had an hour's sleep since I found out. I'm worried out of my mind here. I don't want to step on Ashley's toes, for chrissakes; she's had enough bad times as it is. But if something doesn't give soon with my daughter, you better believe I'll bring in the police. I'll do whatever it takes to get her home safely."

Home, he thought, damn right he'd get his child home. To *his* home. Ashley had fouled up for the last time.

"Look," Robert said. "Keep on this Chris Judge and document every detail you can. We're going to get Lauren back. And when we do, I plan on having her with me. Safely with me. Ashley putting her trust in this loser is just more proof that her judgment is impaired, and I want everything in writing. You understand? Do whatever it takes and I want daily reports."

"No problem, Mr. Marin."

Robert hung up. Of course it was no problem. Money could buy you all the efficiency in the world.

He phoned his lawyer then. "Lenny? You have an hour or so this afternoon? There's something I need to discuss," he said. "Something has happened."

They agreed to meet for a late lunch at The Aspen Club on the east end of town. The club was nestled in the woods above the banks of the Roaring Fork River. The facility boasted world-class spa and health amenities ranging from yoga and aerobic classes to deep tissue massage to the latest in gym equipment and therapy regimens guided by top-notch physical therapists. There were tennis and squash courts, swimming pools. There were shops and beauty salons and a health food bar.

Robert took the Range Rover and dropped Elaine downtown, where she was a volunteer at the Wheeler

Opera House. She sold tickets two afternoons a week
for local theater events and the performing arts—con-
certs and films and ballet. The Wheeler, a restored opera
house dating back to the 1880s, was Aspen's catchall
theater for every imaginable art.

"Pick me up at five?" Elaine asked in front of the
imposing redbrick building. "Maria can't stay past six
tonight, and the baby . . ."

"Five, yes, sure."

"And call me on the cell if you hear anything about
Lauren, honey. I'm so upset. You know she shouldn't
be with Ashley. I *adore* Ashley, don't get me wrong,
but she just lives such a . . . hectic life, and . . ."

"Yes, yes," Robert said. "Be out front at five, all
right? I'm in no mood to wait."

"Yes, dear," she said, and she blew him a kiss.

Leonard—Lenny—Coates was thirty-nine, Robert's
age. But whereas Robert was West Coast born and raised
and still ran his profitable dot com business out of Santa
Cruz, Lenny was a conservative Bostonian, a Harvard
grad who'd first come to Aspen as a college ski bum,
then later, after law school, opened his own office in
town, where he now had three law partners and only
worked two days a week himself. Lenny's favorite expression was, "Retired before forty and loving it." But
Robert had been his first big client in Aspen and he
owed him. Plus Robert Marin had never once complained about his five-hundred-dollar-an-hour fees.

They met and shook hands on the patio overlooking
the tennis courts. "Lunch outside or in?" Lenny said.

"Out here's fine," Robert said distractedly.

They sat at a nicely appointed table under a green
umbrella beneath the green aspen trees. The only noise
they could hear was the white water rushing by in the

river below and an occasional whack of tennis balls from the adjacent courts.

"Hope you don't mind the shade," Lenny said, taking off his sunglasses and tilting his head at the umbrella. "My dermatologist made me promise. Christ, I've already had two suspicious areas treated on my nose. Waiting for the biopsies as we speak."

Sun and skin cancer went hand in hand with outdoor lifestyles at 8,000 feet. Robert didn't mind the shaded table.

They ordered two iced teas with fresh mint and lemon and two salads, one Caesar and one chef's. When their waiter left, Lenny leaned forward. "Okay, Robert, out with it. You sounded like death on the phone."

Robert shook his head and sighed. "I may as well just say it, no point pussyfooting around. But remember, this may be a lunch date, but it's also lawyer-client privilege."

"Always, Robert." Lenny nodded.

"Okay, all right." Robert let out a groaning breath. "It's my daughter. She's been kidnapped."

At first Lenny only stared at him as if he hadn't heard correctly and was trying to figure out what his client had really said. But slowly, while he studied Robert's face, the words sank in. Finally, he said, "Holy shit. Did you really say . . . kidnapped?"

"Yes." Robert waited.

"But . . . my God . . . *when?*"

"A couple days ago."

"My God," he repeated. "But how? I mean, who . . . ? *Jesus.* Stupid question. What I mean is, do the police have any idea . . . ?"

"No police."

"What?"

"You heard me."

"Well, yes, but . . ." Suddenly he banged a fist to his forehead. "Of course. *That's* why you needed the name of a top-drawer private investigator. I wondered, but I figured . . ."

Robert laughed grimly. "I know what you thought. That Elaine was stepping out on me. She's got her figure back; she's fifteen years younger. What else would you think?"

Lenny was strategically silent.

"None of that matters," Robert went on. "What matters is Lauren." He told the attorney everything he knew, starting with Ashley's own abduction and subsequent ordeal to her ongoing struggle with post-traumatic stress disorder and claustrophobia.

The salads came and sat unnoticed, and Robert related Ashley's belief that the same man who'd taken her as a teen now had Lauren.

"All the more reason to notify the FBI, Robert. My God."

"Yes, I agree. But Ashley is right about one thing as far as her own case went. First, the cops, and that includes the FBI, failed to find her twenty years ago. But more upsetting, this creep Potts may be out for revenge. Apparently his father died in prison and this is some sort of sick payback. He's threatened to . . . kill Lauren if her mother brings in the authorities."

"Jesus, oh Robert, oh my God." Lenny kept shaking his head.

"Ashley believes he'll do it."

"Money?" The attorney snapped to attention. "Hasn't he asked for money?"

"Not yet. Not that I know of, anyway. Ashley did tell me that if he wants a ransom I'd have to come up with it. And of course I will. Any amount. I don't care about the money. It's Lauren."

"Of course it is."

"And there's another thing. Ashley has brought in this man to help her. He's an ex-cop. Your investigator told me this morning that this man, this Chris Judge, may even be a dirty ex-cop."

"This just gets better and better, doesn't it?" Lenny said.

"I'm at my wit's end. I promised Ashley I'd hold off involving the police for a few days, but what if I'm wrong? What if . . . what if I get Lauren . . . injured, or worse?"

"No, no, no," Lenny said, "you're not at fault no matter what . . . happens. Lauren is in Ashley's custody till she's eighteen. Your ex-wife is making these decisions." He pursed his lips for a second. "Robert, I think you're right. Maybe, given the circumstances, maybe you were right all along—Lauren would have been better off in your care. Oh, sure, we fought a good court battle to get you custody, but I don't think even I realized just how damaged Ashley's judgment is."

Robert almost said, *I told you so.*

"So what can I do to help? Let me help, Robert, please. Anything."

But Robert waved him off. "I only needed to vent, Lenny. Elaine, well, she doesn't really understand the terrible position I'm in. The last thing I want to do is push Ashley over the edge. Of course she drives me crazy, but I still have feelings for her, and I'm troubled about her instability. What's your opinion? I mean, could Ashley be right about not calling in the police? Should I . . . ?"

"Listen, Robert, ah, hell, I don't know. No one knows

the answer to that. The kidnapper might just mean what he says about the authorities. God knows you read about the tragic results of some of these cases. And you have to wonder, would the victim still be alive if the cops hadn't become involved?"

Robert closed his eyes and leaned his head back. "This is a mess, Lenny, a real fucking mess," he breathed. "And that crooked ex-cop she's got helping her . . . I just don't know. The only thing I can do for now is go along. A couple more days. I'll go along a couple more days. And then . . . And then I only hope it isn't too late."

"You'll get her back. Don't even begin to think you won't. And when Lauren is safe, I swear, Robert, that's it for Ashley. Hell, I love Ashley, too, but this is the last straw. If we have to go all the way to the goddamn Supreme Court we'll win you custody of Lauren."

Robert lowered his head and opened his eyes. "Lenny, I appreciate that. I really do. But right now all I can think about is my little girl."

"I know, Robert, I know, buddy, I know how much she means to you," Lenny said softly.

ELEVEN

Highway 50 took Ashley and Chris past Wellsville and Texas Creek as it followed the Arkansas River. The land was slowly altering on the descent into foothill country, and the temperature was rising, so Chris stopped outside Royal Gorge to put the top down.

"Oh," he said, "I should have asked. Is this going to mess your hair or anything?"

Despite everything, she couldn't help laughing. "My hair? I don't think the wind will bother it, Chris. If I get two minutes a day to fuss with my hair it's a miracle. But thanks for asking."

The top down and secured in the boot, Chris put the car in first and pulled back onto the road. "It looks nice, though."

"What looks nice?"

"Your, ah, you know, hair," he said, and she could have sworn his skin reddened beneath the golden stubble.

Past tourist-jammed Royal Gorge the highway ran through forests of stunted juniper trees and massive red rock formations tossed out of the nether world countless eons ago. Then they dropped again, steeply, into grassland and the high prairie that ran between Colorado Springs and Pueblo.

The land was seemingly empty, stretching down out of the Rockies and running in waves of grass seven hundred miles east to the Missouri River. Seven hundred miles of nothing. Yet hidden on the prairie were NORAD and Fort Carson, ground zero for the nation's defense system. Hidden just as effectively was the state prison complex. You drove along a highway a few miles past Canon City, and if you blinked you might miss the sign in the rolling grasses. But the mammoth complex was there, directly to the south, the many structures tucked carefully away from public view.

"You know," Chris said, flipping on the turn signal to enter the main gate and the Visitor's Center, "Noriega is only a couple hundred yards from us. Not to mention the Unabomber. They all have private suites at Super Max."

Ashley nodded solemnly. Everyone who lived in Colorado knew about Super Max, the state-of-the-art prison that boasted it could break the worst of them. Suites indeed.

But Davey Potts had not been imprisoned in the maximum security structure. He'd been in a youth facility, then at eighteen he'd been moved to a general population state correctional facility on the complex, where he'd stayed for fifteen years until he'd been transferred to a less secure building. There, he'd learned to farm and be a good boy—so good they'd paroled him.

But all that time he'd evidently been working on his plan. Get out and get even.

Chris parked outside of the Visitor's Center. He turned to Ashley. "Okay," he said, "this is as far as you go. You can wait here or wait in the center, where it's air-conditioned."

"But . . ." she began.

"Hey," he said, "I can't bring you along. Think about it. How official would I look?"

"Oh."

"I have to do this on my own. Sorry, but . . ."

"I understand."

He looked toward the Visitor's Center, and she could see a faraway gleam in his eyes, a subtle changing of the planes of his face. He was abruptly unrecognizable. "Gotta go," he said, then he opened his door and tossed her the keys. "If you wait in the car, put the top up or you'll fry. I'll be an hour. Less, if I'm lucky." And then he gave her a curt, impersonal nod, turned on his heel and disappeared inside.

She was stunned. A minute ago he'd been the Chris Judge she'd known for most of her life, an ordinary sort of man, really, strong when he had to be, vulnerable beneath the surface, friendly and competent—her Superman. But now, in the space of a few seconds, he'd mutated into—she searched for the words—maybe a thug, or a cop who wouldn't hesitate to beat a prisoner if his blood was up.

She stayed in the car and mulled over the new Chris. Had he turned into this new man in Newark? And how had he juggled the disparate personas? Husband and father at night—if he'd even gone home at night—and wiseguy during the day. Of course, she reminded herself, he hadn't succeeded. His wife had left him and for what-

ever reason he had quit the police force there. And here,
too, evidently. How did a person live such a crazy life?
One moment a cop. The next day a family man. The
next day a hardened criminal? Good God, she could
barely be herself, whoever *that* was.

She was still thinking about Chris and his role-playing
when he returned, imagining him as a figure in a Greek
drama, the one who donned the comedy mask then the
tragedy mask. Still the same actor inside the costume,
but to the audience completely different.

He slid in next to her, noted that she must be hot as
hell sitting out here. "I was sure you'd wait in the center," he said. Then, without telling her a word about his
success or failure, he nodded at her purse. "I need to use
your phone."

She knew immediately he'd not gotten any information on Potts, that the trip had been a waste of precious
time. Her heart felt like a chunk of lead. "So, he didn't
tell you a thing. Oh God, Chris. Where do we go from
here?"

"Well," he said, "you're right on one score. Williams,
that's the guy I just interviewed, he didn't know a damn
thing."

"You believe him?"

Chris put on his sunglasses. "Yeah. The way I read
it, Williams was close enough to Potts while they shared
the same cell, but not *that* close. But there's good news,
too. Can you hand me the phone?"

She dragged her purse from the floor. "What good
news? I don't see how . . ."

"Okay. Here's the deal. Williams was cooperative. I
maybe let him think I could put in a word with the parole
board when the time came."

"He thought you were a cop." It was not a question.

"Yeah, well, I can still talk the talk. The point is he gave me a name. Guy who's out now and at a halfway house somewhere in Denver, or so Williams thought. Apparently this guy, Jack Fuentes, was Potts's cell mate for years before Williams, and they were real, real tight, if you get my meaning."

"Lovers?"

"Seems so. Anyway, Williams knows Potts and Fuentes have been in touch since Fuentes's release a few months before Potts got out. Fuentes even visited Potts a couple times before Potts was paroled. Williams thinks if anyone knows where Potts is, Fuentes will."

"How do we find him? You said a halfway house, but where?"

"The phone, Ashley?"

"Oh." She handed him the cell phone, and he tapped in some numbers, waited. Several minutes went by before he was put through to his party. "Murray? Chris again. Hey, I'm sorry to bug you, but can you access one more bit of info for me? I'm down in Canon City, and I need you to locate an inmate released on parole to a halfway house in Denver. Name is Jack Fuentes, got out back in March or April." Chris waited again, and then said, "Hey, sure, you bet I'll hang on the line. And thanks, Murray."

"Your friend can get that information right now?" Ashley said.

Chris picked up the keys from the console where she'd put them and started the car, the phone still to his ear. "Sure. The age of information. All Murray has to do is access his files and type in Fuentes. He'll get it, not to worry . . . Yeah, Murray, I'm still here. What? Okay, I got it, on South Broadway just past Gart Brothers. Uh-huh. Thanks again. The favors are piling up here." Chris clicked off. He handed her the phone and backed the car out. "Keep your fingers crossed this Fuentes thing pans out."

"My fingers and toes and anything else I can think of," she said.

"Hey," he said, flashing her a genuine smile, "we're due for a break, right?"

It took an hour and a half to reach the outskirts of Denver where they hit rush-hour traffic. Chris must have read her thoughts; he said, "Doesn't matter. The traffic, that is. If Fuentes is at a halfway house he's got a day job. That's the way it works. We wouldn't catch him before five or six anyway. But if you're going nuts in this traffic, I can pull off the interstate and cut over to Broadway."

"Would you?" she said. "It's just this stop-and-go pace . . . it's so *close*. I almost feel as if I can't breathe."

He put on his directional signal and twisted his head, checking traffic, nosing the Mustang into the right lane. "Hey, I understand, Ashley. You're entitled," he said.

The halfway house where Jack Fuentes was supposedly living was off South Broadway, the main north-south avenue bisecting Denver. Chris parked across the street from the small, dilapidated building and said, "Looks like the place. An old apartment house." He turned to her. "Mind waiting out here again? I'll just run in and check with the den mother, see if Fuentes is around or when he's due to check in."

The den mother. "I'm fine," she said.

Chris leaned close to her and gently placed the back of his hand on her cheek. "Ashley, you're doing great. You honest to God are. Most people would have collapsed. Hell," he said, "you're my heroine, lady."

She couldn't help pressing her cheek into his hand for

a moment, closing her eyes. No one had ever talked to her like this; no one truly understood. But Chris did. He always had.

When he took his hand away, she felt a little like her life preserver was floating out of reach. But he was preparing himself now, putting back on his game face. She recognized the mutation from friend to stranger.

"Now for our pal Fuentes," he said grimly.

She didn't know whether she noticed the man approaching the house on foot first or if Chris did. But something in Chris shifted. He was instantly alert.

"Huh," he said. "Short buzz cut, shoulders like a bull. Could be our man."

"How do you . . . ?"

"Williams described him."

Chris was out on the sidewalk before she could wish him luck. He crossed the street and walked up to the big man who was carrying a thermos. Chris said something. The man paused, eyed Chris, then shrugged heavy shoulders beneath a soiled white T-shirt.

After a minute or so, they walked together toward the front porch steps of the halfway house, and Chris sat on the top one, knees splayed, hands dangling. Fuentes remained standing, arms folded, the thermos pressed into his chest.

They spoke at length. The body language was telling, Fuentes mostly on the defense, Chris at ease. He even smiled a few times, nodding in apparent understanding as Fuentes talked.

The odd thing was that Chris remained seated while Fuentes hovered over him. Was that to lend the man some sense of control? Whatever, she thought, something was working, because Fuentes eventually unfolded his arms and made a few hand gestures. He was doing the talking now. A lot of talking. Her heart, which had already been beating strongly, began to thud.

Oh, Lauren, baby, we're trying, hold on, just hold on.

Chris must've conversed with the man for twenty minutes before he rose to his feet, ducked his head as if in thanks and started back across the street toward the car, tossing a negligent wave over his shoulder.

"Oh God," she whispered, "please, please, please give us a break."

She was interrogating Chris the instant he was behind the wheel. "Did he know anything? Chris, did he . . . ?"

"Yep."

"Oh God, oh please . . ."

"Here's the deal," he said over her pleas. "Fuentes was pretty willing to chat. I got the sense he and Potts were definitely a lot closer than just former cell mates, but when Potts got paroled he dumped Fuentes, told Fuentes on the last time he visited him that he had bigger fish to fry."

"So how does that lead us to Potts?"

"I'm getting there, Ashley. Before Potts came up with what he was terming his coup de grace, he told Fuentes that he was hoping to get paroled, and Fuentes could come live with him at this place he could use in the mountains outside Marble."

She felt as if the rug had been pulled out from beneath her feet. The Marble cabin. But hadn't the place been turned over to the Pottses' lawyer?

She put a hand on her forehead and choked out, "Davey, that bastard. He was lying to Fuentes. Bragging, leading him on. There *is* no cabin anymore, Chris!"

But he was gazing at her with a spark in his hazel eyes. "It isn't the same place, Ashley."

"It . . . isn't? But, how . . . ?"

"Potts told him about the first place, how he and his dad had to turn the deed over to their lawyer years ago. Fuentes said this other cabin is really isolated."

"And Davey has access to it," she reflected, hope springing inside her again. "But . . . but what does that mean? After so much time in prison, how would he . . . ?"

"Beats me. Potts either knows about an abandoned place or he has someone who'll let him use it. Finding it is going to take some digging. Okay, we know that. So we can assume he's somewhere near Marble and we have a starting place."

"Yes," she whispered, "all right, all right. We'll get there. We'll find Lauren. We will find her, won't we, Chris?"

"Goddamn right we will," he said.

It was getting late and he still had one last stop to make. "I need to run by my friend's place and pick up Potts's photograph," he told her, pulling away from the curb.

"The photo the parole officer faxed?"

"Yeah."

"And this friend, is it the man you called from Aspen, this Joe?"

"Yeah, Joe Garcia. We used to work together."

"Oh," she said, and the cell phone rang.

Her pulse took off. Adrenaline shot through her veins, and she snatched the phone out of her purse. She knew she'd never again hear a phone rang without the knee-jerk reaction of sheer terror.

Chris pulled to a curb and said, "Answer it. If it's Potts, don't let him know where you are."

She nodded, tried to still her trembling hands and

pressed the Answer button. "Hello?" she said, her mouth so dry her voice was a croak.

It was him. He began the torment with that horrible twisted pronunciation of her name. "Ash-lee, Ash-lee, you sound stressed out."

Chris scooted close and put his hand over hers, tipping the phone so he could listen in.

"Where are you?"

"At home. I'm at home. I want to talk to Lauren. Please put her . . ."

"No can do, Ash-lee. Your brat is in a cold, dark place, and I can't get to her right now. Does that bother you? *Brr,* it's cold there, Ash-lee."

It was all she could do to keep her sanity. "No, no, please don't do this to her. Please, I'm beg . . ." But he clicked off.

"Goddamn it!" she cried into the dead phone. "Don't you hang up on me, you son of a bitch!"

It took Chris a long time to quiet her. As well as he understood the anguish she was suffering, even he could not comprehend what it was like to be left so alone in the darkness, fingers of cold digging at you day and night, and you didn't even know if it was light or dark out or how many days and weeks or even months had passed. You were buried alive. And Lauren . . . Ashley couldn't breathe.

"Shh," Chris kept whispering, his arm around her shoulders. "Ashley, think about it. He just told you in his own sick way that she's alive. Don't you see that? And I have this gut feeling he's lying. Lauren's not in any mine, she's right there with him."

She looked up into his face. "You do? You really believe that? Or are you just saying it?"

"Hey, you know me. I've never sugarcoated anything with you."

She realized she'd been crying, and she wiped at her cheeks. "Are your feelings usually right? I mean . . ."

"Oh," he said, a slow smile gathering on his lips, "I'm right maybe eighty percent of the time."

"Honest?":

"Honest."

After she took several cleansing breaths, he pulled back onto the road, and she managed to dutifully phone Robert. As expected, he was angry she hadn't called earlier. He was, of course, relieved to hear that they thought Lauren was still all right.

"Jesus," Robert said, "that's at least good news. But have you made any progress at all finding this Potts? Or is this a wild goose chase, Ashley? I want the truth."

She told him what they knew so far, though she had to admit finding an isolated cabin in the Marble area was going to be tough as hell.

"Ashley, I'm not making idle threats here, but if you don't come up with something concrete, and soon, I *will* call the FBI. There isn't any other choice."

"Not yet. Two more days . . . twenty-four hours, I don't care, just please, for God's sake, give us a little more time. We're close, Robert. We are."

"That remains to be seen," he said. "You phone me in the morning. I take it you're driving to Marble?"

"Soon, yes," she said, and somehow she got him off the phone.

"I don't know who I hate worse," she said, avoiding the questioning glance Chris threw her. "Robert or Davey. The only difference between them is money. Past that, they're the same."

• • •

Having been born and raised in Colorado, Ashley was quite familiar with Denver. The Lacouter family had made many trips down out of the mountains into the rush of city life. There had been preschool-clothes shopping trips, Avalanche games—her father had been a big ice hockey fan—her own school trips for museums or volleyball games, Christmas shopping. When she'd been a kid, over twenty years ago, Denver had still possessed the earmarks of a cow town compared to, say, New York or L.A. But the downtown had been totally refurbished. There was the new Ocean Journey, Six Flags amusement park, a huge central park—brand spanking new—two modern stadiums, a giant indoor sports arena, a large campus with three university extension schools. And all this in downtown. Denver itself stretched as far as the eye could see north and south and east. To the west, the Rockies still reigned supreme, hostile to urban sprawl.

Joe Garcia's neighborhood was off University Avenue, all the streets named for institutions of higher learning: Dartmouth, Harvard, Princeton. An older, comfortable area, the houses tidy and small, mostly brick. Each had a detached garage and a driveway to the right of the house. Children played in the street in the waning light, and dogs lay panting on front stoops.

"So Joe was a policeman," she said when they parked in front of one of the houses.

"Uh-huh."

"Are you sure it isn't too late to be dropping in?"

"It's fine. I never call. I suppose I should." He shrugged and opened his door. "Come on, I'll introduce you."

"I'm not in a socializing mood, Chris. Maybe I should . . ."

"Come on, I want you to meet Joe and Charlene. And we won't stay long."

Reluctantly she opened the passenger door. "Just don't say anything about Lauren, you know? It would be too . . . awkward. Okay?"

"I wasn't going to."

He placed his hand at the small of her back as they walked to the front door and knocked. She couldn't remember the last time a man had done that, an innocent, polite gesture that really meant nothing and yet with Chris it did. To her it meant the world.

His hand remained there, and she felt its warmth through her pink linen blouse, and a tingling on her skin. Confusion swept her, but she forgot everything when the door opened and she saw the wheelchair, the man in it. *Joe?* Chris hadn't said a word. Not a single word.

"I should have known it was you at this hour," the man said, and he smiled broadly. "I'll bet you want that picture, don't you? Come in, come in."

"Joe, this is Ashley. Ashley, Joe Garcia," Chris said, guiding her in and around the wheelchair.

"Ashley?" Joe said. "*The* Ashley Lacouter?"

"Actually," she said, "it's Marin now. I was married. But how did you . . . ?"

Joe cut her off. "Are you kidding? I've been Chris's best buddy since we were, gosh, must have been first grade. Of course I know all about you. Hell, I thought Chris was gonna wait till you grew up and steer you down the aisle."

"Why don't you embarrass her to death while you're at it, dear?" came a woman's voice from the next room. She appeared around the corner. "Charlene," she said, taking Ashley's hand in hers. She was round faced, and had beautiful red hair and kind brown eyes. "Just ignore

Joe. He has a real lock on the tactless market. But, really, it is nice to meet you at last."

Ashley didn't have to socialize at all. The Garcia family, who'd all been watching TV in the den, did enough socializing for an army. The two children, Toby and Beth, fought with each other over the remote control for the TV while Charlene got them something to drink, and Joe had to know all about Aspen and how it had changed and did City Market really charge tourists more for food than the locals?

Charlene returned and shooed the kids out. "Go watch TV in our bedroom, and if you mess up the spread your father is going to take you both out to the shed for a good licking."

"Yeah, I can't wait," Joe said, and his daughter gave him a big hug and raced her brother to the bedroom.

"Kids," Charlene said, handing Ashley an iced tea.

Ashley was certain Charlene was going to say, "Do you have children?" but Chris asked her something then and the subject was dropped.

They talked about the heat and joked about global warming. They talked about health insurance and politics and the high cost of colleges now. And then Charlene asked Chris to go into the kitchen to look at the back burner on the stove, which evidently wasn't working, and Chris and Charlene disappeared.

"I used to be pretty handy," Joe said, "then this." He tapped the arms on his wheelchair. "But, hey, I'm coming along. Better than anyone dreamed. I tell you, I sometimes hate doctors. Anyway, Chris has been great since he moved back to Denver. Of course he isn't nearly as handy as I used to be, but beggars can't be choosers, right?"

Ashley smiled.

Then he said something that took her aback. "I'll tell you," he said, "I don't know how Charlene and I would have managed if Chris hadn't given us that money."

She knew, by the gravity of his tone, that he wasn't talking five hundred dollars. But before she could properly phrase a question, Chris was back with Charlene.

"Burner needs new wires."

"I was hoping it was just the plug-in unit," Charlene said. "Oh, well, it's always something, isn't it?"

Ashley put aside her questions for the time being and listened to the conversation. At one point, while Charlene was talking to her about real estate prices in Denver, she overheard Joe saying something to Chris. His voice was low, but she caught a few words.

"Are you sure you're okay? The other afternoon I thought . . ." She didn't catch the rest. But then she heard, "Please, Chris, get some help."

She shifted in her chair and looked from Chris to Joe and back. Something was wrong. Terribly wrong. But then Joe saw her studying them and suddenly he was joking with Chris, who morphed just as abruptly into the carefree good buddy again.

Chris finally spoke to Joe in private. She assumed he was telling Joe about Lauren and getting Davey's photograph. Probably asking for more assistance through Joe's police connections. "Those guys always have something going," Charlene said, sighing.

When the men returned, Chris said they had to leave.

"You driving into the mountains tonight?" Joe asked.

Chris seemed to contemplate the notion. "Too late to accomplish anything. I think we'll head over to my place."

Another surprise piled onto all the rest of tonight's surprises, she mused. Chris's place. She was too tired, really, to protest or wonder or suggest an alternative plan.

They said good-bye at the door, Chris's hand again protectively at her back, Joe in his wheelchair, Charlene absently mussing his dark hair. Ashley was struck by the closeness of this family, the deep, unspoken love that seemed to encase them in an aura of safety. Whatever had put Joe in his chair must have sealed the close bonds.

She thought about the strength it took to overcome seemingly insurmountable obstacles, and for a moment her own troubles paled in comparison. But then she remembered their children in their bedroom rolling around on Charlene's good spread, and she was swept by the urge to feel Lauren in her arms, to draw in her child's special scent. She had to muster her courage and paste a smile on her lips.

"They're very nice people, aren't they?" she said when they were in the Mustang.

"The best."

"And you've really known Joe since you were six or something?"

"Oh, yeah. We even did the police academy together."

And you gave him money, lots of money, she thought.

He turned the key in the ignition and she glanced surreptitiously at his profile, recalling the hushed words Joe had spoken to him, something like, "Please, get some help." The urgency in Joe's voice.

What in God's name had happened to Chris in Newark? Yes, he was the same wonderful, handsome man who'd saved her life and visited her day after day in that hospital, laughed with her, cried with her, even held her. He'd brought her flowers. And a box of candy. And the fur animal that still sat on her dresser and always would.

But inside, deep inside, he was hurting. Every so often his emotions rose to the surface and she'd glimpse the pain. Then he covered it up with insouciance.

She gave him another glance. What in God's name had the system done to this beautiful man?

TWELVE

Chris had rented a place in one of the new buildings that had gone up beyond Coors Field in downtown Denver. Not exactly LoDo, Lower Downtown, which was trendy and expensive, but a newer section of the city center that was a sort of glorified other side of the tracks.

He'd sublet because he had no furniture or belongings, aside from his clothes and personal items, but mostly because he couldn't imagine the future and so he couldn't make any plans beyond paying next month's rent.

Hell, he'd almost splattered his brains on the apartment's bleached wood floor just a few days ago. But he figured the owner would keep his damage deposit, so no real harm done. The guy could hire a cleaning service. But now . . . now he might have to think about next month's rent.

"I haven't been to this neighborhood," Ashley was saying from the passenger seat.

"I don't think it was even here when I left for Newark," he said.

"And where does your ex-wife live?"

"In Wheat Ridge."

"That's a nice area."

"Her folks helped her." He tried to keep the tinge of bitterness from his voice.

"But you pay child support?"

"Yeah."

"Robert pays child support, too. Well, he's *supposed* to, but he's always late, months late. It's not that he can't afford it. He likes to keep me, oh, I don't know, subservient."

"Can you get the court after him?"

She sighed in the darkness. "It's just not worth it."

He pulled into the underground garage at his building and parked. They took the elevator up, and he unlocked his door. A rush of hot, stale air greeted them. He tried to remember if he'd put his dirty laundry in the hamper. As if he'd been thinking about laundry that night. *Jesus.*

Flicking the light on, he said in a faintly sardonic tone, "Home sweet home."

She stood in the middle of the living room, her overnight bag in her hand, looking around. He saw the place from her point of view: a big space, bare blond wood floor, worn furniture in mismatched styles, some bright posters on the walls, the tiled kitchen counter to the left, the short hallway to the bedroom and bath to the right. A large window overlooking Coors Field and LoDo. Dust on every available surface.

"It's nice," she said, as if she weren't quite sure.

He raised his shoulders and lowered them. "Not my doing. The owner's in Los Angeles for six months."

"A man?"

"Yeah."

"It looks like a man."

"It's pretty messy. I'm not much of a housekeeper."

"Oh, I don't care."

"Sit down a minute. Let me go check the bedroom out. It's probably a disaster area."

"Um, Chris . . ." She was staring at him, her dark eyes wide and nervous. "Do you . . . I mean . . . are there any windows that open?"

Christ, her claustrophobia. The hot, dead air, the sealed picture window. He moved to the wall control and switched on the air-conditioning. "Sorry. There's a window in the bedroom that opens."

She relaxed visibly. "Oh, great. I hate to be such a jerk about it, but . . . could I . . . ?"

"Come on. But I warned you."

He led her down the hall to the bedroom, flipped on the light, stepped across to the window and cranked it open wide. She went straight over, dropped her bag and closed her eyes, sucking in the outside air.

"Are you going to be okay in here?"

"Yes, this is fine. But I wish I didn't have to take over your bedroom."

"Don't worry. The couch opens up to a bed." He couldn't help noticing the jumbled covers on his bed, the scattered pillows, the linens that no doubt still smelled of his nightmare sweats. "Uh, let me change the sheets. It's a mess."

"I'll help you. I hate making beds, running around to one side and then the other. It's one of those things . . ." She paused then averted her face. "I'm babbling. I guess I'm a little nervous . . . um"—she waved her hand—"here."

"You don't have to be nervous, Ashley."

"I know, but I am. Dumb."

He started pulling sheets off the bed, bundling them, tossing them into the hamper in the walk-in closet, getting a clean set. Thank God the owner was well stocked with linens. And towels, he'd have to put clean towels in the bathroom.

She helped make the bed. "Just like in Aspen," she said, obviously trying to lighten the situation. She let go of the blanket she was holding, straightened and turned her dark gaze on him. "Chris, how can I ever thank you for dropping everything and helping me?"

Dropping everything, *right*. Dropping his gun? "Don't worry about it, Ashley."

"I . . . I don't know what I would have done. You've seen Robert, you've seen . . . how he is. And I'm so afraid he'll call in the authorities. He could have lied to me and already done it. And then . . . what will happen to Lauren?"

"Let's cross that bridge when we come to it. I'm sure he's just as afraid as you of Davey finding out the cops are involved. He loves Lauren, doesn't he?"

"Yes, he loves her."

"Look, if it were Rich, I probably wouldn't call the cops, either. I have to admit that."

"God, I hope you're right."

"And we could even find Potts tomorrow. It may be over soon."

She shook her head slowly. "If it's only a few days, I'd be so relieved. I don't think I could make it, all those months my mother had to wait. And I worry so much about what Lauren is going through. Look what it did to me."

"From what you say Lauren is tough."

"I hope so. I hope . . . I hope she is."

He hated the pain in her voice. Suddenly he wanted to find Potts and grab him and choke him and choke him until he . . .

"We should make up the hideaway, shouldn't we?" she was asking.

"Uh, oh, I guess so."

She insisted on giving him one of the pillows from the bedroom, fluffed it, tucked in all the corners of the sheets, where he would have stuffed them in haphazardly. A woman's touch. He'd forgotten.

"Are you tired?" she asked when they finished.

He looked at her.

"Well, I just meant, I'm sort of keyed up, and I thought we could maybe talk a little. Do you have any wine, something to drink? To relax?"

Wine. There was a bottle of Stoli in the freezer. But wine? "Do you drink vodka?"

She made a face.

"With orange juice," he hastened to say. "Lots of orange juice?"

"Better than nothing, I guess."

He sat on the edge of the made-up sofa bed; she settled in one of the low-slung modernistic chairs, leaning back, holding the glass with both hands. He'd added juice to his drink to be polite. Usually he took his vodka neat.

"I meant what I said earlier, Chris, I really like your friends Joe and Charlene," she said.

"Joe's a good guy. They've had a bad year."

"The wheelchair?"

"Yeah."

"What happened?"

He rubbed his eyes, leaned an elbow on his knee, hand on his brow. Where to start?

"Was it an accident?"

"Yes. Terrible luck. Joe wasn't on duty, that was the problem. He was home, and he heard the radio . . . A lot of cops listen in at home, you know. Anyway, he heard the call, a burglary, a high-speed chase. The thing was, it was right in his neighborhood, so he got in his own car in his civvies and took off. To make a long story short, there was a real bad crash, the stupid kid's in jail, and Joe . . . Joe's in his chair. Severed his spinal cord. He was so close to dying. . . . It was bad, because I was in Newark, and I couldn't get away; it would've blown my cover. It was a bad time."

"Poor Joe. Poor Charlene."

"You know, they're doing okay now. You saw them. He's amazing, really amazing. Never a word of complaint. And just the other day, he tells me about this job as a building inspector, checking handicap access. A comedian."

"It hurts you to see him," she said softly.

"It shows that much, huh?"

"No, it's . . . it's just that I know you. I can tell. But Joe's accident wasn't your fault."

"No." He raised his head and looked at her. "That part, the accident, Joe's injury, that was bad enough, but he wasn't on duty, so no workers' comp, no pension from the job."

"Oh. Oh, how awful."

"And his insurance maxed out, those bastards, wouldn't pay another cent."

She was silent, taking a sip of her drink, regarding him above the rim of her glass. "Chris, I have to ask you . . ."

"What?"

"Joe said something about money you gave him."

Shit. He hadn't wanted to get near the subject. Damn Joe's big mouth. He turned his glass in his hands, around and around, and studied the flecks of orange floating on the surface.

"I'm being awfully nosy."

He raised his glance. "No, no, it's okay. I told you, I won some money."

"Uh-huh."

"Well, I gave Joe and Charlene some. A loan. No big deal."

"A loan."

"Sure."

"You're a good friend, Chris."

"Yeah, well . . ."

The room was dim, lit by recessed lighting in the ceiling. Ashley was a dark shadow against the pale furniture and floor and walls. Lustrous dark hair and deep liquid eyes and a smooth white neck. And that mouth. The full lower lip. He watched her take another sip of her drink, her lips on the glass rim. *Jesus.* Ashley, here in his apartment, alone with him. On the table next to her chair was the phone, the one that had rung that night, and brought him back from the brink, and on the floor beyond was the pale rectangle of light from outside.

The air conditioner droned, distant traffic noises intruding at intervals. There was, oddly enough, a kind of peace around them, a cocoon in the midst of life's maelstrom.

"I know she's okay," Ashley said into the silence.

"Lauren?"

"Yes, I know she is. Because if she wasn't . . . I'd feel it somehow. She's probably"—a tiny smile quirked her lip—"mouthing off to Davey, driving him nuts."

"We'll find him soon."

She leaned her head back. "I have to believe that."

"You want to go to bed now?" he finally asked.

"No, not yet. It's so nice to be away from home." Her voice was slow, distant, her eyes closed. "It's so quiet here." A pause. "Talk to me, Chris. Keep my mind occupied."

"What do you want to talk about?"

Momentarily she lifted her head, opened her eyes. "Tell me more about Newark. We're friends, aren't we? I care about you, I still do. Strange, but I feel as if you never left, and I know something happened to you there."

"I told you."

"No, you didn't, not really."

He took a gulp of his drink. "Look, Ashley, it's really none of your business."

"So, what does that have to do with anything?"

"Aren't you tired yet?"

"No."

"Jesus."

"You know everything about me. Everything. You know what I'm scared of. You've seen me at my very worst. Your turn, Chris."

"Where's that written?"

She sat up, leaned across the space separating them and laid a hand on his chest over his heart. "Here. Right here."

He felt a thrill, like an electric current pulsating in his chest. He wanted to pull back, he wanted to press against her hand, take her in his arms. And then, abruptly, her touch was gone, and his insides were hollow.

"You know, I see so many kids in high school," she began, and he thought she'd changed the subject for a minute. "And some are so unhappy, so lost. In a town

like Aspen, there are a lot of divorced mothers raising
kids. Like me, I guess. But there are also a lot of rich
kids, and they've had every advantage, but something is
missing in their lives. And I try to reach them. Sometimes I think I help them, a little anyway. When people
hurt they need to talk. They need to connect to someone.
You can't keep it all bottled up inside."

"The last goddamn thing I want is a shrink," he muttered.

"A shrink can help a lot," she said. "You know how
many years I was in therapy?"

He stood up, suddenly restless. God, he didn't want
her to know about his failures or about the cesspools
he'd wallowed in. He wanted her to keep thinking of
him as . . . yeah, as Superman. But she was staring at
him, following him as he paced, still and slim and
lovely, and as obdurate as stone.

"Chris . . ."

"What do you want to know, Ashley? You want to
hear about the nasty stuff, the ugly things I had to do?
The mistakes, the fuckups, the . . ." He went to the big
window, leaned a shoulder against the wall and gazed
out over the city. At night you could almost believe Denver was a glitzy metropolis, but then he'd remember
Manhattan at night, even from across the river in New
Jersey, and he almost wanted to be back there, traveling
the dark alleys, knocking at hidden doors, meeting vicious men, flush with adrenaline. Alive. Not having to
figure out who he was until the sun rose.

He took a deep breath. "I told you I was undercover.
I was on the North Jersey Task Force. We had Newark
cops, a state cop, DEA, an FBI guy. We were the big
shots. Everyone wanted on the task force, more money,

advancement, the works. I was chosen, and I was good. I told you that."

"Uh-huh."

"At first it was great, but then . . ." He stopped and thought: When had it gone bad? When he got in with Sal? When he began respecting the wiseguys? When he found out what was going on in the police evidence room? "I don't know. It started with little things, stuff I found out about. Cops at every level taking bribes and payoffs, guns and drugs disappearing from evidence. Cops lying, outright lying on witness stands and falsifying evidence. I began to get disillusioned, but I was in deep by then."

"You were doing your job."

"Yeah, but you start to think after a while, *why* do the job? You nail someone, twenty more get off and start dealing and murdering in other parts of town and nothing changes. And when you're undercover, you start identifying with the criminals, you start thinking, hey, they're not so bad, just guys trying to make a living. And you . . . *forget.* You forget what you're trying to do and who you are. You lose perspective. You get lost."

"Did *you* get lost?"

He stood by the window, still looking out. Anything to avoid her scrutiny. "I guess I forgot which way was home."

"Did, um, did Joanie know about this?"

"She was gone for the worst of it."

"You were all alone. Oh, Chris."

"She couldn't have helped. What could she do? What could anyone do?"

"I'm so sorry. Oh God, Chris, I know what it's like to be lost."

"Not like this."

"Not exactly, no."

She started to get up from the chair then, and he turned his head and saw her body rise sinuously and move through the shadows to him. She came close and rested a hand on his arm. Said nothing. She was so near he could feel her body heat, feel her sleeve touching his arm, whispering secrets. She smelled like orange blossoms, something light and citrusy.

It would be so easy to turn and draw her into his arms. To feel her skin and bury his face in her hair. Gather in all her sweetness and strength, and maybe, maybe a little of it would seep into him and soothe his pain.

"I saw something in you," she said, so softly he had to strain to hear. "When you came to Aspen. I saw something . . . Maybe I recognize it because of what I've been through. And I know how awful it is to be alone and hurting. Is there anything I can do to help? Anything at all?"

He withdrew from her, needing some distance between them, knowing the folly of allowing any intimacy. He straightened and took a step back, then another, and with each step he felt the anger and resentment grow and fill him like an infection ready to rupture.

"Chris?"

His voice was harsh to his own ears. "You want to help, Ashley? Oh, that's funny. Can you get my job back? Can you erase the past? What, you're some kind of magician?"

She looked at him, frowning. "I thought you said you retired."

"That's right."

"But . . . then, what do you mean, get your job back? I didn't think you *wanted* it back."

"Forget it, Ashley."

"No." Then louder, demanding. "Tell me what you meant."

He held a hand up. "You know? You're a real pain in the ass."

She glared at him, eyes dark pools with glints of light, mouth hard. "You can't just lay that kind of statement on me and then expect me to drop it. I'm not some bimbo you picked up. I'm your *friend*."

He let out an exasperated breath and went to stand in front of a poster of the Maroon Bells in autumn: golden trees, dark rock, white snow. He studied it, arms crossed.

"That's a defensive posture," she said to his back.

He pivoted. "Oh, for chrissakes!" He shook his head in irritation. "All right, damn it. You want the truth, fine. I retired, yeah, my other choice being termination. Not much of a decision."

"Why?" she asked, aghast.

"There was an IA investigation, that's Internal Affairs, and they saw something they didn't like. It's happened before, it'll happen again."

"What did they accuse you of?"

"Oh, it's complicated," he lied, "some technical stuff."

"But you were innocent! How could you have let them . . . *bully* you?"

He almost laughed. *Innocent*. "There's not a damn thing you can do when IA gets involved. They're bulldogs, never let go of your throat until you're dead—or gone. At the time I chose gone."

"Did you have a lawyer?"

"Sure. The police union provides one. He tried but no dice."

"Obviously they had no real proof against you, right? Or you would have been prosecuted?"

"That's right. They had no real proof, but suspicion

is enough. With IA you're guilty until proven innocent."

"That's *terrible*."

He loved her righteous indignation, her complete naïveté. He couldn't believe she hadn't figured it out—the money he *won* gambling and the IA investigation. Ashley, one of the world's true innocents. He didn't even belong in the same room with her.

"Well, I think you should have fought those bastards tooth and nail."

"Um."

"Why should they have all the power? What about *your* rights?"

"It's the way it works. I'm lucky they gave me a choice of retiring."

"*Lucky.*"

"All things being relative."

"Oh, Chris, the whole mess stinks. It's a travesty of justice. They waste their time going after you, when they should be *supporting* you."

"Shoulda, woulda, coulda."

"And you can't get back on the force in Denver?"

He gave a short laugh. "The minute they call my lieutenant in Newark, the cat's out of the bag."

He moved to the table where he'd set his drink and downed it.

"You can't get a lawyer now, a real good one, and still try to fight it?"

"It's over, Ashley."

"Could you . . . I don't know, be a private investigator, something like that?"

"You have to be licensed for that. Background check."

"Oh."

"You think I haven't considered it?"

"Of course you have."

He sank down onto the side of the sofa bed, scraped his fingers through his hair. "I'll figure something out. Don't worry about me. We're not here for me."

"That's like telling me not to worry about Lauren. Well, thank goodness you won that money to tide you over."

He wanted to jump up and shake her and yell, *Can't you see what I really am!* "Yeah, fortune smiles on me."

"Can I have another drink?" she asked.

"Another one?"

"It was mostly orange juice."

He poured a finger of Stoli into her glass and filled it with juice, dropped ice into the glass. He poured himself a stiff one, barely tinged yellow. When he handed her the drink, she touched his arm lightly and gave him a small, sad smile.

They sat and talked some more. Fortunately, she dropped the subject of his retirement, although he was damn sure she hadn't let it go. IA had nothing on Ashley Marin for tenacity.

"How is it being back in Denver?" she asked.

"Well, I get to see Rich a lot, and Joe. That's good. I guess Denver is still home, even if it doesn't quite feel like it. Yet."

"This apartment, well, it's fine, but it's not exactly . . . cozy. Don't you want a house somewhere, or a condo?"

"I don't want to have to think about it. No lawn to mow, no roof that leaks."

"My roof leaks."

"See what I mean?"

She drank, and he saw her long, smooth throat move as she swallowed.

"Chris, what about getting married again? Do you think about it?"

"I don't notice you rushing into matrimony again."

She waved a hand. "I have a very ill mother and a daughter. I have baggage. Besides, I don't have time. *You* have time."

"But no inclination. I'm not a good candidate."

"You're a wonderful, kind person. You're smart and you're handsome and you're terrific at your job . . . I mean, what used to be your job. Oh, damn, I'm sorry. I just . . ."

"It's okay."

She looked at him and tears filled her eyes, one slipping down her cheek. She wiped it away. "I'm very upset about you."

"You have your own problems to worry about."

"There's room inside me for both. When we find Lauren, I'll give you a . . . a testimonial, and everyone will know what a great detective you are."

"Sure, Ashley."

"I will."

"Aren't you tired yet?"

"Yes, I guess so. I'm tired and scared and sad."

"Get some sleep. We have work to do tomorrow."

"I know." She finally stood and bent down to give him a kiss, the lightest brush of her lips, that left a searing trail on his cheek. "Good night, Chris."

And then she was gone, and he waited for the bedroom door to close. But it didn't, and he remembered her claustrophobia. She never closed doors or windows.

He stripped down to his jockey shorts, threw the clothes over a chair and got into bed. Hands behind his head, he lay there, so acutely aware of Ashley down the hall that he was positive he could hear the rustle of the sheets as she got into bed. Into *his* bed.

He'd confessed more to her than to anyone else on

the face of the earth. Joe didn't even know that much. Why? Why her? Why had he come so close, a hairs-breadth from dumping the whole dismal truth in her lap?

She was a princess, a goddamn angel to put up with her lunatic household, her nasty ex-husband, her past. He wanted to protect her, soothe her fears about her daughter, calm her claustrophobic terrors. He had to hold himself back from going to her right now, lying down beside her, clasping her to him like a talisman.

But he was no good for her. He was poison, no good for anyone, not even himself. And even if he found the guts to go into that bedroom, pull away the sheets and make love to her, she'd allow it only out of pity. Was that what he'd been seeking, her pity?

He'd do this one task; he'd find Ashley's daughter for her, and after that he'd be able to let go. It would be easy then, no goddamn phone ringing in the middle of the night, calling him back to the land of the living.

THIRTEEN

She was making the bed when she heard Chris in the shower, swearing through the closed bathroom door. The next thing she knew, he'd opened the door, steam was rushing out, and he had barely secured a towel around his hips.

"It's Rich's birthday. God, I totally forgot till just this minute. Ashley, I'm going to have to run by Joanie's before we leave."

She had a pillow in her hand, and she glanced at the alarm clock on the nightstand. "It's just past seven. We'll make Marble by early afternoon."

"You're sure?"

"I'm sure. But what about a present?"

"I actually did that a couple weeks ago. Got him a new baseball mitt. It's in the trunk of the car."

"I could wrap it."

A smile tilted a corner of his mouth. "Don't you know how men shop? If they don't wrap it, we don't buy it."

She couldn't get the image of him half naked and dripping wet out of her head the whole way over to his ex-wife's house. She felt guilty as hell. It was criminal that she could even *think* about him in that way when Lauren was in such danger. Not to mention that they were on the way to his former wife's house. To meet his son. Yet the picture kept nudging aside everything else, the wet mat of hair on his chest, the way it ran down in a narrow line to disappear beneath the stark white towel. His long arms and nicely shaped legs, the way his hair was plastered to a perfectly shaped head, the ever-present whiskers. He could have dropped the towel and come to her, warm and damp. She would have melted into him, held him inside her for an eternity. Chris. After all this time, after twenty years, her childish fantasies had not dimmed. She ached for him. Even more now, when he was as needy and alone as she was. To feel Chris inside her. To hold him fiercely and tenderly and . . .

"That's the place."

She snapped back to reality with a jolt. "Huh?"

"You okay?"

"Oh . . . oh, yes, sure. I was . . . just thinking." She was thinking, all right.

She wasn't even positive what street they were on, much less what neighborhood. Somewhere in Wheat Ridge outside Denver?

It was a nice area. Middle class, all the houses brick and built close to one another, the trees and shrubs mature. In front of Joanie Judge's house were tidy plots of flowers nestled in a rock garden, lovingly cared for. A sprinkler was whirling in the front yard.

Chris parked in the drive. "I can just run the present in, or if you want . . ."

"I'd like to meet your son," she said, opening her door. And Joanie. Mostly Joanie, she admitted to herself.

His ex-wife was strikingly pretty. She was dressed well, too, wearing an eggshell-white, capped-sleeve blouse, a single strand of pearls and a beige knee-length skirt. High-heeled wedges. She had smooth, fair skin. Her streaked blond hair was pulled back in a business-like bun. She was dressed for work.

In comparison Ashley felt sloppy in khaki twill calf-length pants, brown sandals and a sleeveless green cotton top she hadn't even tucked in. Of course Chris had explained Joanie was a realtor and putting in long hours, but still . . .

"Come in, come in," Joanie said, holding open the front screen door. "The birthday boy is in the kitchen."

Chris introduced them, and Ashley was once again surprised that not only did Joe know who she was, but Joanie did, too. *"Ashley,"* she said. "I can't believe I'm finally getting to meet you. When Chris was in police academy, that's when we met, but anyway, he talked about you all the time. I'm so glad to finally meet you. What an ordeal that was, your kidnapping. I can't imagine if it were Rich . . ."

"It's good to meet you, too," Ashley interrupted, trying desperately not to think about cold, black mines and Lauren. *Not now,* she told herself firmly.

Chris disappeared then to give Rich his present, and Ashley was praying he'd hurry, at a loss suddenly. And then she was dealt yet one more surprise.

Joanie put a slim hand on her arm and whispered, "I am so glad you're with Chris," she said. "We've all been really worried. He's . . ." But she never got to finish, because Chris reappeared with Rich in tow.

The boy—eleven today—was still in his pj's. He

smiled a little shyly and put out a hand to shake Ashley's, then realized he was wearing the mitt. He was a lefty. He laughed and looked embarrassed, pulled the mitt off and shook her hand.

Then he turned to his mother. "This is so great, Mom. It's a real infield mitt. Wait till Coach sees it!"

Ashley could discern both Chris and Joanie in the boy, their best features. He was going to be one very handsome young man in a couple more years. He had Joanie's fair, unblemished skin and her wide mouth. But his eyes were Chris's, beautiful hazel eyes. His hair was certainly his father's, light brown and permanently disheveled.

"I have to run to the office for a few hours," Joanie was saying, "and Mom is due here to stay with Rich and start the birthday cake. But I'll be back by one, and you are both welcome to . . ."

Chris begged off. "You know I'd be here if I could, Joanie." He roughed Rich's hair, then leaned over and said to his son, "I'm sorry I can't make the birthday party, kiddo. But soon as I finish this job I'm on, I'll take you up camping, a whole weekend. Okay?"

"Parties are for kids anyway," Rich said. "It's Mom's idea." He made a face.

They left shortly. In the car Ashley said, "It's a shame about you having to miss his birthday, Chris. I . . ."

"Hey," he said, "at eleven years old all he's interested in are the presents. And I'll try to take him camping, as soon as Little League is over," he added, but something in his tone was off, as if he were merely mouthing words.

"That will be nice. He's a cute kid, Chris. He's going to be devastating in a few years."

"Like his dad?"

"Oh, sure," she said, but then she recalled his ex-wife's hand on her arm and her whispered words. "We've all been really worried," she'd said, disturbingly earnest.

Robert was having a lousy morning. The baby had a summer cold and had kept them up half the night. Then this morning, Maria, who spent five days a week at the Marins', had phoned to say she had a family emergency and needed an extra day off.

Elaine was beside herself, ticking off her busy schedule, which was now ruined because of Maria's nonappearance.

"Honey," Elaine said over breakfast, "we really need an au pair. Maria's great in the kitchen and with the housework, but she's not very dependable."

Then Robert's chief of operations at the dot com company phoned to say they were going to miss street earnings estimates by a penny. The COO was Robert's third since the tech wreck of the year 2000.

Now Robert was going to have to spend most of the rest of the summer in California finagling the corporation's books.

And there was Lauren. And Ashley and this ex-cop she was gallivanting around with.

She had called this morning. Just as she'd promised. He'd give her that. The trouble was he didn't trust the information she was feeding him. He was fairly sure Ashley was withholding important details, details he damn well had a right to know.

After remembering to express concern about Lauren, Elaine took the baby to the doctor at 10 A.M., and Robert closed himself in his office to phone Mark Kingston, the

P.I. who was still digging into the background of Chris Judge.

Kingston was now back from Newark and in Denver. "I was going to call you this morning," he said. "I've got some, shall we say, some strange news."

"Well, let's have it," Robert said, impatient.

"It seems, and I don't have any proof of this, but it seems this Chris Judge is a bit of a Robin Hood. There's this former cop in Denver who's in a wheelchair, and all of a sudden last spring his debts disappear. And he had some big bills, couple hundred thou."

"So? What does that have to do with . . . Oh," Robert said, "*oh*. The missing money from Newark?"

"You got it. This Denver cop and Judge go all the way back to grammar school."

"Robin Hood," Robert sneered. "And that messed up wife, *ex*-wife of mine, is putting all her faith in him? Jesus. I don't know what to think. Sounds like a real loose cannon to me."

"Would you like me to come up there and nose around, Mr. Marin?"

Robert mulled over the idea. "Not yet. I'll give Ashley and this whacked out ex-cop a little more time. I just hope they've been leveling with me."

"You could still make that call to the FBI."

"And I might. I just might," he said.

Elaine hadn't returned, and at ten thirty he drove over to Ashley's. Maybe she was holding her cards too close to her chest, but he was betting her mother would be more forthcoming. If, of course, he caught Pauline in a lucid moment.

He and Pauline had always gotten along fairly well. He knew Ashley's mother had fawned over him because of his money and position. Which didn't bother him. Lots of people did.

He nodded to Luda in the front yard, where she was using a hose to water the hanging flower baskets. Luda eyed him warily, nodded back, and told him Pauline was inside watching TV. Vladimir was not around. At least not in sight.

When he walked in and took off his sunglasses and baseball cap, Pauline looked up and clapped her hands. "Robert! How nice it is to see you."

"Hi, Pauline," he said, hoping her instant recognition of him was a fortuitous sign.

Then Pauline frowned. "Oh, but you missed Ashley. She's in . . . let's see, Denver."

"I know, Pauline."

"And Lauren . . . Lauren is at . . ." The frown deepened. "Oh, my, Lauren is missing. I get so confused, but I'm sure she's missing, because Ashley called and told me she and this man . . . I can't remember who it is . . . But Ashley is going to Marble to look for this other man. It's all about Lauren, I think. Yes, of course it is. Did you know Lauren is missing?"

"I know she is," Robert repeated. "And that's why I stopped in, Pauline. Mind if I sit with you for a minute?"

Pauline appeared delighted and patted the cushion on the couch next her. "You sit right here. I'll get Luda to make you a drink."

"Ah, it's a little early for a drink."

Pauline looked bemused for a moment then shook her head at herself. "What was I thinking?"

"Anyway," Robert said, "do you remember exactly what Ashley told you about her trip to Marble?"

"Of course I remember," Pauline snapped.

"Good, good." Robert smiled. "I don't want to upset

you, I'm just so worried about Lauren. I'm trying to decide if I should call in the authorities."

Pauline's brow furrowed. "Well, they didn't help one bit with Ashley."

"I understand that." He touched her hand. "But it's been days now since Lauren was taken, and I'm afraid Ashley is on a wild goose chase."

Pauline concentrated. "It's that very same man, you know, that Potts. He has my granddaughter. And Ashley . . . What did she tell me? Oh, she thinks he may have her at a cabin. That's it. A cabin."

So far Pauline was for the most part repeating what Ashley had said on the phone. So maybe Ashley wasn't keeping information from him or even exaggerating how close to finding Lauren she and the ex-cop were. *Maybe.* Hell, he didn't know. He only knew he was deeply concerned and felt he was losing control of the situation.

"You know she still can't stand a closed window or close places?" Pauline reflected, and he saw tears spring to her eyes. "Now Lauren, that sweet little girl . . ."

Robert let out a breath.

"Ashley isn't a well person, you know," Pauline went on. "She saw a therapist for years. I don't want Lauren to go through that."

"Neither do I."

"Maybe . . . maybe Lauren should have lived with you. Do you think she would be missing if she lived with you, Robert?"

He wasn't exactly sure how to answer. And Luda had come inside and was straightening the living room, one ear cocked.

He formed his answer carefully. "I don't know, Pauline. I only know Ashley has had a troubled life, and now this Potts is torturing her all over again through

Lauren. Maybe if Lauren had been with me, Potts wouldn't have used her to get back at Ashley. God, I just don't know."

Luda had stopped what she was doing. She stood near the kitchen door, a stack of magazines to be recycled in her arms, and said something.

"What was that?" Robert came to his feet.

"Lauren better off with you. Ashley have problems."

It was none of the woman's business, and he wished she'd keep her goddamn thoughts to herself. He noticed Vladimir rattling around in the kitchen then, putting away groceries. At least he knew his place.

He glanced down at Pauline, who was suddenly very quiet, then up at Luda, who stared at him defiantly. Lauren had said just last spring that she was living in a nuthouse. Robert looked around again, and thought that truer words had never been spoken. And that didn't even count the crooked Robin Hood, apparently the new leader of this band of merry men.

FOURTEEN

Within three hours of leaving Joanie's, they had nearly reached Marble. Ashley always forgot how breathtakingly beautiful the Crystal River Valley was. When they turned off the highway onto the road that wound forty miles past Carbondale and Redstone, she remembered. The bulk of Mt. Sopris to the left, the deep green mountainsides sweeping up to faraway peaks, horses and cattle dotting pastures, red rock rising in surprising cliffs, and the bizarre specialty—huge white marble blocks lying haphazardly alongside the river, tumbled from the trains that once hauled the stone from the quarry.

People fished in the river, picnickers sat under the big cottonwoods that lined the banks. There were a couple of waterfalls, silver ribbons of water dropping off sheer rock walls, a natural hot springs that naked hippies used to loll in, Elephant Mountain, which really did look like a giant tusker, and right outside of Redstone, the antique row of round brick coke ovens, used in the town's coal mining days.

The valley narrowed, the mountains pressing in, and the road turned to bumpy, potholed asphalt, then graded road base.

"Ever been here?" Chris asked.

"Not past Redstone."

"I think my dad took me hunting here once, but I can't really remember it."

"Marble isn't very big, is it?"

"Maybe a few hundred people. No, less."

"If Davey was here, someone would have noticed, wouldn't they?"

"Maybe."

"*Maybe,*" she repeated.

It was a hot summer day, clouds amassing over the highest peaks, the sun shimmering on trees and water, glaring on the road.

The first indication that they had arrived was the sign that read Marble, 7,550 altitude and a jumble of marble blocks lining the route. The aspen and lodgepole pines and blue spruce were thick in the high valley, and the town's buildings were scattered among them, so that it seemed more a camp than a community. There were a couple of bed-and-breakfast inns, a sign announcing quarry tours, the Marble Volunteer Fire Department, the General Store and a community church—a miniature clapboard building with a steeple. There was Fenton's Antler Art, the Gold Pan Gallery and the century-old Marble City State Bank Building. A few houses, some old, some new log structures, and that was the sum of it.

"Tiny," Ashley said.

"Yeah."

"Well, it shouldn't be hard to ask around, should it?"

"Sometimes these people are suspicious of strangers. They like being isolated. We'll have to be careful. Let me do the talking, okay?"

He parked in front of the Marble General Store, a log cabin with a porch; the steps up to it were glistening marble blocks. Inside were two preteenage boys, apparently in charge.

"Hi," Chris said, "I wonder if you guys could help me out some?"

"We can sure try."

"Well, my wife and I"—and Ashley blanched at his easy use of the word *wife*—"are looking for our daughter. We think she may have run off with her boyfriend." He took the wallet-size picture of Lauren that Ashley had given him and the faxed photo of Potts and showed them to the boys. "Have you seen either of them around? Maybe to buy something here?"

"You know what he's driving?" one of the boys asked.

"Sorry, no."

They both studied the pictures. Lauren, pretty and vivacious, smiling for her yearbook photo. Davey Potts, narrow face, the lank, colorless hair, pale skin even more pronounced with his prison pallor. His eyes also colorless in the faxed photo but shrewd and knowing. Scary.

The two boys shook their heads. "Haven't seen them."

"Well, if you do see them around, either of them, could you call me at this number?" He pulled one of his cards from his wallet and wrote Ashley's cell phone number on it. She noticed that the card was an official one, with some kind of seal on it, and Lieutenant prefacing his name. Well, if the card impressed these boys, so much the better.

Chris bought two cold drinks, then he took Ashley outside.

"Your *wife*?" she said.

He hitched his shoulders. "It was easier that way. People are more sympathetic to families." He cut his eyes to her. "You don't mind?"

She felt a flush rising up her neck. All her teenage daydreams and more recent, mature ones. *You don't mind, do you?* "I don't mind, Chris, honestly, whatever it takes. But it . . . I guess it surprised me."

"I never know exactly what I'm going to say. I have to read the people, the situation. So don't be spooked, next time I drop a big one."

They finished their drinks and began to walk the few streets of Marble, knocking on doors, showing the photographs, asking the same questions over and over. They checked at private homes, at the art gallery, the two bed-and-breakfast inns, the quarry tours shack. Most people shook their heads, said they'd never seen either person. One older lady studied the picture of Davey for so long Ashley was ready to jump out of her skin.

"Does he look familiar?" Chris prompted.

"Well now, I'd say so. I swear, my memory's so gol-darn bad these days, but I'm sure there was a man lived here way back looked just like this. Funny name, Mott, Pott, something like that."

"Jerry Potts," Ashley whispered.

"That was it. Sure was. Funny soul, kept to himself. Wife died on him."

"Actually," Chris said, "this is a picture of his son, Davey. Jerry died a few years ago."

"And this"—the woman put a finger on the copy— "this fella run away with your daughter?"

"We believe so."

"Awful, what folks do these days."

"Have you seen either one of them lately?"

"No, can't say as I have."

Ashley slumped with disappointment.

They kept on with their quest, moving out from the center of town, repeating their story so many times it almost seemed believable. A lady at The Inn at Raspberry Ridge raised a brow, stared hard at Davey's picture, and Ashley's heart squeezed.

"I might have seen him," she finally said. "Driving by in an old, beat-up Blazer. I only noticed because I didn't recognize him, and I do know most folk around here, you know?"

"When was this?" Chris asked.

"Oh, couple days ago maybe."

"Do you remember the color of the Blazer?"

"White maybe. I'm not sure."

And Chris gave her his card with Ashley's cell phone number, as he had with all the others.

"Sure hope you find your daughter," the woman said in parting.

They retrieved the Mustang and drove farther out, past Beaver Lake, where they questioned the fishermen, then circled back to the old mill site, where marble plinths still stood, shorn now of their machinery and the huge crane that lifted blocks into the mill. The place, once bustling, the origin of the marble for the Lincoln Memorial and the Tomb of the Unknown Soldier, was deserted, the forest encroaching.

"Do you think that woman really saw him?" Ashley asked.

"I'd like corroboration. One possible sighting isn't enough."

They stopped at the fire department, where they found

a volunteer polishing the big chartreuse fire engine.

"Have you seen either of these people?" Chris asked, going through the routine again. But he was good at it, Ashley realized, patient and earnest, garnering immediate sympathy from everyone to whom he told the story.

The man studied the pictures. "No, I haven't seen them. But I'll be on the lookout, that's for sure."

"Thanks," Chris said. "And can you direct me to East Silver Street?"

"You bet. Straight out of town that way," he pointed, "past Beaver Lake. The road to Crystal City."

"Appreciate it," Chris said.

In his car, Ashley asked, "East Silver Street?"

"That's where the Pottses used to live. Three miles past Beaver Lake, a dirt road to the left. Joe looked it up for me."

"You think he's there?"

"Probably not. Just like he probably wasn't at the mine, but I have to check. Criminals tend to go to ground in familiar places."

"Maybe . . ." She bit her lip. "Oh, this all seems so useless, and he's got Lauren somewhere, and we're floundering around, asking poor old ladies if they've seen him."

"Well, consider this. The entire town of Marble is alerted now. One of them may see him or Lauren and call. We're not wasting time. This is the logical place to start."

He drove past the lake on a dirt road. Crystal City, six miles, a sign read. Crystal City? Did anyone really live there? Ashley thought. Dust plumed behind the car, the sun beat on her shoulder, but she didn't care about that. Lauren was here somewhere in these wild mountains. She was here. Ashley felt it.

"Okay, we've gone three miles," Chris said. "Look for a dirt road on the left."

It was there, a narrow opening in a grove of aspen trees, a bumpy track leading up and up. Then a clearing materialized, and Chris slowed the car to a crawl, rolling to a stop.

"What?"

"Stay here." He reached across her, opened the glove compartment, drew out his gun.

"Oh my God," she said.

"I'm just going to check it out. In case someone's there."

"I'm coming with you."

"Stay here."

She waited. It seemed like hours, but it was probably only ten minutes. She breathed deeply and repeated her mantra and tried to appreciate the pine smell that saturated the air. *Lauren, Lauren.*

Then he was back, silently, opening the car door and startling her.

"Nobody's home," he said.

"What if . . . maybe Lauren's in there?"

"I looked in the windows. It's empty." He started the car, drove a little ways, and she saw the cabin, dappled by sunlight, a snug log house, like a child's drawing, peaked roof, door in the center, window on each side, an outhouse in the rear under a huge blue spruce.

She got out of the car; she had to see for herself. Stood tiptoe to peer in a window. One big room, a bare floor, a woodstove, a set of beds to one side, a makeshift kitchen, a ladder leading to a loft.

"Lauren," she said into the empty room beyond the dusty glass. Then louder, "Lauren!"

"She's not here." His hand grasped her arm.

"How do you know? Are you sure?"

"No footprints, no garbage, no tire tracks. No one's been here for a long time. Months."

"Can we get in?"

"The front door's padlocked."

"Try. Can't you pick it or something?"

"You must think I'm some kind of a magician."

"I do."

"Ashley . . ."

He inspected the exterior thoroughly while she waited. Methodically, carefully, circling the place, head down, squatting, picking something up from the ground, discarding it. He tried each window and examined the padlock again while she waited, watching every move he made. She felt a kind of thrill studying him—he worked with such surety and an animal grace. A predator on the prowl, beautiful and deadly.

She felt that thrill, yes, but the worry over Lauren was still there, the fear, the wondering. Her brain reeled with the conflict: Chris, Lauren, Chris, Lauren.

Finally he came back shaking his head. "Like I told you, the trail's ice cold here."

"Could you break a window and get in?"

"I could, but I really don't think anyone's been here. And I sure as hell don't want to alert Potts if he does show up at some point."

Her heart sank.

"It was a long shot."

"I suppose so."

"We've got to locate the other cabins in the area. If they're all as hard to find as this one, damn, it won't be easy."

"How will you do that?"

"I have an idea. There's got to be a Forest Service

office around here, and some of the rangers will know the country."

"Okay, where?"

A man who was fishing at Beaver Lake directed them: The closest Forest Service office was back in Redstone.

"Redstone," Ashley muttered.

"We can't do another thing here."

"But Lauren isn't in Redstone. She's here. She's around here. I know it. I feel it," she protested.

"And we're going to find her."

They backtracked twenty miles down the highway to the rustic village just off the road, flush with art galleries and souvenir shops and restaurants lining the street along the tree-shaded Crystal River. Above the town on the mountainside sat the imposing Redstone Castle, the turn-of-the-century mansion built by John Cleveland Osgood to impress the likes of J. P. Morgan, John D. Rockefeller and Teddy Roosevelt.

"Pretty place," Ashley said of the town.

"Do you see the Forest Service office?"

"Didn't that man say it was near the turnoff to Redstone Boulevard?"

"And so it is. Right there."

He pulled the Mustang into a parking spot next to the small dark-wood building. "You want to come in?" he asked.

She sighed. "It seems so hopeless."

"Look, I know it does, but try to remember this is what detective work is, checking every angle, no matter how unlikely. You start with the likely leads then go to the less likely."

"And that's where we are, at the bottom of the list."

"You never know. Now, come on, before the office closes."

The burden of their failures that long day rested heavily on her. They'd been from one end of the state to the next pursuing leads for two solid days with nothing to show but an abandoned cabin and an abandoned lover at a halfway house. Davey Potts was an elusive spirit, seen here, perhaps, or maybe there, or maybe not seen at all. And not a sign of Lauren.

She went into the office with Chris, a cramped room, telephones, shortwave radio, detailed topographical maps tacked to the walls. An old schoolhouse clock. There were two men in the office, a high-school-age boy, probably interning for the summer, and an older man in a Smokey Bear uniform.

"Afternoon," Chris said.

"Can I help you, sir?" the boy replied.

Chris explained what he needed, the same story he'd used in Marble, that he and his wife were searching for their runaway daughter, thought she might be holed up in a cabin near Marble, and wondered if there was a map pinpointing cabins and other abandoned structures.

The boy turned to the older man. "Larry, you'd know more about this than I would. Can you help these people?"

"Hm. Well, let me think on this." Larry went to a case behind a counter and pulled out three topographical maps. "I can mark a couple places on these. 'Course, I don't know every single one, but I'll try my best." He spread them out, and he and Chris bent over them, while Larry traced routes with a thick workingman's finger.

"You get up in the backcountry much?" Chris asked.

"Part of my job."

"Been near any of these places recently?"

"Three days ago. Oh, maybe it was four. Went by this one"—he pointed—"near Whitehouse Mountain."

"Any sign of people using it?"

"Not that I saw. But I wasn't looking."

"You would have noticed a vehicle, though."

"Yeah, probably. Can't recall seeing one."

"Lot of people drive these dirt roads?"

"A few. But they can be pretty rough tracks. It's not like a day trip up to see the Maroon Bells or something."

"I'll bet," Chris said.

He showed the photos to the rangers with no success and asked them to keep an eye out for their missing daughter. He gave them his card with Ashley's cell phone number on it.

"Damn crime a young girl like this running off with an older guy," the senior ranger Larry said. "There ought to be a law."

"She's fifteen," Chris remarked. "There *is* a law."

Outside the sun was low in the sky. Ashley was exhausted and disheartened. All they had to show for their day were some Xs on some maps.

"Tired?" Chris asked in the car.

"Yes, tired and hungry and discouraged."

"Let's get something to eat, then we'll decide on the next step."

They ate at the Crystal Club Cafe, a Victorian house turned into a restaurant, painted in pastel colors, tables on its wraparound porch, baskets of hanging flowers along the roofline. They sat outside in the warm summer evening. The menu was pure American, burgers and barbecued chicken and French fries, and the owner herself took their order.

"I know it's hard feeling we're stalled out," Chris said as they waited for their meals. "But this is the way it works, trust me."

"I'm trying," she whispered, eyes downcast, her finger tracing a line on the iced tea glass.

"She's okay. Believe me." He put his hand on hers, and she looked up to meet his gaze, warm and golden, full of such a depth of emotion, and she remembered him looking at her like that before, when he'd carried her out of the mine. And then their dinners arrived, he withdrew his hand, and the light in his eyes was extinguished as if by a switch.

Aspen was fifty miles away, and Chris wanted to make an early start searching the high country, so they got adjoining rooms in a motel just off Redstone's main street.

The Crystal River ran behind their rooms, and Ashley pulled back the drapes and opened her window so that she could hear its soothing murmur and breathe in the cool mountain air. She would have liked to leave the door open, too, but that was foolhardy. She lay on the bed and went through her cognitive therapies: "So what? So what? So the door's shut, so what?"

She took a shower and debated calling Robert. No, not tonight. She was too done in. Then she turned on the television and watched an inane program, which she forgot the moment the credits faded. She thought about Lauren and she thought about Davey. Her cell phone was plugged in, charging. She had an irrational fear that the battery would go dead, and Davey would be trying to phone her with an ultimatum, and she wouldn't be able to receive the call, so he'd do something terrible to Lauren. Kill her. All because of the dead battery. Tomorrow, first thing, she'd buy a spare.

She thought about Chris. She could get up and knock on his door. He'd open it, and maybe she'd go in, brushing past him. Maybe they'd make love on his bed, and she'd be surrounded by his scent, his skin against hers. They'd comfort each other, two lost souls in a chaotic universe. His ex-wife had said she was worried about him. Did Joanie know what had happened in Newark? But, no, Chris told her Joanie had left him by then. Ashley had the impression that Joanie didn't know, yet her wifely instincts warned her that her ex-husband was in some kind of trouble.

"I'm so glad you're with Chris," Joanie had said. As if Ashley could help him. For God's sake, she couldn't help herself half the time, and right now she couldn't help her daughter. What did Joanie think she was?

She dreamed of Lauren that night. Her daughter was returned to her, safe and unharmed. The relief she felt was so overwhelming, so all consuming, yet behind Lauren's triumphant return, there was a dark nagging hint that all was not right. In her dream, she kept trying to deny the small ugliness. She put forth a valiant dream-effort and tried to focus on a happy, smiling Lauren. If she tried hard enough, her dream logic told her, she could make the danger go away; she could save her daughter.

Then she was back in The Close Call—the same horrible, familiar dream she'd had for twenty years—but now, oh dear God, Lauren was with her, chained to a ring in the wall, too. Oh no, it was her fault, she'd let them capture Lauren. It was all her fault. Anguish twisted a knife in her chest. No, not Lauren, too. And her child was crying hideously, "Mommy, Mommy, I'm so cold. Please get me out of here, Mommy."

In her dream she yanked at Lauren's chain in impotent rage, but it wouldn't break. She tried to scream, but no sound came out. Then the walls of the mine, the rough-hewn rock, dark, with glistening mica chips that reflected the light of the kerosene lamp, the walls began to move with an unearthly groan. They began to edge, closer and closer, sliding inexorably together, and Lauren sobbed and clung to her, but she couldn't stop the onslaught of rock. They'd be crushed like bugs, and it was her fault. Lauren crying, the walls moving, the darkness and the cold and there was no air. She couldn't breathe, the walls were squeezing all the air out of the mine. She couldn't . . .

She jerked awake, a scream tearing from her throat. And then, trembling, lurching up, another scream. Oh God, she couldn't stop. She'd scream and scream . . .

"Ashley!" A pounding at her door. "Ashley!"

She managed to rise, to stagger to the door, to unlock it. He burst in, pants pulled on hastily, the waist button undone, no shirt. "What?" he said harshly. "What happened?"

She collapsed on the bed, shaking. "Nightmare," she gasped.

"I heard you. I . . ." He came to her, sat beside her on the bed.

"The mine. Oh, Chris, I was in the mine and Lauren and . . ."

He put an arm around her shoulders, gingerly at first, as if she were so fragile his touch would shatter her. "Okay, it was only a dream. It wasn't real."

She whimpered and rested her head on his chest, felt his arm tighten around her. And then she felt his lips graze her hair. Lightly, so lightly, or was it merely his breath?

"It's always the same, the dream. I'm in the mine and . . . and the walls are sliding in to crush me."

He brushed her hair back with his free hand. Said nothing. Held her.

"But . . ." She drew a quavering breath. "This time Lauren was with me."

"It's natural, isn't it? You're worried about her, so you . . ."

"It was so awful, so . . ." She turned in his arms, and their faces were close. So very close she could inhale his breath. She closed her eyes.

His lips on hers felt as she'd imagined. Soft and warm, his skin scratchy with whiskers, his scent that she knew as well as her own. She sighed deeply and put her arms around him. Wondrous man-skin sliding over muscle. Heat flared in her belly, and she opened her mouth to him, their tongues meeting, tasting.

He drew back, peered deep into her eyes. Touched her hair, her brow, traced a finger down her cheek to her lips. He touched her with reverence, with awe, as tenderly as if she were of the utmost fragility. It was like being embraced by water. She wanted to tell him that she wasn't a princess, a goddess to worship. She was a woman, a mother, a daughter, a lonely woman who needed him, who needed him so badly. But he put a finger on her lips to quiet her and kissed her again, profoundly, lingeringly.

She laid her hands on his chest and pushed him back gently. She cocked her head and studied his face. "You see? You see what a crazy woman you have to deal with?"

"I see . . . I see a beautiful person."

"I never stopped dreaming about you," she whispered.

He shook his head slowly.

"I dreamed . . . I imagined you were always there. You always rescued me."

"Oh Christ," he groaned. "I'm the last . . ."

"No, it's you. It's always been you."

"Ashley . . ."

She placed her head on his bare chest and she could feel his heart beating. "I imagined this."

"You were young, you were impressionable. I'm not . . ."

"Yes, you are." She turned her face, kissed the skin of his chest, breathed in his scent.

He drew her close and kissed the top of her head, turned her face up and kissed her eyes, her lips, moaned with a need she understood only too well. Her hands kneaded his back, feeling his ribs, the knobs of his spine, his smooth skin. He stroked her hair with a featherlight touch, caressed her neck, her shoulders. Careful, reverential, when she wanted ardor and a rough passion to make her forget her nightmares.

"Please, Chris," she murmured against his mouth.

But he didn't reply.

"Make me forget, please."

She felt him withdraw from her even though neither of them moved.

"It's all right," she breathed. "Chris . . . it's what I've always dreamed."

"No," he groaned, and he drew back. "No."

"Please," she tried, "I know what . . ."

"You don't know," he said savagely, and he was on his feet, turning away from her.

"Chris." She was sobbing.

"I'm no good, no good for you. This is . . ." He held a hand up, as if to stop her. "This is *fucked*."

"Why? What's wrong?"

"Just . . . just leave me alone. You don't know me, Ashley. You don't want to goddamn know me." He backed away, came up against the door, whirled, flung it open and disappeared into the blackness.

She sagged onto the side of the bed, curled into a fetal position, clutching a pillow, misery tearing at her with sharp talons.

Oh God, oh God, what had she done? What was the matter? Why? Why?

She lay there as the night wore on, and she knew that he was wrong. They could heal each other, they could help each other, and they could love each other. The three of them, she and Lauren and Chris.

He was wrong, because she did know him. She knew everything about him, had known it for twenty years— he was fine and good and honest.

FIFTEEN

Robert's visit the previous day had thrown Pauline into a haze of confusion. She barely knew what shows ran in front of her eyes on the TV; yesterday, she'd refused to eat lunch or dinner, arguing with Vladimir, convinced she was being held against her will in a strange house by foreigners.

Ashley was gone. She was cognizant of that. But she was certain her child had been abducted again. She had to evade these people who were keeping her prisoner and get to the police. In her mind she could envision the police station. It was in the basement of the Pitkin County Courthouse in the heart of downtown. Right where it had been for years and years.

If she could just get to town. Or just figure out in which direction to walk.

She ate breakfast and tried to go along with her keepers' ministrations. The barrel-chested man with the Slavic cheekbones placed pills in her hand, which she pretended to swallow. The minute he turned his back she spit them into her napkin. The woman came into the kitchen then, her face harshly grooved.

The woman leaned close to Pauline and said, "You have better day today, not make our job so hard."

Pauline said she would. She promised to be good. The woman's reaction was to mutter in an unintelligible language. The big man told the woman, "Pauline okay this morning." Then he, too, said something in the strange language.

She snuck away from them while *The Price Is Right* was on the TV. She'd heard the woman tell Vladimir that she needed help changing the sheets in their bedroom, and when they both disappeared from sight, Pauline stood, walked to the door and was gone within seconds.

Moving along the road rapidly, she waved at a bushy-haired man next door who waved back at her. He was wiping his hands on an oily-looking cloth, obviously changing a tire on a car. One of many cars in his yard.

He even called out to her, "Need a ride somewhere?"

Pauline shook her head vehemently and hurried on. How dare a total stranger try to get her into his car?

At the end of the private road, the hot morning sun beating on her shoulders, she caught her breath and peered up and down the intersection, uncertain. Then she looked up through the trees across the way and over the roof of a house and there was Aspen Mountain. All she had to do was head toward it. Relief flooded her, and shortly she was on familiar turf. Within a few blocks, City Market was on her left and a new upscale complex on her right. On the next block was Scandinavian Design. She darted across the street, took a diagonal short-cut. Past the Elks Lodge—she was puffing now—past

City Hall and there it was, her destination, the beautiful brick courthouse sitting in stately grace on Main Street.

The receptionist at the police station was very kind and told her to take a seat on a bench in the hall, someone would be with her in a moment. The female officer even got her a glass of water. But Pauline didn't want to sit or sip water. She needed to tell the police her daughter had been kidnapped and she herself was being detained by two foreigners.

It seemed as if she waited for hours before she heard, "Mrs. Lacouter? Pauline? It's Terry."

She looked up to see a police officer standing over her. Thank God. And . . . She knew him. Of course. It was her friend Phoebe's son. He was in Aspen High School with Ashley. He was a year or so ahead of Ashley, though, and . . . Pauline's face went blank. When animation returned and she focused on Terry, she saw that his hair was gray at the temples. How could a high school kid's hair be gray? Then she had a definite memory of being at his wedding. Terry and Mary's wedding. And Ashley was already married. To . . . Robert.

"Are you all right, Pauline?" He kneeled down in front of her. "Is Ashley around?"

Pauline gasped, remembering why she was there. "They've taken Ashley! Those men . . . the Pottsses. They've taken her and put two people at her house to watch me. You have to help . . . You . . ."

"Pauline," Terry said gently, and he took her hands in his. "That was many years ago. You remember now? When we were in high school? Has to have been at least twenty years ago."

"No, no." Pauline shook her head desperately. "They have Ashley. It's the Pottsses. They have . . ." Some dor-

mant gear shifted in her brain, a neuron fired and she
blinked.

"Pauline?"

"It's Lauren. Oh my God, they have Lauren, my
granddaughter."

"I see," Terry said. "Well, why don't I give your
house a call and check in? Okay? We'll get to the bottom of this." He rose and smiled at her. "I'll be right
back. You'll wait here?"

"Yes, yes," she said, abruptly bewildered again. Why
had she come here? Shouldn't Vladimir have driven her?
She had walked. She remembered walking here. Why
would she do that?

After making his call, Terry drove her home. He
seemed to be a bright young man, knew exactly where
Ashley lived. Pauline sat in the passenger seat of his
patrol car, a sporty Saab, and asked after his wife and
children and his mother, Phoebe.

When they pulled into the dusty drive at Ashley's,
Vladimir and Luda were waiting out front, Vladimir
looking very upset, Luda's expression guarded.

Terry spoke to them and nodded a couple times toward the Saab, where Pauline still sat wondering just
how she'd gotten there.

Then Terry came back and opened her door. "It's all
right, Pauline, you can go on inside."

"But . . . Lauren? And where is Ashley?"

"It's all right," he repeated, helping her to her feet,
leading her across the drive. "The Rostovs told me Ashley went to get Lauren. So, see, everything is okay now."

But it wasn't. She just knew it wasn't.

Chris pulled the rental Jeep to the side of the badly rutted road so Ashley could take a call on her cell phone.

As always now, on the first ring, her hands began to tremble, and he could see her fighting to breathe evenly.

But the call wasn't from Potts. It was Vladimir. Chris listened while Ashley spoke, one hand holding the phone to her ear, the other on her brow. Then she clicked off, made sure the thing was securely plugged into the dashboard power source and gripped the bar in front of the passenger seat.

"Damn them. Two people and they can't keep track of one sick old lady." She swiveled to look him in the eyes. "Mom walked into town and ended up at the police station. She told Terry—he's a cop, was a couple years ahead of me in school—anyway, she told him Lauren had been kidnapped."

"Oh boy," Chris whispered.

"Well, the good news is that Vladimir only told him I had gone to get Lauren. He knew not to tell the police the truth. Thank God."

"And this cop believed Vladimir?"

"Vladimir thinks so. He said Mom's been really confused. Luda even found her medication rolled up in her napkin. I've never seen Mom this bad."

"Look, think about the events of the last few days. From what I know about Alzheimer's, any little thing that throws a person out of their routine can cause erratic behavior."

"How do you know all that?"

He shrugged. "Took some classes in the academy years ago. Rookie patrolmen run into all sorts of people on the streets, and it helps to know what you're dealing with. Alzheimer's patients have a habit of wandering off and getting lost."

"Don't I know it," she said.

"So give your mom a break. Hell, she meant well. Right?"

"I know she did. Still . . . Oh, well, it's done. And Vladimir at least used his head."

They'd gone directly to a local mountain outfitter that morning and rented the Jeep and all the camping gear they could conceive of. Armed with an extra battery pack for the phone, plenty of water and groceries and the Forest Service map, they were on the road by 9 A.M.

For the first hour they wound through canopies of blue spruce and emerged into a meadow, the breeze running a soft hand over the wildflowers. A gurgling creek meandered along the track, and the silver sagebrush perfumed the air. There were a couple of cabins nestled in stands of aspens and, just in case, they stopped and checked them out. There was no evidence that anyone had been around for weeks. No evidence whatsoever of Potts or Lauren. Ahead of them the Ragged Mountains tore at the blue sky and the valley narrowed.

"Guess we start to climb now," Chris said, nodding at the jagged peaks looming ahead.

Ashley shielded her eyes and looked up. "I'm not the best Jeeper. Heights bother me. You *can* drive this thing, can't you?"

"No problem," he assured her.

After leaving the meadow behind, it was slow going, the old Jeep road badly rutted now, fallen rocks blocking the path in places, other spots so narrow and tilted over hundreds of feet of exposure that Chris had to practically crawl along the route to keep from sliding over an edge of a cliff. Thank heavens there had been no measurable rain in the high country for weeks, and they didn't have to deal with slick mud.

Neither of them had been in this valley before. The

mountains here were particularly close together, and
they were all at least 12,000 feet high. The terrain was
more like Alaska, with massive rock walls pushing
arrow-straight into the sky, and the valley so close there
was barely enough room for a creek and dirt track to
drive on. Meadows were almost nonexistent.

It was magnificent country.

They were following the shoulder of Chair Mountain
now, making slow progress toward Whitehouse Mountain, where the closest old mining camp sat at its base.
Supposedly there were still a couple of shacks alongside
the creek there, and occasionally intrepid hikers stopped
over at the site.

By noon they still hadn't reached the camp. Over the
insistent grinding of the engine, Chris said, "I think we
should stop and eat then push on. Looks like a small
clearing ahead."

They did not take the time to build a fire, just threw
some ham and cheese and mayo in between slices of
bread and wolfed the food down. They drank plenty of
water and took off again munching on apples, the trail
zigzagging up, deeper and deeper into the high country.

It was hard to converse over the constant grind of the
motor, and Chris's thoughts wandered, jumping from
one thing to the next until they reluctantly settled on last
night. No matter how hard he tried, he couldn't shake
those images. He'd summoned every ounce of strength
in order to tear himself away from her. This was the
second time in the space of a few days that he'd behaved
like an ass. Yet he could still feel her in his arms, taste
her, draw in her scent. He wasn't going to lie to himself.
He'd wanted her in his apartment the other night. He'd
wanted her last night. Wanted her right now. He had
always goddamn wanted her.

The truth was he wished to hell the circumstances were different. He wished he and Ashley were merely a couple on a mountain adventure. There would be bottles of wine rattling in the back and they would be enjoying the country but waiting for nightfall, waiting till the sky turned unimaginably black, spangled with diamonds of light that gleamed down on them, billions of stars in an unfathomably enormous universe. The campfire would shoot orange sparks into the blackness, and the air would be thick with the smell of wood smoke and pine. They'd lie on their sleeping bags gazing at the stars, and they'd be a little drunk on the wine in the high altitude.

"Brr," she'd say after a while, and he'd reach over and pull her down bag around her shoulders. He'd allow his hand to linger. After a time he'd lean close, touch her cheek with his fingers, stroke her neck, and he'd finally cup her head in his hands and lift her till their lips met.

He knew how she tasted, and he knew how soft the skin on her belly and hips would feel. He knew that her breasts were small and firm and he knew her hips were wide, a woman's hips made to bear children.

They'd shed their clothes and she'd shiver in the starlight, the fire bathing her in a rich golden glow. And then he would cover her nakedness with his. And he'd be so warm, burning for her. When he moved inside her he knew how she'd feel to him, how her flesh would embrace him.

He knew every inch of Ashley although he'd never touched her intimately. He had known for the better part of his life.

But they weren't on a romantic mountain outing. And they were not carefree souls who could lose themselves to passion. They both came with heavy baggage. There was Lauren waiting for them to find her. There was the possibility that Ashley might come unraveled. He himself was living on borrowed time. Ironically, time Ashley had given him with her phone call the other night. Full circle now. But he didn't know how long he could play her hero. Or when the darkness would engulf him again, and he'd take that gun from his jacket lying on the dusty backseat and shove it in his mouth, pull the trigger. There were no guarantees in this madness.

Ashley was tapping the map with an index finger, her attention ahead to where the dirt road disappeared into a pine forest.

"I think that first cabin is just around this bend," she said. "I can't really tell by the map, but if we're right here"—she held up the map and pointed—"then that has to be the camp at the base of Whitehouse Mountain."

Chris downshifted, braked and killed the engine.

"What are you . . . ?"

"You can hear these things coming for miles. We'll go it on foot. If no one's around, I'll hike back for the Jeep." He reached behind him and picked up his jacket, shaking off the layer of dust that had settled on every available surface in the open vehicle. He took his gun from the jacket's pocket and saw that Ashley's brow was furrowed.

"I'm not about to approach some damn strange cabin without a weapon," he said, ejecting the clip then reinserting it.

"I understand. But what if Lauren really is there? What if Potts has a gun and . . ."

"This is what I was trained to do. I'm not planning to use it, okay? But better safe than sorry." He climbed out of the vehicle. "I'd tell you to sit tight right here, but I know you won't. So stay behind me. I mean it. Don't get cute."

"Cute."

"Yeah, cute."

"You're doing that thing you do," she said.

"Thing I do?"

"Yes. You change. You turn into a tough guy. It's weird. It's not really you."

He hitched his shoulders. Joanie had once said something similar. And she'd genuinely hated him when he came home like that. But Ashley—she seemed more curious than anything.

The uphill hike through the forest took longer than either of them guessed from studying the map. Chris figured that was good, less chance of someone having heard the approach of the Jeep. For a full twenty minutes they trudged up the side of the dirt track, the lodgepole pines casting deep shadows, the odor of pine and rotting deadfall heavy and moist in the cool air. Then they could see a splash of bright daylight ahead. A clearing.

He stopped, put a finger to his lips. Sound had a peculiar way of carrying in the mountains. Someone could take a shot at a deer or elk a hundred yards from you and you'd never hear it. But, curiously, depending on the terrain, you might hear a rifle report from several miles off.

"Let's keep it really quiet now, okay?" he whispered.

They left the road and moved into the forest, coming out into the clearing above the cabin that sat on the edge of the trickling creek. There was no vehicle in sight, but Chris figured one could be hidden close by, even right under his nose, and he might not spot it.

Fortunately, there were no windows on the side or rear of the cabin, and they were able to approach unseen.

Overhead a steller's jay screeched at them, and Chris thought he saw a doe dart into a stand of aspens on the far side of the clearing, but other than that there was no visible sign of life.

He stopped and pressed Ashley soundlessly against the rough-hewn wood of the cabin's side. "I'll go in from here," he whispered. She almost balked, but he gave her a look that quieted her.

Catlike, he moved around to the front of the structure, crouched, his gun held out now in front of him, clasped in both hands.

He was starting to sweat and had to mop at his brow with his sleeve. He paused then, listening, and suddenly the breath held in his lungs—a noise. Something. A scratching inside the cabin.

He snicked off the safety of his gun.

Now his face popped with sweat, his shirt glued instantly to his back. He wiped his forehead again with a wrist.

Another noise. This time a rattling sound. He could almost see the girl inside, bound, trying to free herself. But where the hell was Potts? *Shit.*

The steller's jay screeched again, a magpie answered, and his pulse pounded. If Potts was outside somewhere, gathering wood, God only knew what, then now was the time to get in and out with Lauren. But if Potts was in there . . .

Surprise was on Chris's side. He only prayed the door was not latched.

He duck-walked beneath a small broken window and slowly reached up, testing the rusted metal latch. It moved freely. The place had been occupied recently.

Slowly, he raised the latch with one hand, his gun held straight out with the other, and he burst inside, his eyes barely adjusted to the dimness, wildly swinging the gun from corner to corner.

All hell broke loose. Something ran in front of his line of vision. There was a panicked animal-like snarl. He swung the gun again. Couldn't see a damn thing, nothing. Then there it was, backed into a corner, big and gray and wearing a mask. A goddamn raccoon.

He almost shot the terrified creature; damn near splattered the thing from one wall to the next. His heart was thudding in his ears and sweat was blinding him. He swore and panted, still aiming at the creature as his brain absorbed the scene: raccoon climbs in broken window, rolls old tin can on the floor. Not Lauren struggling against restraints. Not Potts darting for cover, weapon in hand.

He stood slowly from his crouched position and the animal growled at him again. Then Ashley was behind him, moaning something like, "What, what? Is it . . . ?" And the raccoon made a dash for it.

"Watch out, let him by!" Chris shouted. He had to whirl and push Ashley aside before the thing took a chunk out of her jeans on its terrified flight.

"Oh my God," she cried, leaping out of the way, as startled as the animal. It was a minute before she seemed to realize what had happened, and then she said, "Oh God, I thought . . . I was sure . . . A raccoon?"

Chris couldn't help the shaky smile that collected on his face. He put the safety on his gun and secured it in the waistband of his jeans. "Almost a dead raccoon," he said a little sheepishly. "Scared the hell out of me."

"You think you were scared," she said, getting her breath.

They walked side by side back down to the Jeep, moving quickly. It was almost 2 P.M. by the time they drove past the cabin and continued on to the next X marked on the Forest Service map, approximately three miles along the ridge of the mountain near a high alpine lake—three miles that took a full hour.

Again they parked a safe distance away. Again they walked in quietly to the cabin. Again it was empty, no signs whatsoever of recent occupation. This particular place was in shambles, a fire having snaked up one wall some time ago. The remains reeked of acrid wood.

Ashley sank to her knees by the edge of the small lake and splashed water on her face and neck. She looked up at him then, water dripping down her neck to disappear in the cleavage of her blue denim shirt. "We're never going to find her," she said dully. "This country is just too big. Too much to cover. And we don't even know if all the cabins are marked on the map. There could be more. Dozens more."

Chris was standing over her. He reached down, clasped his hands around her arms and pulled her to her feet. "Or she could be in the next place. What the hell are you doing? Giving up?" His tone was rough.

"No," she said. "No. Of course not. I'll never give up."

He dropped his hands. "Then let's not waste any daylight. We can hit two more spots before we'll have to make camp. Let's go, Ashley."

She sighed and studied his face. "Yes, sir," she said, "two more. And maybe she'll be at the next one."

"You got it."

But Lauren wasn't at the next mark on the map or the next, though they did run into a young couple who were hiking over Schofield Pass from Ashcroft to Redstone. They had stopped for the night in one of the cabins near a silver mine that had played out over a century before.

The couple had run into several Jeeps earlier in the day and a few mountain bikers in the White River National Forest. They said they'd come across lots of other hikers. But neither of them recognized Lauren's or Davey Potts's photo. Chris and Ashley drove on, now making a wide swing through the high country that would eventually lead them back to Marble.

Night would fall in an hour. Chris picked a sheltered clearing to stop and make camp. There was a stream nearby and a pine forest that would provide firewood. He unloaded their provisions while Ashley used the cell phone to touch base with Luda. She was worried about the battery, but Luda only spoke to her for a minute, assuring her Pauline was all right. When Ashley called Robert it was a different story. Chris was setting up the two-man tent—thinking he should have asked for two singles—and half listening to Ashley while she brought her ex-husband up to speed.

"No, damnit, Robert, I told you, other than that one woman yesterday who thought Potts *might* have looked familiar, we haven't found a sign of him or Lauren. But we still have a couple more places to check in the morning. . . . No, we're camping. . . . God, I don't know, a couple miles below Schofield Pass, I guess. . . . Look, the battery's going to run down and . . . Yes, there's a power outlet in the Jeep to charge it. . . . Yes, I have an extra battery, but . . . Robert, please . . . No, no more calls from Davey Potts. . . . No, I don't know what that means. . . ."

Chris began collecting wood for the fire. His thinking wasn't that far off from Robert's, he realized—what did it mean that Potts hadn't called in? How long had it been? Almost two days now?

All afternoon he'd been getting that cop's itch under

his skin. Something was not quite right. There was, of course, the off chance that Potts had somehow spotted them in Marble and was lying low. But Chris didn't think that was the source of his uneasiness. There was something else. Something he was missing. He was fairly certain Potts hadn't harmed Lauren. Not yet. He needed the girl alive and kicking if for no other reason than to drive Ashley mad. Potts might even put the girl on the phone for a moment, too, just to prove to Ashley he still had the power.

So why had he gone so silent? Was this another form of torment? But that scenario didn't seem quite fitting, either.

Chris squatted down and dug a fire pit, rimming the shallow hole with loose rock, while Ashley finally got Robert off the phone and plugged it into the power source in the Jeep.

"Damn that man," she was muttering. "As if I'm not worried enough as it is about Lauren, I have to worry about his threats to call the FBI. He just won't let up." She spun around to Chris. "I don't know what more we can do. I don't know what more the FBI could do. I keep thinking Lauren is so close and somehow we missed her . . . somehow . . ."

"We're getting there," he reassured her. "I know it seems like that jerk has had her for an eternity, but it's just been a few days. She's okay, Ashley. Potts isn't going to harm her."

"Why hasn't he called? Why? I know, I know, when he *does* call I go insane. But now . . . This is almost worse. Maybe that's why, to make me even crazier."

"I'm sure that's it," he said, but he was lying. Something was off.

They fixed dinner together. They'd bought a couple

of steaks and packaged potatoes from a small mart next
to the outfitters, and they had a frying pan and a pot to
boil water in, two tin plates and forks and knives and
cups. The outfitter had provided everything in a neat
package—even a cooler. While Ashley started the water
for the dehydrated potatoes, he unfastened the jerrican
from the back of the Jeep and gassed up for morning.

He had his jacket along, and Ashley had purchased a
heavy sweater that morning at the outfitters. She'd
pulled it on as soon as the sun had dipped below the
ridge of Whitehouse Mountain, and she crouched near
the fire now, tending the steaks, her shirttails hanging
out, her jeans grimy from the day in the mountains, her
hair mussed and windblown, pushed behind her ears.
She looked like a real camper, the woman he'd fanta-
sized about earlier that day, who'd lie by the fire with
him after supper, sharing the bottle of wine. God, how
he wished the circumstances were different.

He ate his meat and tasteless potatoes, hunkered down
near the fire as the sky brightened with billions of stars
and a nearly full moon. Even if they found Lauren—
when they found her, he told himself—and Ashley's life
settled back into its normal busy rhythm, he still had his
demons to face. Sure, for the last few days he'd put them
aside, but they'd be back.

He considered telling Ashley everything, about his
discovery that he wasn't such a good guy, that he could
have fallen into the role of wiseguy and stayed there
comfortably if it hadn't been for the bust and the "missing" money. Not that he gave a damn about the money
or ever would care. It was doing someone a lot of good.
He'd do it all over again, too, in a heartbeat. Better paying off Joe's debts than in the hands of some crooked
cops or politician.

Screw the money, he thought, and he looked at Ashley through the leaping embers. She might even understand about the money. But how could he explain about his inability to distinguish between right and wrong? About losing his very identity? Hell, he couldn't explain it to himself. Nor could he explain why blowing his brains out seemed easier than living with the demons.

He washed the pots and tin plates in the nearby stream using grit from the streambed—just like he and his dad had always done. Ashley shook out the sleeping bags. But when she tried to stuff them in the tent and saw the impossibly close quarters, she stood up and appeared ill at ease.

He almost said, "Hey, it's all right, we can handle it," but he knew that, too, was bullshit. Instead, he said, "The tent's for you. I'll sleep by the fire."

"Oh," she said, and he dared for a moment to imagine wrenching disappointment in that single word, "Oh."

He slept poorly. He wasn't cold. The down bag was good for twenty below zero. It was just damn hard being so close to her, hearing her stir inside the tent; the thin nylon walls that were all that was keeping them apart.

But mostly he slept badly because he couldn't get her words out of his head, the words she'd spoken when he'd kissed her last night—all those long years she'd been dreaming about him.

He lay staring at the sky, so clear and crisp he could almost reach up and touch the twinkling lights. He wondered what she'd think, what she'd say if he had the guts to tell her he shared the same dream.

SIXTEEN

She had a million chores hanging over her head when she got back to Aspen the next morning—laundry, bills to pay, her school curriculum to plan. It was good to have things to do, though, a distraction. She hadn't even had time to take a shower yet, and she was still dusty and dirty from two days in the mountains.

Lauren, she thought. *We were close, I know we were. We'll find you.*

The phone rang as she was gathering laundry, not the cell phone, thank God. She was sure it would be one of Lauren's friends, the first of a dozen calls that would come today.

It was Charlene Garcia.

"I hope you don't mind me calling," she said. "We hardly know each other. But Joe told me about your daughter. I hope this isn't a bad time?"

"No, of course not."

"Oh, good. Have there been any new leads? I just

can't stop thinking about the poor child and what you're going through."

"Nothing new. Nothing concrete, anyway."

"I'm so sorry. I can't even begin to imagine."

"It's pretty awful," Ashley said. "And I don't know what I'd have done without Chris."

There was a slight pause at the mention of his name. "I . . . uh . . . look, Joe doesn't know I'm calling. But I wanted to ask you, woman to woman, how Chris was doing."

She hesitated, then she said, "Well, he's been tense, but then we all have."

"No, I mean . . . emotionally." She gave a nervous laugh. "Joe would *kill* me if he knew I'd called you."

"Emotionally?"

"He's . . . well, there have been some problems. We're worried about him."

"What problems?" Luda was rattling around in the kitchen, and Pauline was getting up. She walked into her room for privacy.

"Well, you know, the usual kind cops run into."

"Charlene, I don't really know. I haven't seen Chris in twenty years."

"I guess you'd call it depression."

"I . . . he . . . he did say something about New Jersey."

"Yes."

"He didn't want to talk about it."

"Of course not. Men."

She sat on the edge of her bed, cradling the phone, holding it close. "What was it, Charlene? What happened to him there?"

"I don't know, honestly. Neither does Joe. Something happened, though. His ex-wife is worried, too."

"She mentioned it, but I . . ."

"Be good to him, Ashley. He hurts a lot."

"God, Charlene, I'm having enough trouble staying sane myself."

"I can imagine. I just thought, well, you know, men won't talk."

"No kidding."

"Well, sorry to bug you. I know he'll find your daughter. He's the best, the very best. Our thoughts and prayers are with you, Ashley."

She hung up, pensive. Curious. No one had any answers, though. What was Chris holding on to, where did his pain come from?

She was finally starting the load of laundry, and Chris had just come from the apartment over the garage, his hair still damp, mussed by a towel, when her cell phone rang. Her eyes met his at the sound, and she was torn between relief and the now familiar surge of terror. Davey was finally checking in.

"Answer it," Chris said, and she pressed the button.

"Ash-lee," came that voice. "How are you, Ash-lee? It's been too long."

"I want to talk to Lauren. You have to let me talk to her. How . . . how do I even know you have her?"

He chuckled in reply.

She tried a new tack. "Look, if you want money, my ex-husband will pay anything you ask. Whenever you want, however you want. We won't tell the police, and you'll be rich, and . . ."

"It's not about money. I don't want your goddamn money."

"Then what do you want?" God, she hated the quaver in her voice.

"I got what I want."

"What? Me suffering? Okay, yes, you have that.

Okay? Now can I have my daughter back?"

"Not just yet, Ash-lee."

Then Lauren was alive, her mind screamed. She was *alive.* "Listen, you son of a bitch. If you touch her, if you hurt her, I'll hunt you down till my dying day. I'll get you. I'll get you, do you hear me?"

"Ooh, tough stuff. Did your boyfriend tell you to say that, Ash-lee?"

She hesitated a heartbeat too long. "What are you talking about?"

"You know damn well."

"I don't know. What do you mean?"

"I might be watching you right now. Think about that."

Goosebumps rose on her skin, and she suddenly felt dizzy. Then rage flooded her. "You bastard! I'll find you. I'll hunt you down. That's a promise, Davey!" Without thinking she pressed the end button and sat there, panting with fear and fury. Defiantly, she raised her head and looked around. Her mother was staring at her and nodding over and over; Luda had come out of the kitchen, a dishtowel hanging from her hand, and was regarding her with frank respect. And Chris—his expression was unreadable.

What had she done? "I'm tired of him torturing me. I'm sick of it. I . . . I just don't want to put up with his *crap* anymore." Then she put a hand over her mouth. "Did I . . . did I do something awful? Will he . . . ?"

"It doesn't matter what you say," Chris assured her.

"I should have groveled. I should have begged."

"Don't beat yourself up. At least he called. Now we know he's still out there."

She blinked, remembering. "He knows about you."

"What?"

"He said something about my boyfriend."

"How in hell . . . ?"

"Could he be watching us?"

Chris thought, shook his head. "Doubtful. Too risky. There hasn't been a sign of him. I'd have noticed."

"I don't know, maybe he has been. I don't know anything. I . . . oh God, I want this over! I want my daughter!"

"Ashley, hey, it's going to be okay."

She straightened her shoulders. "Yes, it will be. It has to be. I will not let him destroy Lauren or me. I'll get him." She could hardly believe the fierce determination taking root in her. A step above fear, a step above apathy. Anger. She closed her eyes and willed her strength to Lauren. *Hang on, baby, we're coming.*

Robert drove up in his silver Range Rover after lunch. "Any news this morning?" he demanded, striding into the house. "You were supposed to be in touch."

"He called," Ashley said. "He says he doesn't want money."

"No? Then what *does* he want?"

She lifted her shoulders, let them drop.

"Well, what did you find out on your mountain excursion?"

"Nothing."

"In Marble?"

"I told you, a woman might have seen him driving an old white Blazer."

"*Great.* That's the sum total of your research? Nothing in Canon City, nothing in Denver, a possible sighting in Marble?"

"It takes time, Robert."

"My daughter may not have time." He straightened, pulled in his stomach, and rearranged his belt. "I think this farce has gone on long enough." He stood in the center of the small living room as if he were presiding over a boardroom. "Your time is up, Ashley. I'm taking over. I gave you your two days, and it's stretched into a lot longer. You and your pal Judge haven't made any progress, and I'm not waiting anymore."

"Robert . . ."

"No, no more time. I'm going to have your calls ring on my cell phone. Don't worry, it's all legal. Lenny Coates is handling everything. The order's in with the phone company. *I* will monitor the calls from Potts, and *I* will arrange for my daughter's release."

"Oh God, Robert, he'll . . . we don't know what he'll do if you get involved. He told me . . ."

"I don't give a rat's ass what he told you. He's committed a federal offense, and he's got my daughter, and I'm going after him."

She swayed, her face drained, all the blood pooled in her belly, and she was sick with dread. The walls of her house lurched, nausea rose in her throat; the walls began to slide in toward her, to move . . .

"It's okay," she heard dimly through her panic. "Ashley, listen, you're okay."

Chris, yes, his voice low and soothing, and she was outside in the sunshine and the summer breeze, his arm around her. She was cold but wet with sweat, trembling.

"See?" Faintly she heard Robert behind them. "See what I mean? She's not well. I should have handled this from the beginning."

And Chris replying, his tone low and hard. "Listen, you pumped-up asshole. If you step in and fuck things up, if you think your money can solve this . . ."

"You know what? You're fired, buddy." Robert aimed an index finger at Chris.

"I work for Ashley."

"What she wants is no longer a concern of mine."

"Get in that fancy piece of tin you drive and get out of here."

"You can't talk to me like that," Robert blustered.

"I can't? Funny, thought I just did. Now get the hell out of here."

She heard footsteps crunch across gravel, his car door opening and closing, the engine starting its expensive throaty purr, the sound growing fainter.

"He's gone," Chris said.

"Can he do that?" she implored. "Can he get the calls on his phone?"

"With the help of his lawyer? Probably."

"Chris, we have to do something. We have to . . ."

"Not much we can do right now."

"Chris," she cried.

"Yeah, I'm still here." His arm tightened around her shoulders till her trembling subsided.

That night, unable to sleep, she sat by her open bedroom window and breathed in the night air. The moon was rising behind the house, over the shoulder of Smuggler Mountain, casting an otherworldly glow that lit up the eastern sky and dimmed the stars.

She was bitterly ashamed that she'd fallen apart in front of Robert. Giving him more ammunition. Giving him even more of an excuse to take over. Her weakness could seal her daughter's fate, and she'd never forgive herself for that. She may have survived her own ordeal twenty years before, but she wouldn't survive causing Lauren's . . . She shut the thought down.

She sat there, her forearms resting on the windowsill, chin on her arms. The familiar silhouette of the mountains lay like scissored shadows against the incandescent moonlight, the night punctuated by a dog barking, a car on the road, someone laughing next door at Jay's.

She could see a corner of the garage from her window; a light was on in the apartment. Chris, too, was awake.

With effort she pushed aside the image of him and thought about the day, Robert barging in—the nerve of him—and then earlier, when she'd felt an annoying itch below the surface of her consciousness. What exactly had precipitated the sensation? That morning, before returning to Aspen, they'd located two more cabins, both abandoned, one with a caved-in roof. There had been nothing remarkable about either place or, for that matter, any of the other backcountry cabins they'd come across. So why was she uneasy? Could she have subconsciously noted something?

Out of possibilities, they'd turned in the Jeep and camping gear, picked up Chris's car and driven home. She'd been disheartened after their failure in the mountains, but Chris seemed impervious to disappointment. He went on, undeterred, undaunted. Failure was not in his vocabulary. But then Lauren wasn't his child.

She stared unseeing at the trees and the mountains and the glaring crescent of the rising moon, and she went over the sequence of events: They'd gotten back to Aspen, Davey had called almost immediately, as if he were indeed spying on them; Robert had arrived with his officious pronouncement, and she'd sleepwalked through the rest of the day.

She prayed that her blowup on the phone hadn't endangered Lauren. She was truly losing control—screaming at Davey one second, collapsing in front of Robert the next. Chris was her only anchor. Chris, who was probably sitting in the old armchair right now, devising new schemes to find her child. Despite Robert, despite *her*, despite everything.

Davey Potts. Why *hadn't* he called for two whole days, when he'd called every day before that? How had he known about Chris? What did he want from her? What did he really want? Kidnappers *always* wanted money. Or something else concrete, like the release of political prisoners or asylum or *something*. Her own abduction had been an aberration. Davey did not want Lauren as a servant. No.

But he had said several times that the kidnapping wasn't about money. "I got what I want," he'd said. Did he mean Lauren? Or did he mean her own agony? Or was she misreading his motives entirely?

She sighed and rolled her forehead across her folded arms. She was tired but full of questions. Nothing made any sense. *He had what he wanted.* His voice, in every call, gloating, as if he knew something she didn't. And how had he learned about Chris? Something didn't fit, something wasn't logical, like a wrong value in an equation, so that no matter how long you calculated, it wouldn't come out right.

She didn't know she'd made the decision until she picked up a sweater from the back of a chair, drew it around her bare shoulders and padded through the darkened house and out the front door. Across the brightly moonlit yard and up the stairs at the side of the garage. Tapping quietly at his door.

She didn't hear him approach; the door opened, and he was there, a shadow against the light within.

"Ashley?"

"Can I come in?"

He stood aside, barefoot, wearing jeans and a white T-shirt, his hair mussed, his eyes darkened with surprise.

"I saw your light on," she said.

"Uh-huh."

"I wasn't asleep, either."

He stood there warily, as if unsure how to react.

"I was thinking. About Davey and the calls he's made, what he said, the way he sounds. And him knowing about you." She hugged herself. "We're not seeing something."

He stared at her.

"I mean, it's like he knows things we don't, he's a step ahead of us."

"Yeah?"

"What is it, Chris? What are we missing?"

"I don't know. Yet."

"And this business with Robert . . ."

"Huh."

"It's driving me out of my mind. How did Davey know exactly when and where to grab Lauren? How does he know so much? It's like . . . it's like he's playing cat and mouse with us."

"Yeah, it's occurred to me, too."

"My mind keeps going around and around. Could Lauren have known him? Did he befriend her, something like that? It's crazy, I know, and I can't imagine her even looking twice at a man his age. God, no, he'd scare her. I *think*." She put her face in her hands, and her sweater slipped off her shoulders. She was aware of Chris picking it up, standing there with it in his hand, his glance trailing along her skin. Then he draped the sweater around her, his fingers lightly brushing her arm.

She raised her eyes. "It's almost as if . . . it's a hoax. The whole thing. A trick. But why? Am I insane?"

"No, you're not insane."

There was only one lamp on in the room, and it cast

a sickly circle of yellow light compared to the moonlight that flooded through the window. Brilliant, silver-white light from an impossibly huge moon.

She couldn't see his features clearly. His face, eye sockets, hollowed checks, mouth, all were deeply shadowed. The amber tone of his voice was at odds with the enigmatic sculpture she was trying to decipher.

"Chris? Maybe there is no connection with Lauren. Maybe I'm grasping at straws."

He shook his head wordlessly.

"Do you think . . . do you think the police or the FBI can really figure it out?"

He gave a short laugh. "Not goddamn likely."

"But Robert, he's going to call them in. Maybe he already has."

Chris twisted his mouth. "We'll do our best to co-operate, and then we'll ignore them."

"So you won't stop helping?"

"No, Ashley, I don't give up that easily."

"Thank God," she breathed.

"Do you want something to drink?" he asked. "You know, to calm down? I found an opened bottle of wine in the refrigerator."

"Okay, yes. Anything." She suddenly became aware that she was in a nightgown, a pale blue cotton one, with eyelet straps, and she was barefoot. She pulled the gray cardigan tighter, holding it together in front. "Uh," she said to his back, "on second thought, maybe I should go."

He turned, one eyebrow raised quizzically. "Are you afraid of me?"

"No, no, of course not. It's just that it's late."

He came toward her, two glasses of wine in his hands. After a moment she took one.

"Sit down." He gestured.

She knew she should put aside the glass and leave. Coming here in the middle of the night had been foolish. But she didn't leave—she held on to the drink and sank onto the couch, curled her legs up under her, one hand clutching the sweater, the other the wineglass. A signal in her brain flashed on in warning.

He sat next to her on the couch, not in the chair as she'd expected. He smiled, a slightly sad quirk of his mouth. "You're scared to death."

"It's Lauren and Robert and . . ."

"Uh-huh."

She looked down at the ruby liquid in her glass, biting her lip. Yes, she was afraid. Of herself. She was so in need of comfort, of forgetfulness, so terribly vulnerable right now. And she hadn't been with a man since a brief encounter with another teacher just after her divorce. It had been so long. She ached to be held, to be loved, to give love. The thought of Chris touching her made her belly coil with yearning.

She raised her glance. "I am afraid," she whispered. "I'm afraid you don't want me. Not like I want you, not nearly as . . ."

He put his glass down—she heard it click on the table—and he pulled her to him so suddenly the air left her lungs, his mouth covering hers, his hands everywhere. She heard him groan against her lips, "Don't be afraid," then the kiss deepened again.

She moaned and pressed against him, her arms snaking around his torso. He kissed her with a sweet violence then drew back and studied her face and kissed her forehead, buried his face in her neck and placed his lips on the place where her pulse beat.

She banished all thought, all pain, and immersed herself in sensation. She craved him as if she were an addict, his smell, his feel, his closeness, the sound of his smooth resonant voice, the way they melded together—where she was soft, he was hard, where she was needy, he fulfilled.

Her nightgown bunched up, and she felt his hand on her knee then stroking up her hip and down again, warm and insistent on her flesh. His caresses moved to the inside of her thigh, the soft flesh. Ripples of longing fluttered in her, and her breath came in shallow pants, her skin dewy and hot. His hand traced upward along her inner thigh, and she was mad for him to touch her even higher.

She heard herself whimpering, "Please, please, oh God, Chris." Her voice was not her own.

They sank down on the cushions, his body heavy on her, a welcome weight. He tasted her bare skin, one hand still on her thigh, the other pulling aside the strap of her nightgown, and he pressed his lips to her breast. She gasped and clung to him. "Yes," she whispered, "please."

She'd always known how his skin would feel beneath her fingers, satiny and firm, and that the texture of his hair was coarse so that all the combing in the world would never get rid of the cowlicks. She ran her hands down his head to his shoulders and up again, clutching at him hungrily, knowing him, yet surprised at each touch and scent and sigh, feeling his mouth on her breasts, whispers of longing on her lips, her heart ready to explode from beating so madly.

Then something infinitesimal altered in him, in the pressure of his mouth on her skin and the rhythm of his hand where he stroked her thigh. A hesitation?

"I . . . can't," she heard him groan. "I can't do this to you."

Then his weight was off her, abruptly, and as if from a long distance she heard him swear.

"What is it?" she breathed, confused, lost. As cold as if she were in that mineshaft again. She gripped the sweater around her.

He was in a corner of the room, bracing himself against the wall, head hanging between outstretched arms.

She got up shakily and went to him, tentatively put a hand on his back. He flinched. "No," he said.

"No?"

"Go to bed, Ashley."

"I thought . . ."

"Leave me alone."

"But . . ."

He whirled, and his eyes were damp. "Get out."

"Chris, what is it? Can I help? Anything. You know I'll . . ."

"Go back to your house," he said tiredly.

Her shoulders slumped. What was wrong? What had she done? She started to leave, took a step, took another, then she halted and without turning said, "Will you be all right?"

Silence.

"Chris, will you . . . ?"

"Yeah, sure. Go on."

She went. Out the door, closing it very carefully behind her, down the stairs and across the yard, her moonshadow moving slantwise with her, the earth stark in silver and black. Into the house and her bedroom, her skin cold and clammy now.

What had happened? What tortured him so? He knew

precisely what tortured her, but she knew so little about him. She knew the man, his soul, his innate humanity, but she understood so little of the forces of life that had buffeted him. He'd told her some. Not enough.

What was he hiding?

She slipped into bed and curled up, her body still throbbing with need. Frustrated. Physically and mentally and emotionally frustrated.

She was empty, frightened of his reaction, not for her. For *him*. His actions bespoke a man weighted down with pain, who felt undeserving of any pleasure or closeness. Yet she knew how good he was, how brave and full of integrity.

Since that long-ago bleak November day when he'd rescued her, it had always been Chris she wanted and dreamed about. And she knew that her judgment of him was not tainted, her dreams not based in fantasy.

The moon rose higher, a huge silver globe pock-marked with dim craters; it shone in her open window and spread over her like a blanket.

But was he the same man she'd first known? Had torment and disillusion altered him beyond redemption? She lay there alone and she yearned for him and she was afraid for him, terribly afraid. For the both of them.

SEVENTEEN

Chris barely had time to beat himself up over his performance last night when the apartment phone rang. He was in bed, had just woken. He glanced at his watch, 7:08, and scrubbed his hands over his face. What now?

Robert Marin was on the line.

"Look," Chris began, "Ashley isn't here. Call her on the cell . . ."

Marin cut him off. "It's you I want to talk to," he said.

Thinking how much he'd like a cup of coffee or two under his belt, Chris said, "Thought we *talked* yesterday."

"What I want to say is between us. *For now*," the man added. "I want you off the case. I don't want you within a mile of Ashley or anyone else remotely connected to me, buddy."

"Really," Chris said.

"I'm not the fool my ex-wife is. I had you checked

out, and I sure as hell didn't like the report I got back."

Chris waited.

"I'm talking about a suitcase full of drug money that disappeared last year in New Jersey."

"Newark," Chris said helpfully.

"Don't be a wiseass. We both know exactly what I'm getting at. I haven't discussed this with Ashley, but I will unless you pack your shit and go back to whatever rock you crawled out from under."

Chris was silent.

"Are you listening?"

"Yeah, I hear you."

"And you don't have anything to say?"

"Sure I do," Chris said. "Fuck off." He hung up, and he wondered how long it would be before Marin told Ashley about the money.

By eight he was showered and talking to Vladimir in the kitchen over coffee and toast. He heard Ashley's voice down the hall where she was trying to reason with her mother who, evidently, was refusing to get dressed and leave her room. The tension in the house was palpable, mounting every day. It was only going to get worse until Lauren was safely home.

He poured himself another cup of coffee, turned and leaned against the kitchen counter while he drank. "So, Vladimir, how does the visa thing work?" he asked casually.

"The visa thing?" Vladimir looked up from his breakfast.

"You know, how long do you get to stay in the States on a work permit?"

The Russian was shaking his head. "My English not so good. You ask how long I am here?"

"How long is your *visa* good for?"

"Have few more months. Ashley, how you say, file for new one then?"

"Um," Chris said. "Been a tough week here, I bet, with Pauline having a hard time understanding about her granddaughter."

Vladimir nodded morosely. Maybe he hadn't caught all of what Chris had said. In any case, he was a hard guy to draw out. The Russian rose from the table then rinsed his plate in the sink. He seemed to be in a hurry.

Luda passed her husband on the way out the back door, and they said a couple words to each other in Russian. Probably, *this place is a madhouse,* Chris thought. Then Ashley came into the kitchen, saw Chris and blood rushed to her cheeks. He'd been trying his damnedest not to analyze last night, not to wallow in guilt or self-pity or even consider how baffled she must have been by his behavior—or lack thereof. Whatever was going to happen to Lauren would happen soon, and one way or another he'd be out of Ashley's hair for good. If she knew the real him, she'd thank her lucky stars.

She would know about the money soon enough anyway. That asshole Marin was going to tell her. Maybe she'd believe him and maybe she wouldn't. Maybe she'd leap to Chris's defense. But if she put two and two together she'd eventually realize Chris had gone bad. At least then she'd understand why he couldn't hold her and comfort her and maybe even love her.

"Good morning," she said tentatively.

"Morning."

"Did, ah, Robert reach you? He called and got the number in the apartment."

"He reached me."

"And?"

"And nothing."

"He tried to get you to leave again, didn't he?"

He gave a negligent shrug.

"I thought so. Oh, Chris, I feel as if I'm spinning my wheels. I'm no closer to getting Lauren back right now than I was a week ago."

"I disagree."

"Oh? You suddenly know something I don't? Something new this morning? Or is it one of those *gut* feelings you have?"

He wished to hell he could tell her, *promise* her everything was going to be okay. But he didn't know that. All he really knew was something about this case smelled, and that something was like a lost word on the tip of his tongue. Maybe if he quit thinking so hard about it he'd get it. But he could provide no guarantees for Ashley. Right now he had nothing to offer her, either personally or professionally.

He set his coffee cup on the counter and turned to her. There were tears swimming in her eyes, and she was pale, agitated, her hair lank. As if she were ill. A terrible feeling of futility swept him, the same feeling he'd had when facing the mother or wife of a victim, the feeling a cop had to squelch or go mad. But this was Ashley, not a stranger, and the stab was close to being mortal.

And last night. Christ, he'd acted like a goddamn ass when she'd needed him the most. She hadn't asked for a thing, only the comfort of another human's touch. And he didn't even dare give her that.

"Well?" she said.

"Ah, yes." He shut down the internal chatter. "It's the gut feeling. I admit it sounds stupid as hell to you, but . . ."

"I'm not arguing, Chris. I'm *praying* you're right. It's

just that I know Robert. He's probably on the phone right this minute to the FBI. And if Davey finds out . . . You *heard* that maniac yesterday. I think he's been watching me since the first day. He'll know, Chris, he'll *know* the cops are here, and it won't matter whether I called them or Robert did. Lauren . . . Oh God, everything's flying apart around me and there's nothing I can do, nothing . . ."

The urge to hold her was overwhelming. If he were a whole man, a *good* man, he would press her to his chest and stroke her hair and whisper comforting words into her ear. Make her nightmare go away. But he was only a hollow figurine, a fake copy of a man, and Marin was going to tell her about the money, and he wouldn't be able to bear her disappointment or her disgust.

That morning while Ashley did laundry and showered and tended to her mother, he phoned the Hodgeses and asked if he could stop by. When all else failed, it was time to go back to the beginning of the trail and retrace the steps. Maybe Hayley or her mom would remember something, no matter how insignificant, *something* that would unlock the closed door of his brain.

"Hayley's called several times," Ashley said when he told her his plan, "and Luda just says Lauren's visiting her grandparents. What are you going to tell the Hodgeses now when you go over there? You can't tell them the truth, Chris. My God, they'd call the police . . ."

"It's not a problem. I'll just say I'm finishing up the police report for the files. They don't know I'm not a cop. And all they know about Lauren is that she's at her grandparents."

She thought a moment. "But I don't know what else they can tell you."

"Neither do I," he admitted.

He did not learn much at the Hodgeses'. Nothing new or illuminating. When he said he was cleaning up a time disparity in the police report from last week, Mrs. Hodges mentioned that she thought she remembered looking at the kitchen clock when she told Lauren it was time to meet her ride out front.

"I keep that clock a few minutes fast, you know, so the kids are on time for the school bus or whatever."

"*How* fast?" Chris asked.

"Oh, five minutes maybe."

He left the Pitkin Green home chewing over that tidbit of information. It told him that Lauren was most likely out in front waiting for Vladimir either a few minutes early or right on time, even if she and Hayley had goofed off for a minute or two before Lauren walked out the driveway.

He drove up Mill Street and turned onto Main, passing the Local's Corner gas station a block down on his right. Vladimir had either filled Ashley's Cherokee with gas right here or at the other station in town, a couple of blocks away. Damn, he should have asked him which one. He drove slowly, trying to retrace Vladimir's route in his mind: from Ashley's house to one of the gas stations, waiting for the tank to fill, impatient perhaps because he was going to be late to pick up Lauren. Putting the hose back, tightening the gas cap, paying for the gas . . .

"*Jesus.*" Chris banged his palm on the steering wheel. "Of course." Vladimir probably paid with Ashley's credit card, but even if he used cash, there'd be the receipt. And all the receipts had the time of purchase stamped on them. Jesus, he hoped Ashley saved them.

He crossed the bridge over the Roaring Fork River then drove up Ashley's road, waved at the ever-busy mechanic Jay, and parked next to the Cherokee. Vladimir had been out front watering the patch of lawn when Chris had left an hour ago. But no one was in sight right now. Chris hated to sneak. . . . If he were lucky, though, the slips would be in the glove compartment or center console. Where most people stuffed them. And maybe Ashley didn't bother looking at them, maybe she trusted Vladimir.

He opened the passenger door to the Cherokee—nobody locked up in Aspen. He looked in the glove compartment. Just registration papers and maps, a Chap Stick and utility flashlight. He glanced at the front door to the house. No one around. Then he checked the center console.

Well now. There were several receipts mingling with a few CDs and a box of Kleenex. He looked through them. City Market. No. Ace Hardware. No. Local's Corner. "All right," he said under his breath.

He *could* have asked Ashley about receipts. He could even have asked for the original ones from the owner of the gas station. But this was so much easier.

There were several slips. And one dated the day Lauren had been snatched.

Four-thirty-five P.M. it read. Not a few minutes before five. Not even close.

He sat back against the car seat as if pushed. How could Vladimir have been so off in the time? And even if he had not been aware of the exact time, then he still would have arrived at the Hodgeses too early. Unless he'd run another errand. But he'd *said* he hadn't.

So where exactly had he been when Lauren walked out to meet him at five?

The stench Chris had been getting all week suddenly enveloped him.

Vladimir? But how? Why? He couldn't possibly know Davey Potts. Potts had been in prison up till a month ago, and he'd been there the entire time the Rostovs had lived in the States.

What was he missing here? Where the hell was the connection? If there was one. Maybe he wasn't thinking straight, or maybe everyone's timing was off about the five o'clock meeting.

Potts and the Russian couldn't possibly have met. Plus Potts had probably been planning to snatch Lauren even before he'd been paroled. The two men could not be connected. Another thought struck him then—this could sure explain how Potts had gotten Ashley's cell phone number. Vladimir. But where was the goddamn link?

He pocketed the receipt, closed the car door. No point bothering Ashley with this. *Yet.* However, he now had something to go on and someone to watch. He should have checked out Vladimir's time line a week ago. He felt like kicking himself in the pants for the oversight. He only prayed his stupidity didn't cost Lauren her life.

The tension ratcheted up another notch late that afternoon. No sooner had Marin and his lawyer Coates walked in, than the cops arrived and, on their heels, two special agents from the Denver FBI office. Robert Marin was at least as good as his word.

Lenny Coates greeted the two agents as if they were long-lost friends. He introduced them to Ashley. "Special Agent Freed, Special Agent Parker, my client's ex-wife, Ashley," Coates said.

Chris eyed the feds, ordinary-looking fellows, Freed bony and dark, Parker round-faced and fair. They were dressed in khakis and polo shirts, tennis shoes. At least they weren't wearing department-issue dark suits.

Ashley introduced Chris as an old family friend. He shook hands with both agents, met their scrutiny squarely. Hell, they were only doing their jobs.

"Mr. Judge *used* to be a policeman," Robert put in meaningfully.

Both agents turned on Chris, and the questions began. It occurred to him that Robert might dump his dirty secret in front of them, but he didn't. Saving his ammo, no doubt.

"Retired?" Freed said. "Interesting."

"Undercover work burns you out," Chris replied. True enough.

Parker took Ashley into the kitchen to question her. Chris could hear her voice in there, murmurs, then the agent's deeper voice. On and on. Pauline sat beside Chris on the couch, asking querulously over and over, "Who *are* these men?"

"Newark, you say?" Freed began again. "Rough place."

"We had a couple of your guys on the task force," Chris said. "Good men."

"Get any indictments?"

"A few."

"Two years, you say?"

"That's what I said."

"And you left how long ago?"

"Six months."

"Uh-huh."

Marin was listening, sitting nearby on a chair, foot clad in an elegant tasseled loafer crossed over his knee. The gloating smirk on his face made Chris want to smash a fist into his mouth.

When Freed went into the kitchen for coffee, Chris

said, "Hey, you'd make a great wiseguy, you know that?"

"Go screw yourself, you goddamn thief," Marin retorted.

By 6 P.M. another agent had flown in with electronic surveillance equipment. He set up his equipment to monitor the phones while everyone in the house was questioned at length, after which one of the agents drove to the Hodgeses' house to interview them.

Davey Potts's parole officer was located in Glenwood Springs and was interviewed by phone. Then the agent who'd driven to the Hodgeses turned around and drove forty miles down valley to Glenwood Springs and questioned Davey's cousin, at whose house Davey was supposedly living.

As the evening proceeded, Chris could tell Ashley was losing control. He noticed her distracted manner, the way her face grew white and tense and her shoulders hunched. He was sensitive as hell to her body language, recognized every nuance of her expression as if she were part of him. Shit, he knew her *better* than he knew himself.

It made him crazy to see what the feds and Marin and that damn lawyer of his were doing to her. And he was helpless to stop the torture.

She finally stood up in the center of her living room, her hands clenched into fists at her sides. Her voice was shrill, shaky, and the agents, one on his cell phone, two others talking quietly in a corner, turned to stare at her.

"I didn't ask you here! I want you out! Robert had no right to call you. I have custody of Lauren! You haven't done a single thing we haven't already done. And my mother . . . Can't you see what this is doing to her!"

"Ashley, my dear girl," Lenny Coates said in honeyed

tones, "we're all here to help you find Lauren."

"You'll get her killed! You'll get her killed, and you'll all be guilty as sin, and . . ." Her voice clicked off.

"You see what I have to deal with?" Marin said softly to his lawyer.

Chris wanted to strangle the man. He closed his eyes and drew in a deep breath, then he took Ashley's arm and led her out front and tried to reason with her. Not that she wasn't right. Nevertheless, Marin and Coates had taken charge, and short of a court intervening—which wasn't likely to happen—there wasn't a damn thing Ashley could do at the moment.

"But Davey is probably watching right now!" she cried. "And you know he threatened if I brought in the cops he'd . . . he'd *kill* her. Oh, Chris, oh God . . ."

"Take it easy," he said, putting an arm around her shoulder, "all kidnappers say that. He's not going to hurt Lauren. And besides, he's probably gotten to know her and that's good. He's even less likely to harm her. Potts isn't a murderer, he's a screwed-up ex-con playing a sick game with your head."

"Yes, but . . ." She sniffed. "But he'll panic now, won't he?"

"So maybe he'll just release her and take off into the mountains. He can stay lost forever."

"You don't really believe that he'll just let her go?"

"Hey, why not?" he said, but even he could hear the lack of conviction in his voice.

Ashley finally retreated to her mother's room, where both of them tried to get some rest.

It was obvious that Lenny Coates was growing impatient. Nothing was happening; things were moving too slowly to suit him, Chris guessed. And at his hourly rate, Marin was crazy to keep him hanging around.

At ten-thirty he announced he was leaving. He put an avuncular hand on Marin's shoulder. "Any developments, call me right away. You hear me, Robert? We'll get to the bottom of this. We'll find Lauren, don't you worry."

"Right, Lenny," Robert said.

"This never should have happened. Terrible thing. When we get her back, Robert, there's going to be a review of her custody. You can count on that. The whole thing's inexcusable."

His tone was so officious that even the FBI agents ducked their heads in discomfort.

Luda and Vladimir tried to stay out from underfoot, Luda furtively picking up take-out containers and plastic foam coffee cups while she muttered in Russian. Vladimir helped her, doing dishes and taking out the trash. Chris watched him move silently and tensely around the house, as if he wished to be ignored by the special agents. Typical Russian distrust of law officers.

At a few minutes before midnight Ashley's main phone line rang. She raced out of her mother's room, still fully dressed in jeans and a T-shirt. Agents donned earphones, hand signals were given.

"It's not him," she said. "He always uses the cell phone."

They monitored the call anyway. It was a wrong number, some drunk looking for his girlfriend.

Chris watched the action with a jaundiced eye. He studied Vladimir, who'd appeared in his bathrobe, wakened by the commotion. Watched his stoic Slavic face, picked up nothing but the usual suspicion of the world. Then the Russian went back to bed. As did Ashley.

The house quieted. Marin was still there. Chris wasn't about to retire to the apartment and leave Ashley alone with him and a roomful of grim strangers. In any case, he couldn't have slept. He needed to find the missing piece of this crazy puzzle so he could slip it into place. Vladimir and Potts. Something didn't mesh.

For a while, around two in the morning, he sat out on the top porch step, staring at the inky sky and then into the black woods across the road. Was Potts watching the charade at the house? Chris didn't think so. It didn't feel right.

Hell, he thought, nothing about this case felt right.

EIGHTEEN

Davey's cell phone rang, and for a moment he looked at it, mesmerized, still amazed at the technology. The hunting cabin had no electricity. His cousin had dug a well years ago, but the water was supplied only to an outdoor hand pump that had to be drained every autumn after elk season or the damn thing froze up. Yet here was a battery-powered connection to the entire world, its signal bounced off satellites circling the globe. His cousin had told him he could even have a wireless connection to the Internet. All the way up here. Hell, the Internet hadn't even been a household word when Davey had been put behind bars.

The brat stared at him over the gag he kept in her mouth. Big dark brown eyes like her mother's. But this one was more defiant than her mother had been, full of sass. He had to work to scare her. But he managed. Oh yeah, he'd learned the hard way how to intimidate people. You had to in prison.

He could see that the ringing phone caught her attention. She was curious; maybe this call would be her salvation, she was thinking. Right.

He'd love to kill her. For lots of reasons. He thought
about it, savoring the images, imagining her father and
mother, their reactions. The beauty of pure sweet revenge. But he wanted more money first. He deserved the
goddamn money. To get both, the coup de grace—that
would be perfect.

He checked the gag in her mouth as the phone rang
a fifth time. Her hands were already tied. He kept them
tied most of the time, ever since the first day when she'd
scratched his face.

He finally picked the unit up and walked outside so
the girl couldn't hear. He knew who was calling. The
big day had arrived. But wait till the caller heard the
new plan. Wait till he found out who was really in
charge.

"Yeah?" he said into the tiny mouthpiece.

"It's time," the man said. "Let's go over the details
again. I don't want any screwups."

Davey snickered to himself. "Well, see, we've got a
change of plans here," he said.

"A change of plans? What the hell . . . ?"

"I've made up some new rules."

"New . . ."

"Just shut up and listen. You want the kid back it'll
cost you double."

There was a short pause, and then the expected explosion. "Who do you think you're dealing with?!" Pure
rage.

"Double or nothing," Davey said, wallowing in his
mastery of the situation.

"Now just a goddamn minute . . ." the caller said, but

Davey severed the connection. Let the asshole stew.

The girl's eyes fixed on him, followed him as he came back inside. She probably wanted to know who'd called, when she'd be ransomed. But he wouldn't tell her—keeping her ignorant was his most effective weapon.

He glanced round the cabin, the empty pizza boxes, soda cans littering the rough wooden table, the Mc-Donald's bags and candy wrappers on the plank floor. "You're a slob," he said.

She glanced at him. *If looks could kill.* No doubt she'd spit out some four-letter words if he took the gag off. He'd had to smack her a few times when she cursed him. Now he just left the gag on, and she could only shoot daggers of hate from those big brown eyes.

He kind of liked to talk to her, though. A captive audience. It got boring up here alone with only her. And Davey liked to talk.

"You're going to clean this place up. Make yourself useful, you little snot."

She tilted her face down and shot venom at him from under her brows. She looked like a goddamn devil. He gritted his teeth, goaded, even though she couldn't say a word. And in his fury he made a slip. One he'd carefully avoided all week.

"You're worse than your mother, you spoiled brat," he said without thinking, and he saw the instant confusion on her face, saw the way vertical lines appeared between her brows as she tried to make sense of his statement. Then comprehension dawned. He could tell. Her features froze and her eyes grew big as plates.

He was pissed as hell. At himself for talking too much and at her for getting to him. He felt as if she'd stolen part of his power. *Shit, shit, shit,* he thought.

But it was too late to take back his words. He kicked

at a soda can and it struck the kid on the shin. "I want this place cleaned up, you hear me?" he shouted.

She sat quietly studying him.

"You fucking hear me!" he yelled, forcing her around and yanking at the ropes to free her hands. He was furious but not so much that he forgot to stay out of range of her fingernails. He knew she wanted to pull her gag off, but last time she'd tried he'd backhanded her good. So she just stared at him with narrowed eyes.

He shoved her down to her hands and knees. "Pick up the goddamn trash."

He could kill her now. When she finished cleaning up. It would be easy. But his brain stopped him—the money, the money. The big kahuna had to see that she was okay first, then he'd fork over the rest of the money. Unless Davey came up with an even better plan.

The money. When he had it in his hands, he'd be history. Mexico first, no trouble crossing the border. Then maybe that country with the rain forests and howler monkeys. He'd seen it in a *National Geographic* in the prison library. Costa Rica. He'd never seen a rain forest or a real live monkey. Never even been to a zoo. Truth was, he'd never been out of Colorado. You bet your ass he'd be gone, and no one would see or hear from him again.

Costa Rica, here I come, he thought, and he felt like a million—exactly what he was going to try to disappear with, a cool mil. But if he couldn't get it all, then he'd make do with what he already had. He'd still live like a king.

She rose to her feet and dusted her hands on her jeans, hurled hateful looks at him. A tough little thing. He could almost admire her. And he remembered what it was like to be a teenager. She was near the same age he'd been when his father had snatched her mother. He remembered feeling that you were bulletproof. Everything was an adventure. Until, of course, you wound up in a youth correctional facility, then state prison. And someone took your virginity and you cried yourself to sleep every goddamn night till you became numb. To this day he'd never had a woman, doubted he could handle the experience. Nobody gave a shit. Nobody cared when your old man had to sign your house over to the idiot lawyer who'd gotten you locked up in the first place. Nobody cared when your old man got emphysema and lingered for years. They let you visit him once on his deathbed in the prison hospital. Then some sadistic asshole guard hands you a death certificate, says, "Oh, didn't you know, your old man died on Wednesday?"

But you played their game and you went up in front of the parole board dutifully every year with your public defender and told the stupid old farts you were reformed, you'd changed. Hell, you'd found God. That one always got them. All the while you plotted and schemed because the world owed you. That bitch Ashley owed you. Had they even hurt her? They'd offered her a good clean life with them, a better life living off the land, away from that crazy ski town where all anyone did was fly around in their screaming jet planes and snort drugs up their noses.

Maybe Ashley had hated the mineshaft, but they'd fed her good and let her have a sleeping bag and a lamp, and it had only been for a short time till she got her head straight and realized they were doing her a favor, liberating her. But that hunter had come along and stumbled across her and ruined the whole thing. A couple more weeks and she would have come around. His father knew what he was doing. His father had been a smart man. Best man Davey had ever known.

His thoughts dwelled on Chris Judge for a time. He remembered him real well from the trial, testifying so cool and calm, being treated like a big hero for saving Ashley. He wondered if Ashley had been seeing him all these years. Maybe even seeing him when she was married. Hell, maybe the spoiled brat kid Lauren wasn't a Marin at all, and maybe that was why the ex-cop had come running to Ashley's side the day after her kid disappeared. Yeah, could be. He guessed, though, none of that mattered. Not to him. He was gonna have his money and get back at the bitch at the same time. And get back at Marin and maybe Judge, too. For years he'd been trying to figure it out, and then that power-hungry big shot had walked into his cousin's house in Glenwood Springs and dumped the solution right in Davey's lap. A miracle.

The brat made a noise behind her gag, cutting into his thoughts. She was hungry.

"Yeah, I'm going to get some food. Hold your horses."

He assured himself her hands and feet were tied tightly, then he felt his pockets for the car keys.

"Back soon. Don't do anything I wouldn't do," he quipped over his shoulder on the way out.

Locking the door with the heavy padlock, he smiled to himself. Let her stew, just like the moneyman was stewing. He had them all under control. And pretty soon, tomorrow, in fact, she wasn't going to be giving him those vicious looks anymore. She'd be too busy screaming.

• • •

Elaine and Maria were in the kitchen making a grocery list for tonight's cocktail party. The dog was madly scratching at the hardwood floor in the living room, tearing up a corner of the Navajo rug. Outside the tall window, the birds swooped from aspens to cottonwood trees, and across the valley, tourists rode the gondola up the face of Aspen Mountain to lunch at the Sundeck Restaurant.

Robert was unaware of his surroundings. His brain was reeling with panic. He paced his office, his heartbeat hammering in his ears. He hadn't counted on this, hadn't factored into his scheme Davey Potts's sudden stab at control.

Was Potts just pushing him? Robert tried desperately to concentrate and consider all the angles. The ex-con *might* be bluffing, but even if he were, Robert didn't dare risk Lauren's life by calling the bluff. He'd have to pay up. The trouble was, Potts still might harm her; not as an act against Robert, but as revenge against goddamn Ashley.

He paced, and dread spread through his body as if he were diseased. Where had he gone so wrong? How could he have so badly miscalculated Potts? He had always been able to read people. His ability was a gift, whether in business dealings or social affairs. His sixth sense had always given him the edge. So what had he missed that day at the cousin's place in Glenwood when he'd laid out the plan?

He collapsed into the chair behind his desk, head in his hands. The FBI were in place at Ashley's, everything was on schedule—*had* been on schedule, that was, till Potts pulled the double cross.

He took several deep yoga breaths and reminded himself to stay calm. Things had a way of working themselves out. Hadn't he learned that in the dot com industry? Sure, everything sought its own level.

But no matter how many positive thoughts he drilled through his mind, one ghastly notion kept surfacing—Potts might come out of this a rich man and still murder his daughter.

"Honey?" Elaine tapped on the office door and pushed it open. "We need to pick up the dry cleaning. My dress? I thought if you were going to the post office you could stop at the dry cleaners. Maria and I will be hours at the store."

He looked up. His airhead wife had gone ahead with this cocktail party despite his daughter—*her* stepdaughter's kidnapping. Gone ahead with the arrangements because her sister was in town and leaving tomorrow. As if Robert gave a good goddamn.

Yesterday he'd said, "Do you have any idea how inappropriate a party is under these circumstances?"

And she'd replied, "You don't have to yell at me. What am I supposed to do, call seventy-five guests and cancel? Tell them that your daughter, *our* daughter, tell them she's been abducted, when you yourself told me not to breathe a word?"

She had him there. He hated to admit it, but she'd been right. Nonetheless she didn't have to be enjoying her social arrangements so much. And now this sudden disaster with Potts. What was he supposed to tell her, that he'd offered to pay the kidnapper to take his daughter and keep her hidden safely and comfortably for a week? While he watched Ashley sabotage her chances of retaining custody of Lauren, especially when he himself rescued her. Naturally the kidnapper would escape with the ransom money, but Lauren and the world would be witness to Robert's extraordinary heroism.

How could he admit to Elaine that Potts was turning the tables?

"The dry cleaning, Robert? Could you stop and . . ."

Coldly he appraised her. "No, I can't pick up your fucking dry cleaning. Now get the hell out of my office and don't ever barge in here again."

She burst into tears and left. *Thank God,* he thought. *Now calm down and think, do what you do best, analyze the situation.* But his head was pounding furiously. His young bitch of a wife—mistake number two—had done this to him.

Maybe he was putting too much stock in Potts's threats. Maybe it was all hot air. The plan was still on track, really, except for having to pay double. By design Robert had warned Ashley repeatedly to call the FBI, he'd deliberately consulted his lawyer, he'd finally called the authorities himself. Yes, all according to his master plan.

He'd given that white trash Potts a chance to be rich and free, and the little shit had turned on him. Was Davey even in the cabin where he was supposed to be? Maybe he'd gone somewhere else, called Robert to taunt him, and he had never planned to return Lauren at all. *Jesus.*

He picked up the cell phone that belonged to his wife—no reason anyone would trace the calls on her phone—and punched in Davey's number. He'd stay cool and businesslike but try to let Potts feel as if he had the upper hand. Agree to a million. Set up the time to meet in the morning—he'd have to sell stock and . . . Christ, hire a courier to deliver the cash, because no damn bank in this tiny town would have so much on hand. The meeting would have to take place in the late morning then . . .

"Yeah?" came Potts's voice.

"All right," Robert said, forcing humility into his tone. "I'll get you the extra half a million, but it will take till at least eleven tomorrow morning to get the cash here. And then I have to drive up there. I only hope the FBI doesn't catch on. We were supposed to have made the exchange today, you realize."

"Not my problem."

Robert put his temper in tight check. "You'll still be at the Avalanche Creek location?"

"Oh, sure."

Was Davey lying? "And Lauren's okay?"

"Snug as a bug in a rug."

"Just one last question then. How do I know you'll make the exchange and not hold out for even more money?"

There was a pause, then, "Guess you have to trust me on that." Davey Potts broke the connection.

Robert sat back and felt oily panic ooze out of his pores. He knew people, always knew how to read them, even on a business call halfway around the world. "Have to trust me on that," Potts had said, and Robert knew without the slightest doubt the man was lying.

NINETEEN

She pushed through the screen door, stood on the porch with her hands on her hips and sucked in so many deep breaths she grew dizzy.

Chris, who was leaning against the Mustang in the drive, talking to FBI Special Agent Steve Parker, gave her a concerned look. "To hell with them all," she breathed, her throat scratchy from repeating her darkest fears over and over to those jerks who'd taken over her house. Didn't they get it? Just their presence was a threat to Lauren. And what had they done to conceal themselves? Moved their big black Suburban a few feet down the road? As if Davey wouldn't spot it.

"You don't know that he's been watching this house," Special Agent Freed had said.

"And *you* don't know that he isn't!" she'd fired back.

Her only touchstone for the past twenty-four hours was Chris. Throughout her anger and tears and outbursts of dread, he'd remained unflappable, talking her down, forcing her to go on short walks, gaining the grudging respect of the agents, because he was the only one who could keep her from flying apart. But for all his quiet strength he couldn't make Davey call again or find her child for her. She was beginning to despair that no one could.

She sank down onto the top step and dropped her head into her hands, half listening to Chris and Parker chew the fat as if nothing was out of the ordinary.

Parker reached into his pocket while they talked and pulled out a pack of cigarettes, lit one. "Just went back to these goddamn things a month ago," he said, taking a drag. "Wife took the kid and moved in with her mother."

Chris nodded, and Ashley got a whiff of the acrid smoke. She would have gone back inside, but she couldn't deal with the agents in there. Or her mother. Or Luda or Vladimir or any other damn thing.

"You ever been married?" Parker asked Chris.

"Oh yeah. Divorced."

"It's hell." Parker ambled slowly along the edge of the drive, smoke trailing behind him. "Divorce, that is." He smiled wryly.

"Sure is," Chris agreed, and she could tell he liked Parker. He'd even said to her last night that the man was okay for a fed.

Pauline's open bedroom window overlooked the front yard, and Ashley heard her mother's voice. "I don't want to eat in here. Why am I being held in this room?"

And Luda: "Staying in here *your* idea, Miss Pauline." Ashley could tell the woman was about out of patience.

And where was Vladimir? Conveniently and studiously avoiding the entire mess, either locked in his side of the duplex or about to run another errand, fetching take-out for the agents when he should be helping Luda with Pauline.

"You have kids?" Parker was asking Chris, and he stamped out his cigarette butt on the driveway, only picking it up when he saw Ashley's expression.

"Yeah, a boy."

"You miss him?"

"All the time. But I see him. Little League and weekends, when I can."

"I hate that weekends-only shit."

"I know," Chris said, "me, too."

Chris was crazy to have given up police work, she mused. No matter how awful his experiences had been, *this* was him. The camaraderie between cops suited him; even the waiting, the eternal waiting for a break in a case didn't get under his skin. To her he was . . . so much more than a friend. To Pauline he'd become a buddy, cajoling her into eating her lunch with him, getting her to reminisce about the good old days in Aspen, and how things had changed now, with presidents visiting and world-renowned musicians playing in the big music tent and scientists meeting all summer long at the Aspen Center for Physics to argue the origins of the universe while Friday night brawls still broke out in the downtown saloons.

He was tough with Agent Freed, telling him to go screw himself when the officious man had barked at her an hour ago. He lent a sympathetic ear to Parker right now. He even tolerated Luda and her snide remarks. As for Vladimir, he exchanged cool glances with the man when he bothered to show his stoic Russian face. He was there for everybody. She wondered yet again why he'd sent her away the other night. Couldn't he have met her needs then, too?

Chris. A man for all seasons. An undercover cop. A *former* cop. Yes, he was wrong to have given up. And he was wrong to have rebuffed her. She craved him. And she was certain he felt the same.

Parker eventually went back inside, and Chris shrugged at her, then joined her on the steps. "You doing okay?" he asked.

"No."

"Dumb question, huh."

"Yes."

He was quiet for a moment and then, as if weighing his next words, said, "Can I ask you something without you losing it?"

"What sort of question is that?" she said tiredly.

"An important one."

"Then, yes, ask away."

"Let's walk. I don't want our pals inside to overhear," he said, and he took her hand and tugged her to her feet.

Somewhere down the road plaintive violin music carried on the air—a music student practicing somewhere—and she felt the notes drift into her, soothing, the late-day sun hot on her face till they crossed the gravel road into the shade.

Chris kept walking. He finally cleared his throat and said, "Is it possible Vladimir ever met Potts?"

"What?" she said.

"At, say, the last parole board hearing before Potts's release? Did Vladimir drive you there?"

"No. Why?"

"Just thinking."

"Oh, bull. I know that look. What is it?"

He stopped then and studied her.

"Come on, Chris. What are you getting at?"

"Something in Vladimir's story doesn't fit," he said.

"Oh God, you've interviewed him, and even the FBI have gone over that ground at least three times."

"True. But I found the receipt for the gas in the console of your car."

"So?"

"So, Vladimir lied. He's got twenty-five minutes missing from his timeline."

Her brow crinkled. "Twenty-five minutes? But . . . I don't understand." She looked down at her feet then back up. "You think . . . you're thinking Vladimir is somehow involved?"

He nodded.

"But . . ." Her frown deepened while the aspen leaves shivered in the warm breeze and stippled shadows moved across her face. "Chris, he couldn't be involved. I mean, he came back here with the car. How could he have done anything with Lauren? And besides, we know it's Davey. *I* know it's him."

"I'm not arguing that. I'm saying Vladimir isn't dumb. Twenty-five minutes is a long time. He could have met Potts and led him up to the Hodgeses. Potts drives off with Lauren. Vladimir arrives back here with his cock-and-bull story."

She was shaking her head. "It doesn't make sense. There's no way Davey and Vladimir could know each other."

"I agree."

"You think, wait, let me get this straight, someone else planned this and involved Vladimir and Davey?"

"It's a theory."

"I . . . my God, in my house, all this time . . ."

"Don't let on to Vladimir. Just act the same. Can you do that, Ashley?"

She paled. "I . . . I'll try."

"Good girl."

"Why?" she implored. "Why would he do that?"

"When we find the link we'll know," he stated.

Suddenly her eyes were brimming. "How could I have misjudged him so?" And on the heels of the tears came a hot spurt of fury. "That . . . that bastard!" she began, whirling and staring at the house. "I'll . . . I'll . . . No, *you* talk to him. You do whatever it takes. I don't care if you have to beat it out of him, just . . ."

"Hey," he said. "Think a minute. The agents aren't going to let me beat the info out of Vladimir. Come on, Ashley, we play this out to the end."

"You want me to . . . to just pretend I don't know?"

"It won't be long."

"How the hell do you know *that*?"

"I just do," he said, and as if to punctuate his words they both heard tires crunching on the road below Jay's house, and then a Range Rover was rocking toward them. Robert's car.

"Oh no," she breathed.

But Chris was curiously quiet. He watched the vehicle approach, his expression shifting into neutral. Ashley wasn't as sanguine, though. Her mind spun. *Vladimir*. If only she could sort everything out, but now Robert was here, and he'd bluster and tell everyone what a terrible mother she was, and none of his posturing was going to do a bit of good—he was just as incapable of finding Lauren as the rest of them.

He got out of his car appearing haggard, pale. Her heart almost went out to him when she realized that for all of his chairman-of-the-board manner, he was suffering just as much as she was. When he saw her he seemed to pull himself together, and his expression hardened. *Same old Robert.*

"You're still here," Robert said as he strode up, and he pointed a finger at Chris's chest. His hand was shaking, though. Robert, shaky?

Chris reached up and eased Robert's hand away. "Don't push your luck," he said.

Oh God. "Look, Robert," she began, "please don't make things worse."

He turned his attention to her. "How could I make things fucking worse than they already are?" he sneered, and despite the force of his words, she recognized that something rang false.

She looked to Chris for help, but he was studying Robert. *What in God's name . . . ?* she was thinking, when she saw a look on Chris's face, the dangerous cop look, his eyes sparking, his mouth a hard line.

Chris took a step toward Robert. He thrust his face close—only inches separated them. "I think your ex-husband has something to tell us," he said flatly.

"What?" Ashley said, but neither of them acknowledged her.

"Get the hell out of my face." Robert stepped back.

"So, what went wrong, Marin? Potts wants more money? Or is it Vladimir?"

"I don't know what you're . . ." Robert blustered.

But Chris cut him off. "So you blew it. Can't be the hero of the day now. Come on, did Davey ask for more money?"

"Go to hell," Robert said.

"I'll bet Vladimir came cheap. Right? Let's see, a little cash and maybe a promise to get him and Luda permanent residency."

Ashley listened in disbelief, her mind trying to absorb the words, her heart thudding a heavy cadence. The violin music drifted lightly by her, an insane counterpoint to the exchange between the two men. Robert? Involved in Lauren's kidnapping? *Impossible*. Chris had to be wrong, recklessly groping for answers no matter how far-fetched.

But Chris was never reckless.

Without realizing it, she'd drawn close to the two posturing men and placed a hand on Robert's arm. "Do you . . ." she began, "do you know where Lauren is, Robert?" She couldn't believe she'd even asked. He was Lauren's father. He'd never . . .

"Go ahead," Chris was saying, "tell her. Hasn't she suffered enough?"

She kept staring at her ex-husband, shaking her head in denial. This was impossible. But the more she studied him, the more she could see something was hideously wrong. He seemed desperate, but there was something else. . . .

Abruptly she sucked in air. Chris had said, "Can't be hero of the day." Could Robert . . . ? *Could* he have set this whole thing up in order to rescue Lauren?

"Robert," she whispered, "is it true? Did you . . ."

But he shoved past them and barged into the house. She turned frantic eyes to Chris, who only raised a brow and said, "He's going to feed the feds some bullshit story. But it's too late."

"You believe he really did this?" she said.

"Oh, he's up to his ears in it, all right."

She broke then. She felt as if she'd been holding hot liquid inside her for a week, and suddenly she could no longer contain it and it all gushed out.

"Ashley, now listen, let the FBI . . ." Chris began, but she was already rushing after Robert, banging open the screen door and searching for him in the room of faces. Then she was in front of him, and she grabbed his arm fiercely. He raised it to fling her off, but she held on.

"Do you know where Lauren is?" she hissed. "Tell me, you bastard! Goddamn it, tell me!"

He tried again to shake her off, but she placed herself between him and the door. She was wild, hysterical. Blinded by rage.

"Mrs. Marin," one of the agents tried. She didn't even hear him. Agent Parker rose, then he frowned and hesitated.

She was beyond hearing anyone. She flailed at her ex-husband with her fists and screamed, "Tell me, tell me! Tell me the truth! Where is Lauren?"

He began to breathe rapidly, then suddenly he crumpled. He turned away from her and buried his face in his hands. His shoulders shook, and he weaved so badly one of the agents made a move to steady him.

"Oh God, oh God," he was sobbing. "Oh God."

"Where is my daughter?" she cried, standing there, still now, arms hanging, face sheet-white, her chest heaving with exertion. *"Where is she?"*

"Mr. Marin," Freed said. "What's going on here? I have to warn you . . ."

No one paid him the slightest attention.

Robert felt behind him with one hand and sank blindly into a chair. "It's not my fault," he stammered, "not my . . . my fault. It's Potts. Oh God, forgive me."

And finally Chris stepped in. "What does Potts want, more money?"

"Yes," Robert got out.

"You had a deal with him and he double-crossed you?"

"Oh God, yes."

"Have you paid him anything?"

No reply.

Chris reached out and grabbed a handful of Robert's hair and yanked his head up.

"Hey now, Judge, you can't . . ." Freed protested.

Chris ignored him. *"Did you pay him any money?"*

Robert nodded. "Half," he groaned.

"When were you going to pay him the rest?"

Robert swallowed. "Today . . . today . . . but I was afraid . . . and I knew . . . oh God, I knew . . ."

Ashley put a hand on Chris's arm then went to stand in front of her ex-husband. Her voice was razor sharp. "Where does he have Lauren?"

Robert looked up, his face contorted, his nose running. "Avalanche Creek," he croaked. "A cabin."

"Where, Robert? *Exactly where?*"

"A mile . . . a mile from the river . . . the Crystal. On the Avalanche Creek Road."

"Thank you," she bit out.

"Mr. Marin," Parker said. "Are we to understand that you planned your daughter's kidnapping?"

But he just sat, collapsed, shaking his head over and over.

"Mr. Marin, I'd like to clarify your statement. You know where your daughter is?" Parker attempted.

No reply.

"He did it so that he could rescue her and blame it all on me and get sole custody of her," Ashley said in a high, clear voice.

Three heads pivoted toward her.

"And you might want to interview Vladimir Rostov," she added.

"Holy shit," the third agent said.

"I want to call my lawyer," Robert muttered. "I want to call Lenny. I have to speak . . . to speak to him."

The agents seemed confused. Parker pulled his cell

phone out and spoke urgently into it. Freed handed Robert a phone and stood over him scowling. The third man ran out front then rushed back in again. "Avalanche Creek?" he asked Ashley. "Where the hell is that?"

"There's a map in my car," Chris put in helpfully.

"A map, sure, okay. Where's your car?"

"Out front. The Mustang."

Ashley met his eyes; he didn't have to say a word. She read his mind as if it were her own. She snatched her car keys off the hook on the wall, and they walked out though the front door, leaving raised voices and disorder behind. They strode swiftly to his car, Chris grabbing his jacket, then to the Cherokee, Chris to the driver's side. She tossed the keys to him in a perfect arc, the sun glinting off them as they dropped with precise accuracy into his hand.

They were racing against time. Chris drove as quickly and skillfully as possible, but the rush-hour traffic leaving Aspen in the late afternoon was as bad as usual. Stuck in an endless line of vehicles on a two-lane road, the only way out of town, she quivered with frustration. She directed him to shortcuts whenever she could, parallel roads that only locals knew, but they were winding and congested and slow, too.

Lauren, hold on, we're coming, she thought silently over and over. Then her mind would flip to Robert, Lauren's *father,* once her husband, and each time she suffered a new death.

Finally, finally, they reached the four-lane highway, and he picked up speed. Past Woody Creek and Old Snowmass, Basalt and El Jebel. The now-familiar turn up the Crystal River Valley.

Chris said little, concentrating on driving. His profile

was determined, his eyes checking the road ahead, the rearview mirror, passing cars on the winding road whenever he could.

For an instant, she had a vision of Lauren sitting in the driver's seat a few weeks ago. Ashley had been letting her practice driving on their private road. Her daughter's shoulder-length blond hair had been streaked with red that she'd just put in, her skin smooth and unblemished, her midriff bare, her jeans so tight it was a wonder she could breathe. Her face set in concentration, her fingers with all her silver rings gripping the wheel. Determined to get her license the minute she was old enough. *Lauren.* Still her baby.

She forced the memory aside, shut her eyes for a moment, drew in a deep breath. "Do you think," she said as they left Carbondale behind, "do you think those agents could get there before us? Get a helicopter or something?"

"No," he said, pulling out smoothly to pass a truck. "It'd take too long to get a chopper to Aspen. They'll drive."

"So they're behind us."

"Got to be."

"Robert," she couldn't help saying. "Robert planned it all."

"Damn right."

"I can't believe it, but I know it's true. I knew, I knew, the minute you looked at him."

"Uh-huh."

Dusk was falling as they approached Redstone, Venus bright in the western sky, rain clouds hugging the mountaintops ahead, shrinking now that the earth cooled.

"I tried so hard to convince the parole board to keep Davey in prison," she said.

"Parole boards are goddamn useless, any cop'll tell you that."

"Do you think . . . do you think Lauren's okay?"

"Potts wants money. You heard Robert, he wants even more now."

"But when Robert didn't deliver it . . ."

"Let's hope Potts thinks Robert is having trouble getting the cash. Let's just hope Potts wasn't watching him," he said grimly.

He didn't have to finish the thought; she knew exactly what he meant. If Davey had been tailing Robert, he'd know Robert had no intention of paying him and had instead gone to her house, to the FBI. And then he'd kill Lauren. She felt chilled, a sick lump in her chest. Fear, paralyzing fear.

"What if he's not there?" she asked to relieve the pall of silence.

"Not at Avalanche Creek?"

"Yes, what if . . . what if he got nervous and moved Lauren?"

Chris merely shook his head.

Darkness was gathering as they reached the turnoff, a dirt road that led up the cleft between Mt. Sopris and Mt. Daly. She reached into the glove box, took out the utility flashlight and map, which showed the dirt road turning into a Jeep track after three miles then a hiking trail. But Robert had said the cabin was only one mile from the highway. The lights of the Cherokee pierced the night; the car bounced on the bad road. Chris read off the odometer: half a mile, six-tenths, seven-tenths. After a couple of houses, there was nothing but trees and rocks and the pale, dusty track ahead.

At eight-tenths of a mile, he pulled to the side of the road and killed the engine.

"What are you doing?" she asked. "We have to get there, Chris."

"I don't want Potts alerted. He'll hear a car, he'll see the headlights. We walk from here."

She saw him check his gun in the light of the full moon. Saw him pull it from his jacket pocket, eject the clip, snap it back in place and slip the gun, barrel down, in the waistband of his jeans. Then they hiked, searching for the cabin. The brightness helped, but it could help Davey as well.

Chris led her along the verge of the road, in the shadow of brush and trees. The night was silent but for the distant sound of vehicles on the highway, crickets in the underbrush. An owl. The air was pine scented and cool and crystal clear, mountain air. Sound carried.

She searched both sides of the road as they walked. For a driveway, an opening in the brush, a light from a window, the linear, unnatural shadow of a manmade structure in the wilderness. But there was nothing.

Chris stopped short and clasped her arm, holding her back.

"What?" she whispered.

He pointed.

She peered into the night. Yes, there was a darker shadow against the trees.

"Stay here," he ordered.

"But Lauren . . ."

"Stay here." He drew the gun.

"No, let me go, please. She might be . . ."

"Stay here, Ashley."

She had to wait, alone in the immensity of the night, shivering, straining to listen, waiting, waiting, her heart thumping like a wild thing against her ribs. Finally, she couldn't bear another second—she had to move, she had to do something. She started toward the structure, slowly, trying to move silently, eyes searching, ears alert to any sound.

She reached the short driveway to the cabin. Where was Chris? She stopped, listened. Nothing. No lights, no movement, no voices. Oh God, the cabin . . . was it empty? Was Davey gone? Had he taken Lauren somewhere else? Or was she . . . ?

She shut down the thought when she saw a shadow detach itself from the darkness and move stealthily to the front door. Chris. Gun held in front of him, a phantom. He made a quick move, she heard a sharp clatter, a crash, and the door slammed open, Chris following it in.

Lauren, Lauren. She found herself running breathlessly, bursting into the cabin, uncaring of herself, of anything. *Lauren.*

"Chris? Chris?" she called out.

"Right here," came his voice. "Now, stay where you are." He switched on the flashlight, skimming the beam around the room.

"She isn't here," Ashley panted, and disappointment swept her like a drowning tide.

"They're gone," he said. "They're fucking gone."

The flashlight beam touched soda cans, pizza boxes, paper plates crusted with food on a makeshift table, picked out frame bunk beds in a corner, bare, stained mattresses, a wood stove, cold as death. She looked around for a sign of her daughter, anything. She stepped forward, bent to pick up a crumpled napkin, but Chris held her back.

"This is a crime scene," he said.

"A crime scene," she repeated dully, moving back to the door. She couldn't see very well, only bits and pieces wherever the light touched, crazed impressions, the shadow of Chris behind the brightness.

"Yeah, we can't contaminate possible evidence. There'll be fingerprints, hair. We need to keep the integrity of the evidence."

"I don't care about the integrity of the evidence," she ground out. "I want my daughter back. Maybe there's something here, something to tell us where they went."

"I'll check it out, don't worry."

"Hurry," she said, her voice catching, "if he's moved her, he knows about Robert and the FBI. He knows, Chris."

"Yeah, he knows."

She was trembling; she hugged herself, willing it to stop. Chris shone the light on her, and she couldn't do a thing but shiver and gulp air. He came to her then, put his arm around her, and she sagged against him with a sob torn from deep inside her. He held her, and he murmured, and he stroked her hair in the smoke-tinged darkness of the cabin.

"We'll find her," he said. "I swear to you we'll find her."

Gradually she calmed down, and the panic began to subside. "I'll help you look through this stuff," she said against his chest. "Please, let me *do* something."

He released her, but he would not let her set foot past the threshold. "I mean it," he said, his cop voice now, "don't touch a thing."

So she had to stay put while he moved slowly and methodically around the small room, focusing the light here, sweeping it there. Everything he touched he picked up by a corner then replaced. And all she could do was watch the writhing shadows and the sudden brilliance of the beam on a silver can or foil or bright red paper.

"Fast food from a Subway in Carbondale," he said, holding a wrapper by an edge, putting it down. "Two receipts from City Market." Then he crouched, picked up a small item. "Matchbook. Looks generic." He returned it to the floor. "McDonald's wrapper."

There were soda and beer cans lying helter-skelter around the place. Pizza boxes from a Pizza Hut. "Where's the closest Pizza Hut?" he asked.

"Glenwood Springs."

"Our boy gets around."

"Maybe his cousin, you know, the one he was supposed to be living with, brought it here."

"Um. Maybe."

"What's that over there? No, in the corner. That's it."

"Torn-up newspaper." He held it up gingerly. "*Aspen Daily News*. Dated yesterday."

"You can pick them up anywhere in the valley," she said.

"Huh." He stood up and swung the flashlight beam. "Huh," he said again, aiming it at more crumpled papers. He picked one up. "In and Out House," he said. "Looks like a receipt."

"What's the date on it?"

"Ah . . . It's faint. Looks like yesterday. Yeah, it is."

"Oh God," she said.

"What?"

"The In and Out House is in Aspen. He was there."

Chris let out an audible breath. "So Potts was watching you. Or maybe Robert. He knew Robert went to your house, he knew about the FBI. He came back here and got Lauren and took off."

"Then he was right ahead of us," she said. "Damn him." She heard the shrillness of her voice, but she repeated the words anyway. *"Damn him."*

"He can't have gone too far," Chris said.

"But where? Where's he taken her?"

He finally said, "At least there's no sign of a struggle."

She knew what he was getting at. She squeezed her eyes shut a moment and took a rattling breath. There was no sign of a struggle here, true, but that didn't mean . . . *No*, she told herself, *don't even think that*. What she had to do was concentrate fully on where Davey had taken Lauren. Someplace neither Robert nor the FBI could predict. Not the cousin's house then. And probably not out of the Roaring Fork Valley, because Davey had rarely ventured from his home—except for his time in prison.

So where had he gone then? *Where?*

She stepped aside as Chris passed on his way to check the outhouse. "Oh dear God," she was whispering, when he began slowly sweeping the beam over rocks and a stand of lodgepole pine beside the outhouse.

Where was Lauren?

Time began to press on her, heavy, an enemy sapping her strength and her will. *Think. Think!* She knew Davey better than anybody, didn't she? But it was so hard, so much at stake. So little time . . .

It came to her as she turned toward Chris, a flare of sharp clarity.

"Chris! Chris!" she called out, half stumbling, righting herself. "I know where she is! The mine. She's in the mine!"

"The mine?"

"The Close Call Mine. Where he kept me!"

Chris was silent for only a second, and then he whispered, "Jesus, of course," and he was already hurrying her to the car, the flashlight beam skittering along the rough ground ahead of them as if it were alive.

TWENTY

It took half the night to drive back up the valley and Castle Creek Road to Taylor Pass, then to negotiate the steep, rutted dirt road that led to Chris's old hunting camp. Thank God there was a full moon.

She'd had the errant thought, as they sped past Aspen Valley Hospital, that she hadn't been beyond this point in twenty years, not since Chris had rescued her.

The night was a kind of blessing, cloaking the memories. She wondered how she'd react when they reached Taylor Pass, when the sun would rise on that forgotten yet always-present horror. But she had to be strong.

"How far is it?" she asked for the hundredth time.

"The hunting camp is just ahead," Chris said. "But we'll need to walk from there."

"You're sure you can find the mine?"

"Oh, yeah, I can find it. I was just there, remember?"

"But it's dark."

"I can find it, Ashley."

She grasped the dashboard with stiff fingers, leaning forward as if that would propel them through the night faster.

"Do you think the FBI agents have found the cabin yet?" she asked as the Cherokee bumped up the road in four-wheel drive.

He shrugged. He was concentrating on a steep, washboard pitch.

"But they won't find us here," she went on.

"Hell, no."

"Maybe, oh God, maybe we should alert them. I could call on my cell phone, call the police, something. Maybe . . ."

"No."

"They'd think I was crazy, wouldn't they?" She looked down and shook her head. "Maybe I am. Maybe Davey isn't here at all, and I've wasted our time, and Lauren is somewhere else, and . . ."

"You're not crazy."

Her fingers curled into fists, and she pressed them into her stomach. "I'm scared."

"I know. Me, too."

"I mean, I'm scared for Lauren, yes, but I'm scared of going back to that awful place."

"You don't have to go inside."

But she knew she did.

The white shape loomed out of the darkness, an alien object in the wild, until every detail of it was clear in the headlights.

"The Blazer," Chris said, "the goddamn white Blazer."

"He's here! Chris, I was right." And she burst into tears.

"Hey, Ashley, it's okay. It's good. You were right." He reached over and stroked her bent back.

"No, no, I'll be fine. I'm just so . . . so relieved." She straightened and wiped at her cheeks, took a deep breath.

"You can wait here, you know."

"You're kidding, aren't you?"

He tried a wry smile. "Yeah, kidding."

He led the way, the flashlight beam jittering ahead of them. It was cool, so cool that the brisk walk erased her exhaustion. It must have been nearly four in the morning, she figured, but she wasn't tired anymore. Her mind sparked and twisted and tested her fear. Bearable, just bearable. So far.

"How long?" she panted.

"A quarter mile or so. You okay?"

"Yes. Hurry."

The night made the scene unfamiliar. Stars and blackness—the moon had set, the mountains were shadows against the dark sky. A stream gurgled somewhere close by, and a coyote yipped higher up among the peaks.

The beam of light hit mine tailings, then ran across wooden beams, a pile of weather-beaten, splintered wood that had been a shed, and she knew they'd reached the mine. Her heart burst, and sweat gathered under her arms, on her forehead and upper lip. Her teeth chattered.

Chris switched the flashlight off. She felt panic assail her and clutched at him.

"It's okay, Ashley. I don't want him to see the light."

"Yes, yes . . ."

"I'm going in, all right?"

"I'm coming with you."

"You sure?"

She clenched her jaw to stop the nervous spasms. "Yes."

He turned the light on, aiming it down, his hand shielding the beam. She focused on the circle of light,

one step at a time. She could manage if she did that—
not looking up, one step at a time.

The mine engulfed them; the instantly familiar damp-
ness and cold, mist hanging in the air like dust, the smell
of mold and wet earth and a peculiar kind of rot. *So
what?* she repeated inside her head. *It's only a hole in
the ground. So what?*

He held her arm as they moved; she concentrated on
the pool of light and the warmth of his hand and her
daughter, somewhere in this terrible black maze. *I'm
coming, baby, I'm coming for you.*

She fought panic. Her throat seemed to close, and she
couldn't catch her breath. *So what, so what?*

He stopped, pressing fingers into her arm. "Light," he
whispered.

She peered ahead. Yes, there was a faint, diffused
glow, the barest glint of light on rock. She stiffened.

"Careful," he breathed, clicking the flashlight off.

They crept ahead, toward the glow. One step at a time,
her hands curved into claws, the walls of the cave closing in on her, moving, creaking. Just like her nightmare.
The damp, the clammy cold, the incessant drip of water.
*So what, so what? Damp can't hurt you, cold can't hurt
you, water dripping can't . . .*

A sound. Not water, not the echo of their own footsteps, not the scurry of a rodent.

She snatched at Chris, missed, grabbed his jacket.

"What?" he whispered.

"Listen."

They stood frozen, and she strained to hear, but her
heart was beating so hard, and the walls were grinding
in on her.

"Yes," he hissed and moved ahead.

Then she heard it again, a curious piping sound in the

bass profundo of the cavern, echoing, high frequency sounds. . . . A voice. A young girl's voice? Vast joy shot through her, and she started to run, but Chris grabbed her. "No," he said against her ear, and she could feel him sliding his gun from under his jacket. "Easy now."

They moved on, so slowly now she thought she'd scream. The sounds came louder, detaching themselves from the background. Then she heard another voice—Davey's. And Lauren, yes. A snatch of sound, words. ". . . can't keep me . . . they're coming . . ." The deeper tones—curse words, angry.

Chris's lips against her ear again: "Okay, this is it. I'm going to get his attention, make a noise, make him follow me into that tunnel we passed. When he leaves her, you go, get her, get out."

Her teeth clicked together uncontrollably. She nodded, but he couldn't see her. "Yes," she managed. "But what if he used a chain? What if Lauren's chained like I was?"

"Then just wait there. I'll be back for you. But if you can, get her out. Okay?"

"Okay, yes."

"Keep the flashlight off till you reach Lauren."

The flashlight. He was pressing it into her hand.

"No, you keep it. There's light up there. A lantern, maybe. Chris, you keep it."

"Can you do this, Ashley?" His breath brushed her ear.

"Y . . . yes."

"That's my brave girl." He took her face in his hands and gave her a quick, hard kiss.

"Chris," she whispered, holding him tightly, "be careful. Be careful."

He melted away into the shadows, and she was alone. Shivering, trembling, sucking the heavy wet air. The voices . . . Yes, Lauren. She was okay, she was alive. *You can do this, you can.*

Then there was a crash, loud, the sound thundering in the closeness, bouncing and rumbling off the stone walls.

Chris, luring Davey. Had Davey heard? Would he check the noise out? She waited, flattened against a depression in the pitch-black, praying Davey would not see her when he went past. The echoes deafened her, the sharp rock dug into her back, her hands pressed against the cold greasiness of the wall. Holding it back so that it would not crush her.

Footfalls, sharp, echoing, pounding. A shadow moving past her, silhouetted against the glow for a heartbeat then gone. Receding steps.

She ran then, stumbling, hands outstretched, splashing through puddles, tripping over the old rails, pulse pounding in her ears. Screaming silently. Shoulder careening off a rock wall. What? A curve in the shaft, running on, into the light, the flow becoming a yellow explosion, a circle of brilliance that made her pupils contract. Blind, she was blind. But no, there was the lantern, the rock walls, the floor, scraps of bags and paper, the rusted iron ring in the wall. The ring she'd been chained to.

"Mom?" she heard.

She swiveled, tried to focus. There, a movement.

"Mom? Oh my God, Mom!"

A step, two, tottering, staggering, her arms out, then touching, then holding fiercely. Her child, her flesh and blood. "Lauren," she moaned.

Someone was crying. Sobbing. Was it her? No. Lauren was crying.

"Are you all right?" she rasped, frantic. "Did he hurt you?"

Between sobs. "I'm okay. Mom, how did . . . ? My hands are tied."

Rope. Not a chain. Ripping at the stubborn knots, tearing fingernails. It was taking too long. Panting, terrified Davey would come back.

A rolling, thunderous crack. They both froze.

A shot? A gunshot? *Chris.*

"Who was that?" Lauren gasped.

"My friend. He's been helping me." She tugged at the rope; an end came loose. Quickly, quickly.

The rope fell away. Lauren flexed her arms.

"Can you make it out?" Ashley breathed, trying desperately not to think about the gunshot. *Chris is all right, he has to be all right.*

"Can you stand up, honey?"

"Yes, oh Mom, I can't believe . . ."

"Let's go."

She clutched Lauren's hand and grabbed the kerosene lantern and headed for the mine entrance. How far was it?

They ran as fast as they could, dodging rocks and rubble and the rusty ore train tracks. Running, holding onto each other. Past the entrance to the side shaft where Chris and Davey were. A blast of sound beat at their eardrums as they ran—another shot, then two more in rapid succession.

Part of her desperately wanted to stop, but she kept on, clutching Lauren, rushing out of hell toward the illuminated circle that was their salvation.

Propelled into the world, the pearly light of dawn, the misty mountains and trees. Reborn.

Lauren's face was dirty and tear streaked, her clothes torn and stained, a filthy man's sweatshirt over her jeans and T-shirt.

"He didn't hurt you?" Ashley asked shrilly, holding her daughter, then pushing her out to arm's length, then pulling her close again, feeling her face, her hair, her shoulders, her hands fluttering over her daughter like moths around a flame.

"I'm okay, Mom, honest. He was kind of rough a few times."

"That bastard, that bastard," Ashley ground out.

"How did you know where I was?"

"I knew. I just knew."

"And that man, he never told me his name, but he's the one, isn't he? He did that to you?"

"Yes."

"Oh, Mom," Lauren cried. "You went in the mine. Mom, you went in after me."

"Shush. Of course I did. You're my daughter."

Then Lauren looked round. "Your friend?"

"Oh God." A new stab of fear. "Chris."

Lauren's eyes grew wide. "Do you think Davey shot him?"

"Davey had a gun?"

"Yes, he liked to show it off, like he was going to shoot me." Scornfully.

"Baby, I have to go back. I have to leave you and go back," Ashley breathed.

"I'll go with you."

"No." She took her daughter in her arms and held her tightly for a moment. "You need to be strong for me right now. You can do it. And when I get back we can both fall apart. Okay?"

"Okay," Lauren whispered.

"I love you so much."

"Me, too, Mom."

"Now call 911. Call the police, tell them it's The Close

Call Mine on Taylor Pass, to look for the hunting camp. There're two cars there, my Cherokee and that Blazer. White. Tell them . . . we need a helicopter, there may be injuries." She thrust her cell phone into Lauren's hand.

Then she gave her daughter's arm a last squeeze, prepared herself mentally. *It's a mine, a hole in the ground. So what?*

She left Lauren there in the morning sunlight, holding the cell phone, starting to punch in the call for help. She marveled, wondered at her child's courage and resilience, then she turned, scooped up the kerosene lantern and plunged once more into her nightmare.

She started shaking instantly. Her stomach turned, her mouth went dry, she labored to suck air into her lungs. Picking her way this time, not running, looking for the entrance to the tunnel on the right. Yes, it had been on the left when she and Lauren ran by.

She was well aware that there had been no more gunshots for some minutes, and no one had come out of the mine. She had no idea what that meant, but she knew it was not good. And she'd left Chris in there, alone, to face *her* nemesis.

Please, God, please let him be okay.

She moved on, deeper into the inky darkness. Where was the shaft? *Where?*

There. She held the lantern up and lit the black hole on the right. She stopped, listened. Nothing. Made herself move.

She almost tripped over a body. Drew up with a muted scream. Raised the lantern to see. It was Davey, lying on his back, a gun in an outflung hand, black blood soaking his jacket. Unconscious? Dead? She didn't care which.

She straightened, took a quavering breath and swung the lamp from side to side. "Chris?" Her voice probed the darkness, echoed back to her: *Chris Chris Chris.*

Louder. "Chris? Where are you?" But only her own voice reverberated back.

Oh God, why wasn't he answering? Was he . . . ?

A sound. Not an echo.

She hastened toward it, the lantern swinging crazily. A moan. The scuffle of movement.

He was there. Yes, lying in a heap, there, by an old ore wagon left to molder away.

"Chris!" She ran, dropped the lantern, kneeled beside him, felt his face, down his arms.

He mumbled something. She bent close. "Shit, it hurts."

Hysterical laughter bubbled in her chest, threatened to erupt. "Chris, where are you hurt?"

"Leg."

She looked. His pant leg was soaked with blood, there was a dark pool under it. So much blood.

He groaned again. "Lauren?"

"She's okay. She's fine. Calling 911. I have to get you out of here."

"Lost a lot of blood."

"They'll send a helicopter. Chris, stay with me, don't close your eyes, just stay with me."

"Potts?"

"Dead. I don't know." She felt panic shuddering in her brain, in her heart. "We have to get you out."

"Leave me."

"No!" The walls squeezed closer.

"Can't walk."

"I'll help you. I'm strong. Get up, Chris, please try to get up."

He pushed himself up on his arms, grunting with the

effort; she squatted, put a shoulder under one of his arms. He was heavy, God, he was heavy.

"Does it hurt?" she asked stupidly.

"Feels great."

"Oh God, Chris."

"I'll . . . live."

But would he?

He finally made it to his feet, hunched over, groaning, leaning on her, his wounded leg dragging. They hobbled forward, one step, then two. She couldn't hold the lantern and him, so she left it. Darkness swallowed them, but she could make out the dim light ahead, a beacon. It drew her on, the way people who'd been brought back to life described dying—moving toward a bright light.

He groaned and sagged, and once he almost fell, but she wouldn't let him stop shuffling, even though they moved excruciatingly slowly.

"Lauren!" she yelled when they neared the light.

"Mom?" Scared, a white face in the entrance. Just a few yards away, a few yards.

"Help me!"

It was better with two of them. They got him outside in the sun, laid him carefully on the cool, moist ground. Blood smeared her hands, her clothes.

"Oh, Mom . . . ?"

"It's his blood. His leg. Did you call?"

"They're coming. The stupid woman started asking questions, but I told her we needed help. I've been watching for them."

Ashley was kneeling next to Chris. She knew some first aid. All teachers did. Direct pressure to stop bleeding.

"Chris, can you hear me?"

His face was gray, dotted with beads of sweat. He mumbled.

"A helicopter is coming. Hang on."

She found the bullet hole near his groin. It must have hit an artery—there was a big artery there, she knew. Blood still welled form the hole. It had obviously pumped earlier, but now it only seeped. How much blood had he lost? Shock . . . he must be in shock. If you lost too much blood, your organs shut down and you died.

She pressed her hand on the area over the bullet hole. Direct pressure. He jerked. *Sorry, sorry, but it has to be done.*

"Where's the damn chopper?" she cried.

"Is he going to . . . ? I mean, is he . . . ?" Lauren asked at her shoulder, her voice thin.

"Not if I can help it." Then she leaned forward and kissed him on the lips with a kind of desperation. "Hang on, Chris. Stay with me. Do you hear me?"

His eyes opened, glazed. "Yeah. Jesus, that hurts."

"Soon. They'll be here soon."

"Unh." His eyes rolled back, his head lolled.

"Chris, Chris." She laid a hand on his cheek. "Stay with me."

It seemed as if hours had raced by, but she knew it was early morning, cool, the sun still low, the shadows long. Where was that helicopter?

Lauren heard the sound first and cried out. Then Ashley heard it. She jerked her head around to face the direction from which it was coming: the distinctive *whoop-whoop* of blades beating at the air.

It appeared then, from over the shoulder of the mountain, a tiny insect flying up the valley toward them, and the sun glinted off its whirling rotors, winking at them as it grew bigger and bigger.

"Thank God," Ashley wept fervently. Lauren started waving her arms and screaming, and the chopper stopped then, dipped in a salute and began to drop.

TWENTY-ONE

Davey Potts drew his last breath in the helicopter on route to the hospital. Chris was rushed into emergency surgery. He was still in surgery when Ashley got there with Lauren.

"Is he going to be all right?" Ashley begged the nurse in the emergency room.

"I'm really sorry, but you'll have to wait until Dr. Whitcomb finishes, and then he'll talk to you."

Lauren was admitted, her filthy clothes taken away to hold as evidence; she was put in a hospital gown and checked over by the ER team. She kept saying she was fine, but Ashley had been advised by the EMT on the helicopter to have her examined. He'd explained apologetically that they'd have taken her in the chopper if there'd been room.

Exhausted and frantic with worry over Chris, Ashley held her daughter's hand. She hadn't had time yet to feel relief, to sort out what had transpired or what would transpire. She had no idea yet what had happened to Robert or Vladimir—she didn't have room in her head to care.

She slipped out into the hall, as Lauren was being poked and prodded, and tried to find someone who could tell her Chris's status, but she learned nothing except that he was still in surgery. She took a moment to visit the ladies' room, to meet her haggard eyes in the mirror, to splash water on her face and run her fingers through her hair. To pray.

Back to the emergency room, where Lauren was growing impatient. Her eyes filling one minute, then holding on to Ashley, then turning teenage sarcastic. But not terrified, not traumatized. *Thank God.*

"How's your friend?" Lauren asked, dangling her legs off the side of the hospital bed. "What are they doing to him?"

"He's in surgery. I can't get an answer yet. I guess they have to repair the bullet hole. And give him blood." She bit her lip, trying not to let Lauren see her anxiety.

But her daughter wasn't fooled. "You're really worried about him."

"Yes."

"He saved me, right?"

"Pretty much, sweetie."

"But, Mom, you did it, too. You came in the mine to get me."

"I was pretty darn scared."

"But you did it anyway, Mom."

Ashley tried to smile. "That's what mothers do for their kids."

"You're really, really brave, Mom. Wait till Dad hears about it."

Robert. Good God, she'd have to deal with Lauren

learning that her own father had been behind her kidnapping. There would be no way to keep that from her, no way at all. He'd probably be prosecuted—everything would come out. Damn Robert, damn him to hell.

But it wasn't the time to consider that. Now was the time to revel in the fact that Lauren was unhurt and to await news of Chris.

"I saw you . . ." Lauren's cheeks turned pink and she looked away. "I saw you . . . um, kiss Chris."

Oh boy. How to tell her little girl? She sat on the edge of the bed next to her daughter. "Chris and I are very old friends." She plunged on. "Remember when I told you about the friend I had in Denver, the one who rescued me from the mine?"

"Uh-huh."

"Well, that was Chris."

"Oh."

"I called him when you were kidnapped. I didn't know what else to do. I knew he was a policeman, and he drove right up."

"You like him, Mom?"

She took Lauren's hand. "Yes, I like him a lot. And if he's okay, if he comes out of this, I'm going to do everything humanly possible to keep him in our lives."

"You mean like marry him?"

Ashley had to smile. "Let's not get ahead of ourselves here, okay?"

"Mom, do you know they told me the police want to—what'd they call it?—take my statement?"

"Yes."

"So I just tell them what happened?"

"Yes, everything."

"But that man's dead. They told me he was dead."

"They still need the whole story."

"Mom, did I do anything wrong? I mean, like everyone's always saying don't talk to strangers, don't get in strange cars, but I couldn't help it. He grabbed me and . . ."

"You did nothing wrong, Lauren. Nothing. Don't blame yourself for a second."

Lauren's eyes filled. "He was horrible, and my hands were tied up, and I was hungry all the time. And it was freezing in that mine."

Ashley hugged her child, held her and rocked her back and forth as she had when Lauren was a baby. These were small things, Lauren's concerns; the edges of her memories would soon dull. Mostly Lauren was angry. *Angry.* How amazing. How wonderful.

"Mrs. Marin?" came a voice.

A lean-faced doctor in green scrubs, his surgical cap pushed to the back of his head, a mask dangling around his neck.

She stood up too quickly, felt the blood leave her head, swayed. Put a hand out to steady herself.

"Mrs. Marin?"

"Yes . . . *Chris?*"

"He lost a lot of blood. But we've got that under control. We removed the bullet, sutured up his femoral artery, and I think he's going to recover nicely."

She put her face in her hands, and tears burned her eyes. "Thank God," she whispered.

And then she felt her daughter's hand on her back, patting her, and a fifteen-year-old voice, trying to comfort her. "It's okay, Mom. Don't cry." And that made her cry even harder.

They went home that afternoon. Chris hadn't regained consciousness yet, but one of the nurses promised to call the minute he did.

Relief and dread filled her equally. What would she find at home? What had happened to Robert, to Vladimir? How was her mother? And she was tired to the bone, running on autopilot.

Luda was there with Pauline—a panicky and contrite Luda. "They take Vladimir in for questioning. Terrible thing. I know nothing, Mrs. Marin, I swear. I say to him, 'you stupid man, you don't get green card renewed, you go to prison.'"

"All right, Luda. Just take care of my mother. We'll talk later, okay?"

Luda grabbed Lauren in a bear hug. "So glad you back, so much worry. Poor baby, poor little thing." She even kissed her.

Pauline was confused, retreating into her bedroom, reacting testily to everyone but Lauren, whom she wept over, even as she was unsure exactly why she was weeping.

Then Ashley had to call Charlene and Joe Garcia to tell them about Chris. A harrowing phone call, Charlene sobbing on the phone, then Joe asking a million questions in a curt cop's voice.

"Keep us informed," was the last thing he said. "We can be up there in a few hours."

She took a shower, stood under the water until the hot water heater was empty. Let her tears mingle with the spray, felt herself giving in to weariness, relaxing her vigilance a fraction. Until she remembered Chris, and then adrenaline surged in her chest.

She fell asleep on her pastel-colored bedspread, slept a deep sleep filled with swirling images of mineshafts and dark tunnels, but it was not a nightmare, simply a harmless re-creation of where she'd been.

And she woke to the shrill ringing of the phone.

"For you, Mom," Lauren said, holding out the phone, her eyes meeting Ashley's.

"This is Janey Cornish at the hospital. He's awake."

She threw on clothes—jeans, a white shirt that she didn't bother tucking in, sandals—and drove too fast through town to the hospital. Surprised to note that it was growing dark, the sky streaked orange and fuchsia and smoke gray where the setting sun shone through layers of clouds. Parked, ran into the hospital.

They told her at the front desk he was in room one-twenty-one. Her feet carried her past the nurse's station, reading room numbers. One-nineteen, twenty, twenty-one.

He was alarmingly pale against the white sheets, an IV hooked to his arm, eyes closed, the thin blanket raised in a tent over his injured leg. She moved close, feasting her eyes on his features, his hands lying so defenseless at his sides, whisker shadow smudging his cheeks.

"Chris," she whispered, bending close. Her voice trembled.

His eyes opened slowly, lids fluttering.

She couldn't help the smile that curved her mouth. "Chris?"

"Yeah, I'm here," he said, licking dry lips.

"You're going to be okay, you're going to be fine."

"Don't feel so goddamn fine."

"You will." She took his free hand and gently rubbed her thumb up and down its back.

"Lauren?" he asked.

"She's home. She's good."

His eyes closed.

"You did it, Chris."

His lids raised and he looked at her. "No, *you* did it."

"Davey died."

He moved his head, a slight acknowledgment.

"Do you want anything?"

"More of that pain medication," he half joked.

"Oh . . . oh, should I tell the nurse?"

"No," he said, "stay here for a minute. Just a minute."

She sat on the plastic chair by his bed, holding his hand, watching his face as it relaxed and he slid into drug-induced sleep again. Holding onto him, loving him, so grateful that he was alive. So very grateful.

Her days turned into a routine: Mornings were for Lauren and Pauline, afternoons for Chris. Two days after his surgery he got out of bed and used crutches to walk to the bathroom. "A small step for mankind, a giant step for me," he quipped.

His color returned, and he took to hobbling to the outdoor patio of the hospital for sun. She brought him desserts and fresh fruit, homemade lasagna. Ben and Jerry's ice cream. Luda sent borscht and pickled herring: "For to grow blood," she said.

It was Ashley's turn to take care of Chris, to be at his side, to support him, as he'd supported her all those years before. It felt good to return the favor.

He grumbled at times; some days he seemed depressed, quiet and turned inward. But there was an unspoken intimacy between them that thrilled her to the core.

The FBI interviewed him as soon as Dr. Whitcomb allowed it, and she barely had time to talk to him that day. When the agents were done he was so exhausted, he could barely eat dinner. She fretted and fussed, but he fell asleep practically in the middle of a sentence.

She sat and watched him sleep, brushed his lips with hers before she left.

Lauren visited him two days later, a little embarrassed, shy, watching with proprietary curiosity as her mother kissed him on the cheek.

"You're a trooper," Chris told her. "You're one tough little lady."

Lauren squirmed, grinned.

"Just like your mom," he added.

"Yeah." Lauren blushed.

But the best times were when they were alone, Chris in his chair, his leg out straight, her close, touching him, talking, just talking. And yet, there was something he was holding back. Something she still couldn't fathom.

"The FBI took her statement?" he was asking.

"Yes, one whole day."

He moved, grimaced with discomfort.

"Do you want a pill?"

"No, hell, go on. What'd they do?"

"Took Robert and Vladimir in for questioning. I really don't know much more. I gave my statement, too."

"Does Lauren have any idea what her father did?"

"No . . . not yet. I told her he was involved in paying her ransom, that's all. I'll . . . I guess she'll find out anyway."

He regarded her gravely. "Better she hears it from you."

"I know. God, I know. But she loves him."

"You'll handle it. When the time's right."

"When the time's right."

Joanie, Chris's ex-wife, and Joe and Charlene called constantly. Ashley came into Chris's room one day and heard the tail end of a conversation.

". . . getting pretty fed up with the hospital. Oh, sorry,

I didn't realize you were the hospital expert. Yeah, well, I can sympathize now, you jerk." He saw her, smiled, told Joe he had to go. "Nurse Ratched is here."

"Hi," she said, "how are you doing?"

"Great, just great. I hurt like a bastard, walk like an old fart, and they're kicking me out of here next week."

"That's wonderful."

"Yeah, great."

A small question ticked inside her. "Have you . . . ah, thought what you're going to do?"

"Not really. Joanie offered to fly up and drive me home."

Home? "You can stay with me . . . us. I'd . . . I'd like that, Chris. Lauren would like it, too."

He looked away, and his features fell into harsh lines.

"Chris?"

He made a dismissive gesture with a hand.

"What's the matter? I know . . . I know something's been bothering you."

He kept his attention on the window, the green hills that rose behind the hospital.

"Tell me," she whispered.

"You think you know me," he said slowly. "You think I'm this great guy who saved you. But I'm not that person, Ashley."

"Who are you then?"

He turned his gaze on her. "You don't want to know."

"Don't tell me what I want. Damnit, Chris, I think we've been through enough together."

"This has nothing to do with you or what we've been through." His voice was tight.

"So it's about you. Okay, I'm listening."

He shook his head, moved in his chair, grunted with pain. She waited.

"Look, I was on the task force," he finally said. "Shit, I told you all about it. Except for one little detail."

"Go on." She folded her hands in her lap and watched him.

He regarded her steadily, and she saw his mouth twist bitterly. "I was a dirty cop. I took money, drug money," he said flatly.

Her pulse beat in her ears. She forced her expression into neutrality. *Wait*, she thought, *don't judge. Wait.*

"There was a big deal going down. A raid, get the goods on the head of the New Jersey family. All set." He wiped a finger across his upper lip, stared into the middle distance. "I was sick of it. I'd been undercover for two solid years. It fucks with your head. You get screwed up. The money was there, in the trunk of a car. Cash." He shrugged. "So I took it. What could the wise-guys do, complain to the cops?

"So I took the money. A lot of money. And my task force leader got suspicious. To make a long story short, they couldn't pin anything on me. But I was asked to resign."

"I see."

"Now you know, Ashley." The resignation in his voice was palpable. "You know what a goddamn big hero I am."

"What did you do with the money?"

"It can't be traced, if that's what you mean."

She shook her head. "No, I mean . . ."

He cut her off. "Look, this is between you and me, okay?"

"Sure."

"I gave it to Joe."

Of course. The loan to Joe.

"I figured, Jesus, all that money. Some other corrupt

cop would take it. I figured it'd do more good with Joe."

"It probably did," she said quietly.

He looked at her, frowning.

"You *are* the man I know, the same one I've always known. I won't judge what you did. I can't."

He scrubbed a hand over his face. "Shit," he said softly. "You don't get it. I'd take the money all over again. That's the problem. I don't feel one goddamn bit of remorse."

"Oh, Chris," she sighed, "you made a mistake, but you did it for a good reason. Can you forgive yourself for the bad and learn to live with the good part?" She leaned forward and touched his knee. "We all have good and bad in us."

"You don't."

"Good God, I can be the most selfish bitch in the universe."

"Bullshit."

But she waved him off. "There are times when I resent my mother so much I could smother her. And after my divorce I didn't have time for a life of my own. I was so angry. And I was impatient with Lauren. Sometimes I think my panic attacks were some kind of sick manipulation. Chris, none of us is a saint."

"You make it sound simple."

"It's not simple. You wonder how you can go on."

It was a long moment before he spoke, then he said, "I didn't know myself anymore. I felt like a schizophrenic. I let everyone down, my family, the force, Jesus, even Sal." He paused. "Myself, that was the worst."

"You didn't let Joe down."

"He's the only one."

"You didn't let me down, either. Or Lauren."

He didn't reply, and she forged ahead. "You owe too

many people to take the chicken's way out. You've got great friends who love you and worry about you, and you've got a wonderful son who, by the way, is coming to see you tomorrow. It's all set. His mom is dropping him off with us for three days, and Lauren's promised to show him the town. You have to pull yourself together for Rich."

"Yeah, well, what if I can't?"

"You will."

"How the hell do you know *that*?"

"Because I'll help you."

"Ashley . . ."

"I've loved you for so long I can't remember not loving you. I won't give up on you."

"You might be making a big mistake," he began, but she laid the back of her fingers on his cheek and merely shook her head. This was one of the few *right* things she'd done in her life.

The following days in the hospital melted together for Chris. Joanie delivered Rich then she left. Rich and Lauren rode bicycles across town to visit him at least once a day. He'd been worried about his son's visit, because it seemed wrong for the boy to see his father laid up and hurting, but Rich was too busy to even notice. Then Joanie drove back up to fetch him home, but not before Lauren promised to take him snowboarding next winter on the coolest slopes in the Rockies.

The media had a heyday with the story of Lauren's kidnapping, especially because of the remarkable parallels. The hospital staff did an excellent job filtering well-meaning visitors from the press, but a couple got through anyway.

"Christ, they're like pit bulls," he complained.

"More like kids in a candy store. I can deal with kids," she said.

Ashley was amazing. Of course, he read the local papers every morning and knew the latest on Robert Marin and even Vladimir, but still he listened to Ashley's version of the news, which was usually closer to the truth.

"Robert's been released on a hundred-thousand-dollar bond," she told him, when the papers had reported a five-hundred-thousand-dollar figure. "And Vladimir's case is still up in the air. He may be deported. The police aren't sure they have enough to prosecute him, and Robert, of course, isn't talking to anyone about anything."

"The papers said Vladimir was being shipped out next week."

Ashley shook her head. "That's only one option. God, these reporters."

"How is Lauren taking the news about her father?"

"Not great. She just can't seem to grasp what he did in order to get custody of her."

"Yeah, well, it's a tough one for anyone to figure. Do you think she needs counseling?"

"We're talking about it. I don't want to push her. Still . . ."

"You'll do what's right. You'll know when the time comes."

"Maybe I will."

"You will."

Outside his window the brush on the mountainsides was showing the first signs of fall. Although it was still August, the underbrush was changing to orange and ochre and red, and even a few aspen trees high up had turned so that their leaves shivered in the breeze, reminding him of golden coins.

Autumn.

Soon Ashley would be back at work. He'd had job offers himself, amazingly, from a couple of home security outfits in the valley. Not knowing what to say, he'd merely told them he'd be back in touch. He hadn't let on to Ashley, either, and he wasn't sure why. Maybe he felt that if he even considered a job offer in the area she'd be obligated, feel as if they needed to make some sort of a commitment.

He got a packet and letter from the ex-FBI man who Marin had hired to investigate him. A curious letter, the private detective obviously feeling guilt for not recognizing the truth behind Marin's request to document every last thing he uncovered about Chris Judge rather than trying to help find Lauren.

Chris read the letter. Set it aside and pulled out the contents of the packet. It was pages and pages, everything Mark Kingston had learned about Chris. The last page was a note to him. It read: *Burn this if you want. Regards, Mark.*

Chris did ask Ashley to get rid of the damning report, but he also asked her to read it first. "So you'll know."

"I *do* know," was her reply.

The long period of recovery, as he hobbled around the halls on crutches, was a monumental task, but he had time to consider Ashley's theory of life. At times he felt she'd opened his eyes to some great truth. At others he figured she'd just been trying to placate him.

The evening before he was to be discharged, they sat on the outdoor patio in the waning light. He could walk with one crutch now, could shower by himself, even get dressed without help. Progress.

But he still hadn't decided what to do. Things were moving too fast. The last he remembered he was going to eat his frigging gun and now ... and now he was a hero, with a woman, job offers, a possible family. A goddamn *family*.

She seemed nervous that evening, a little distracted.

"Is Lauren okay?" he asked.

"Yes, sure, she's fine for the moment. Getting ready to go back to school. Buying out the Gap. She'll be a sophomore."

"Your mother?"

"Okay. She had a good day today. Maybe that new medication is working. She asked about you."

What was wrong then? "Robert?" he ventured.

"He's canned Lenny and hired the biggest name lawyer he could. Elaine took the baby and went back to San Diego to her folks."

"Well, well."

"I know."

She fidgeted in her chair. What the hell . . . ?

"Chris," she began.

Shit, here it was. The kiss-off. *Sorry, Chris, but I don't think it'll work out.* A kick in the balls. "What's on your mind?" he said carefully.

"Well, you know, school starts in ten days. I have to go back to work. I love teaching, and I want to keep it up . . ."

"Yeah?"

"I'm a little . . ." She looked away. "I'm a little, um, on tenterhooks these days. Not exactly knowing what's going to . . . uh . . . happen between us. I'd like . . . I'd really like to have my mind clear so I can concentrate on my students."

"Okay."

"What I mean is . . . God, this is hard." She drew in a breath. "What I'd *like* is a commitment from you. *If* you can give it, if you *want* to give it. I . . . I just would like to know. . . ." She halted, looking down at her clenched hands.

He was stunned. His mind groped uselessly for a moment until he processed what she'd said. "Are you proposing to me?"

She glanced up. "Sort of."

He felt the most astonishing thing happen—his eyes filled with tears. Jesus, he hadn't cried since . . .

"Chris?" Beseechingly.

"You're sure?"

"God, Chris, I've been sure for twenty years."

"Damn."

"You know I love you. I haven't exactly made a secret of it. But I don't know about you. I don't want to pressure you. But I . . ."

"You really want me? Warts and all?"

"Oh yes."

He couldn't say a thing. He was afraid his voice would break. He took one of her hands and lifted it to his lips, kissed the back then turned it over. God, he was going to lose it. And if he did, she'd still be teasing him when they were old and gray.

A guy had to salvage some pride, didn't he?